## BAD BLOOD

"Get your butt out of my house, and I mean now!" he yelled.

She screamed back, "You've always been a son of a bitch, but I won't leave without my friend."

Anger gripped him, his finger tightened on the trigger, and abruptly, gunpowder blasted the room. The woman instantly dropped to the floor, her face turned toward the wall splattering it with blood. Blood poured onto the carpet as he rushed to check her pulse. Nothing. The bullet had torn into the corner of her left eye, destroying her eyelid and cornea until only a dark space stared back at him.

## REAL HORROR STORIES!
## PINNACLE TRUE CRIME

**SAVAGE VENGEANCE** (0-7860-0251-4, $5.99)
By Gary C. King and Don Lasseter
On a sunny day in December, 1974, Charles Campbell attacked Renae Ahlers Wicklund, brutally raping her in her own home in front of her 16-month-old daughter. After Campbell was released from prison after only 8 years, he sought revenge. When Campbell was through, he left behind the most gruesome crime scene local investigators had ever encountered.

**NO REMORSE** (0-7860-0231-X, $5.99)
By Bob Stewart
Kenneth Allen McDuff was a career criminal by the time he was a teenager. Then, in Fort Worth, Texas in 1966, he upped the ante. Arrested for three brutal murders, McDuff was sentenced to death. In 1972, his sentence was commuted to life imprisonment. He was paroled after only 23 years behind bars. In 1991 McDuff struck again, carving a bloody rampage of torture and murder across Texas.

**BROKEN SILENCE** (0-7860-0343-X, $5.99)
The Truth About Lee Harvey Oswald, LBJ, and the Assassination of JFK
By Ray "Tex" Brown with Don Lasseter
In 1963, two men approached Texas bounty hunter Ray "Tex" Brown. They needed someone to teach them how to shoot at a moving target—and they needed it fast. One of the men was Jack Ruby. The other was Lee Harvey Oswald. . . . Weeks later, after the assassination of JFK, Ray Brown was offered $5,000 to leave Ft. Worth and keep silent the rest of his life. The deal was arranged by none other than America's new president: Lyndon Baines Johnson.

*Available wherever paperbacks are sold, or order direct from the Publisher. Send cover price plus 50¢ per copy for mailing and handling to Kensington Publishing Corp., Consumer Orders, or call (toll free) 888-345-BOOK, to place your order using Mastercard or Visa. Residents of New York and Tennessee must include sales tax. DO NOT SEND CASH.*

# TRIANGLE

Irene Pence

Pinnacle Books
Kensington Publishing Corp.
http://www.pinnaclebooks.com

Some names have been changed to protect the privacy of individuals connected to this story.

PINNACLE BOOKS are published by

Kensington Publishing Corp.
850 Third Avenue
New York, NY 10022



First Printing: February, 1998
10 9 8 7 6 5 4 3 2 1

Printed in the United States of America

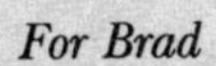
*For Brad*

# ACKNOWLEDGMENTS

This is Sandra Underhill's story. Without her, this book would not have been written. Through over 40 interviews that spanned nine months, I learned about her life of unconscionable twists. Thank you, Sandra, for your honesty, and sharing the pain that frequently comprised a good deal of your life.

Carri Coppinger loved to write poetry; several of her poems are printed in this book.

The following people generously shared their expertise: Dr. Gary Sisler, Tarrant County assistant medical examiner; Sergeant Paul Kratz, Tarrant County homicide supervisor; Detective Eddie Neel, homicide investigator; and Officer Philip Woodward of the Fort Worth Police Department. Many thanks to the Fort Worth police for the crime scene photographs.

My sincere appreciation to the very cooperative Judge Don Leonard, and the Tarrant County Appeals Court including deputy district clerks Nancy Gilliland and Mickie Millerd. Many thanks also to Mansfield, Texas, Assistant Police Chief Steve Noonkester. David Nunlee of the Texas Department of Criminal Justice arranged for my prison visits for which I am grateful. I am indebted to Assistant Prison Warden Major Reeves and Lieutenant Breed at the Men's State Penitentiary, Ramsey Unit I, Rosharon, Texas; Sergeant D. Klepak of the Georgetown County Jail; and Sergeant Benson from Gatesville Women's Prison.

Thanks to Beth Bennett for expert information on the long-term results of child abuse, Franci Moses for her colorful descriptions of west Texas, Helen Ann Alspaugh for her knowledge of St. Louis county, Mike Lester for his help, and to the many people who gave me time and information but requested anonymity.

Kudos for the fine-tuning and suggestions from my incomparable gang and writers all: Julie Benson, Dan Hurwitz, Jim Loose, Heiko Mueller, and Alpha Ward-Burns.

My sincere gratitude to my resourceful agent, Janet Wilkins Manus, and the wonderful people at Pinnacle Books: Editor-in-Chief Paul Dinas, editorial assistant Katherine Gayle, Amy Morgenstern, assistant production editor, and my hardworking and patient consulting editor Karen Haas.

Dialogue has been extracted from the murder trial, court documents, and the author's interviews. Some scenes have been dramatically recreated to portray episodes that occurred.

The author has chosen to change names of some individuals to afford them privacy. Any similarity between the fictitious names used and those of living persons is entirely coincidental.

# PART I

# Chapter One

The dead have their own way of communicating. The decomposing body had sat for three days inside a barrel; first in a garage, and now on a patio under a relentless July sun. The odors emanating from the corpse refused to be silenced in the steamy 100-degree temperatures that dipped no cooler than 90 at night. Literally, the woman inside was cooking.

By now her skin had slipped, leaving the top of her head bald. Gases bloating her body forced her tongue and right eye to protrude. Her left eye was missing.

They had argued three days ago. He ordered her out of his house, as he had many women, but she refused to go. The baseball bat he used to threaten her still lay by the side of the bed. He angrily stomped out of the bedroom only to return with a gun.

Then he had yelled, "Get your butt out of my house, and I mean now!"

She screamed back, "You've always been a son of a bitch, but I won't leave without my friend!"

Anger gripped him, his finger tightened on the trigger, and abruptly, gunpowder blasted the room. The woman instantly dropped to the floor, her face turned toward the wall, splattering it with blood. Her blood poured onto the carpet as he rushed to check her pulse. Nothing. The bullet had torn into the corner of her left eye, destroying her eyelid and cornea until only a dark space stared back at him.

He ran from the room, down the stairs, and into his garage. He grabbed one of two blue plastic barrels sitting there and hauled it upstairs.

Laying the open barrel on the floor at her feet, he gradually slid the vessel up her legs and past her hips, pushing her down all the while until her lifeless legs folded. He shoved her body deeper into the three-foot tall container until she had coiled into a fetal position.

Perspiration rolled from his body as he struggled to set the barrel upright. After he had pressed her head down so it would clear the barrel's top, he reached for the white plastic lid. A metal band encircled the lid and connected to a gasket. After fitting the lid in place, he securely locked the ring.

He learned the meaning of "dead weight" when he tried to pick up the barrel. Finding that impossible, he dragged the container out of the room toward the carpeted stairs and turned it on its side. Bumping each stair, he slid the drum down the winding staircase, then rolled it out to the garage where he stood it upright, lest too much pressure push against the lid.

After making a couple of phone calls, he hurried to his bedroom to take a shower, change clothes, and douse his face with Brut. Then he walked downstairs and into his garage, trying to avoid the barrel. His two Mercedes awaited him there—one a yellow sports coupe, the other a red sedan. He climbed into the coupe, backed out of his garage, and closed the door.

But he would return. The woman would not let him forget her. Soon she would call to him with an acrid aroma he couldn't ignore.

# Chapter Two

The Fort Worth, Texas, emergency operator received the 911 call at twenty minutes past two on Saturday morning, July 16, 1994. A woman had called to report that her best friend had been murdered and stuffed into a barrel. The call originated from the Residence Inn on the Trinity River.

Officer Brian Raynsford, a young, dark-haired Fort Worth policeman with five years' experience, manned the 11 P.M. to 7 A.M. shift. His patrol unit, the first line of defense for any emergency in the city, received the call from the police dispatcher.

Raynsford hurried into the hotel's lobby to see a shaking, crying woman who held a small baby and identified herself as Sandra Underhill.

"My best friend, Carri Coppinger, is dead," Underhill reiterated. "She was shot last Wednesday and she's in a barrel at Miles Bondurant's duplex over on Collinwood. Miles went there now to commit suicide."

With that information, Raynsford ran to the two-way radio in his patrol car and summoned Sergeants Gary Morris and Chris Beckrich. "Meet me at the Residence Inn," he told them. "I've got a woman here who's giving me info on a murder."

Once the additional officers arrived at the hotel and questioned Underhill, they decided they all should go to Collinwood Avenue. But first they went to secure Room 813, where Bondurant and Underhill had been registered and briefly stayed. The police considered the room a crime scene and wanted no one tampering with it.

Sergeant Morris asked Sandra Underhill for Bondurant's house number, then called police headquarters and told them to contact a judge to issue a search warrant.

"I'll consent to a search," Underhill offered.

The men appeared to consider the possibility. "Do you own the house?"

She shook her head.

"Don't worry," Morris told her. "We'll get a warrant."

Also patrolling the streets on that stifling night were Officers Philip Woodward and James Burchfield. They too had pulled the midnight shift, which so far had been uneventful. As they cruised their northwest territory, they listened to calls crackle over the police radio and watched the computer screen in their squad car display Sandra Underhill's story.

Soon they picked up on Raynsford's conversation with their patrol sergeant, Officer Chris Beckrich. They heard Beckrich say, "No need using up police radio air time. Let's switch to talk channel."

Woodward switched to the channel officers use to more fully discuss a serious situation. "Probably some damn nut case," he said to Burchfield, thinking how absurd the story sounded. "We'll go out there and find some dead dog in a barrel." Then Woodward heard Beckrich say, "We need to get some officers out to that house."

As Woodward leaned closer to his computer screen, the names "Bondurant" and "Collinwood" captured him. "That's where I've been dragged out a couple times on domestic disturbance calls.'' He broke into talk channel, ''Officers Woodward and Burchfield here. We can get there in five minutes. I'm familiar with that house.''

Beckrich answered, ''Great. You two go, see what you can find, and call me back.''

Immediately, they steered their patrol car toward Collinwood Avenue.

The sophisticated, quiet neighborhood lay in darkness except for a spattering of street lights when Woodward and Burchfield parked their squad car in front of Bondurant's home. They were the first to arrive and they trudged over the grass of the vacant lot that bordered the duplex. After shining flashlights along the side of the structure, they easily found the fenced patio.

Remembering his prior visits, the size of Bondurant's duplex impressed Woodward. ''This neighborhood's too rich for my paycheck.''

''Yeah. We don't often find someone wasted in this part of town,'' Burchfield said.

Just as they headed toward the fence, a breeze kicked up. ''Smell that?'' Burchfield asked.

''I've smelled decomposing bodies before,'' Woodward said, ''but this one's different. It's like someone's tried to cover it up with Glade.''

The whirl of fans greeted them as they neared the patio. They squinted through the narrow spaces between the wooden slats made visible by a light coming from the house. Woodward shined his flashlight through the slender openings and caught a glimpse of the blue barrel.

''Give me a hand,'' he said, ''I need to see over the fence to make sure.'' Burchfield knelt down and cupped his hands in a foot hold for the 200-pound officer who threw his muscular arms over the top of the fence. Immediately, Woodward's flashlight found its target. ''There's the barrel, just as advertised. You ought to see this mess. It's covered with freshners. Containers of insect repellent are sitting around. There's a bunch of white powder on the concrete around the barrel. Smells like the rug cleaner my wife uses. And there's a charcoal broiler with a couple fans on it."

"Where's that light coming from?" Burchfield asked.

"Through French doors leading from the house to the patio." He jumped down to the ground.

"Looks like somebody's home. We better start securing the scene."

Sergeant Beckrich's call woke Homicide Detective Eddie Neel at 2:38 A.M.

Neel's nine years in homicide had conditioned him to instantly wake up from a deep sleep, especially when he received a call about a possible murder. "Check to see if anyone's in the house and verify that Ms. Underhill's a resident. It would be good to get authorization to search the place from both her and Bondurant."

The officers knew that they could enter the property if no one answered the door in case someone inside needed medical assistance. But before they could touch any evidence they'd need a search warrant.

Detective Neel would be the lead homicide investigator on the case. The detective had grown up with investigations by following in the footsteps of his father, who retired as a lieutenant after 30 years with the Fort Worth Police.

Neel immediately dialed Sgt. Paul Kratz, who headed homicide, to alert him to the possible crime.

By now Raynsford, Morris, and Beckrich had joined Woodward and Burchfield. The most senior officer was Morris, who had worked his way into commandeering the midnight shift after 15 years on the force. "We need to get inside this place, and fast. His girlfriend told us he might commit suicide," Morris warned.

Woodward walked to the front of the house and knocked

on the door. He waited, then pounded again. No one answered. He called to Raynsford, "I think Bondurant's in there. Get his phone number and give him a call."

Miles Bondurant stopped speaking into his tape recorder when he heard someone at his front door. He heard voices outside and car doors slamming. He hurried to his front window and saw police roaming his yard. Flustered, he rushed back to his den, dropped the recorder on the sofa, picked up his cellular phone, and dialed Calvin Jacobs, his business attorney of 12 years. He glanced at his watch; almost 4 A.M., an awful hour to call anyone, but surely his attorney would understand. When no one answered, Bondurant left a message on the lawyer's recorder after he heard the beep: "This is Miles Bondurant. I was hoping I could talk to you because I intend to take my life—"

"Miles?" Jacobs interrupted. "I'm here. What on earth is wrong?"

Bondurant told him about his suicide plans.

"Hold on, Miles. Tell me what's happened."

"Sandra's killed that lesbian who's been living here with us."

"Oh, my God."

"Yeah. She put her body in a barrel and it's been sitting in the garage for a couple days. Everything's such a mess. I just wanted you to know so you can take care of everything."

"Miles there's no reason for you to—"

Bondurant told the attorney to hang on and answered a beep that signaled another call coming in.

"Hello?"

"Miles Bondurant? This is Officer Raynsford with the Fort Worth Police Department. We're parked in front of your house. We need you to come out and talk with us."

"What's the problem?" Bondurant asked.

"Sir, this is the Forth Worth Police Department. We are asking you to come outside immediately."

"Okay. In a few minutes."

He transferred back to Jacobs and told him about the call from the police.

"Listen to me," his attorney pleaded. "Go outside and cooperate. And, Miles, for heaven's sake, there's no reason to kill yourself."

Sandra Underhill sat in Sergeant Morris's squad car in front of Bondurant's house. Feeling so nervous she could no longer sit still, she picked up her 5-month-old son, Cody, in his infant seat, grabbed the diaper bag, and went outside, finally settling on the curb across the street. The sultry night had moistened her short dark hair, which now stuck to her head. She pulled out her cigarettes and watched the officers string yellow crime tape around the house.

One squad car after another, red and blue lights whirling, screeched to a halt in front of the house. In minutes, seven police cars lined the street. Officers, crime scene investigators, and homicide detectives hurried out of their cars.

Thanks to their police scanners, television crews from two different channels showed up almost as fast as the police, their interest heightened by the description of the victim's peculiar coffin.

Awakened by the lights, neighbors started filing out of their homes to gape at the scene. Underhill didn't speak to them. When she had first moved in, word filtered through the neighborhood that she had been in prison. She had always felt that she didn't belong in this neighborhood and suspected her neighbors agreed.

The police still didn't have a search warrant and considered letting Underhill sign a consent form. But first, following Detective Neel's directions, they needed to make certain she actually lived at the Collinwood address. They called Bondurant's landlady, Christine Logan, who lived in the adjoining duplex.

When Logan's phone rang at 4 A.M., she looked at the digital clock on her nightstand and picked up the phone.

"Ms. Logan, this is the Fort Worth Police Department."

"Do you have any idea what time it is?"

"Yes, ma'am. We're sorry to bother you, but we need to ask you some important questions."

"How do I even know you're the police?"

"Look out your window, ma'am."

Logan got out of bed and went to her front window. She saw all the squad cars snaked along her front curb, accompanied by over a dozen police officers. She also saw Sandra Underhill holding the baby. She hurried back to her phone and told the officer she'd be right down.

Minutes later, Logan ran out of her duplex dressed in pink slacks and a matching blouse, while combing her hair with her fingers. She asked what all the commotion was about.

"We've had a report that there's a dead woman in a barrel in there," he said, nodding toward Bondurant's duplex.

Christine Logan's hand flew to her mouth. "Oh, no!"

"Do you know Sandra Underhill?" the officer asked.

Logan looked in Underhill's direction. "I know who she is. She's lived here on and off for a couple years." Then she shook her head. "Whatever possessed a man like Miles to take her in is beyond me."

Bondurant's phone rang again. "Mr. Bondurant, this is Officer Raynsford. Are you coming?"

"Yes, sir," Bondurant said, at the same time he emerged

through the front door, still talking to the officer on his cellular phone.

The police ordered Bondurant to put his hands in the air. Bondurant obeyed and held the phone high. Camera lights flashed and television cameras whirled. A colored photograph of Bondurant at his door would appear Sunday morning on the front page of the *Fort Worth Star-Telegram.*

"Put your phone down, sir," Raynsford ordered.

Bondurant placed his phone just inside his entry and again raised his hands. Raynsford and Woodward hurried up to him. Woodward patted him down. Although Bondurant appeared calm, Woodward would later say he could feel Bondurant shake as he searched for weapons.

Raynsford said, "We need to talk with you, Mr. Bondurant. Please accompany us to our car."

Officers Morris and Beckrich stood by the car as Raynsford placed the tall suspect in the backseat on the passenger side. Then Raynsford sat behind the wheel, but left the door open so Morris and Beckrich could hear. Raynsford pulled out his Miranda card and read Bondurant his rights. "Mr. Bondurant, we've been advised that there's a dead body in your house. We need to check out the story," he said, looking at Bondurant who still seemed extraordinarily calm.

Raynsford handed him a form. "Would you be willing to sign this?" Bondurant squinted in the car's dim overhead light at the consent to search.

"Let's read it in the headlights, sir," Raynsford suggested. The three officers stood with him in front of the police car.

As Bondurant started to read, he said, "Should I call my lawyer?"

Raynsford nodded to Morris and Beckrich, indicating he wanted to talk with them out of Bondurant's earshot. Standing behind the squad car, Beckrich said, "If he wants to get a lawyer instead of signing the consent to search, let's back off and get one from a judge."

When the officers returned, Bondurant said, "Okay, I'll sign the form."

They placed their suspect back in the car and called two officers to guard him.

Then Raynsford raised his arm and pointed to the duplex, signaling to all the police that they now had permission to enter.

Twenty uniformed men and women ran up the sidewalk and dashed inside. The detectives turned on all the inside lights and the crime scene experts brought their own portable floodlights to scan for evidence. Police crime photographers flashed more lights as they snapped pictures of the scene.

Beckrich called Detective Neel again to report that he had Bondurant's signature on the consent form. Neel told him to verify the barrel's contents.

Woodward, who had seen the barrel first, followed the crime scene investigators to the patio and waited until photographs were taken before touching the barrel.

Although only 25, Woodward had been walking in on decomposing bodies for years. His father, a police officer, had taken young Philip along to investigate calls from people concerned about relatives who didn't answer the phone or doorbell for days at a time.

Despite having lived through his father being shot at, stabbed, and at one time immobilized for a year in a body cast, Woodward followed his father into the Fort Worth Police Department. He did not, however, become a "motor jock" like his dad.

After the photos were taken, five police officers and two crime scene experts milled around the small patio, staring at the three-foot tall cylinder.

"Boy, even with bulging sides, it looks incredibly small to have a person inside," Sergeant Morris said.

Woodward agreed, and Morris glanced at him. "Looks like you're the youngest here. Probably real eager. Right?"

Woodward knew what was coming. His father being Supervisor of the Crime Scene Division never made his job any easier.

"Okay. I'll open it," Woodward said, and reached for his gloves. He didn't trust the police-issued thin latex, powder-coated ones. Instead, he bought the kind worn by the medical examiners. Pulling on the blue, thick rubber gloves, he took hold of the barrel, pivoting it toward him to find the clasp on the metal band. When he freed the clasp and broke the dried caulk, air gushed out with the swoosh of a newly opened can of coffee—a sound and odor he would never forget. From how it smelled, the barrel may as well have been filled with rotten eggs. He took off the band and looked up at his fellow officers. All eyes were on the barrel, and all of those eyes were large. Woodward grabbed the sides of the plastic lid and tried to remove it, but it wouldn't budge. After twisting it back and forth, the lid finally broke free. Glancing at its underside, he found hair and skin clinging there, and realized what had kept the lid in place.

Woodward looked down into the barrel and Carri Coppinger stared up at him. "Hey, man," he said, "There *is* a body in here." When he raised his head, the other officers had vanished. The two crime scene experts had stayed, but his sergeant was throwing up in the begonias.

As the crime scene investigators moved in to photograph everything, Officer Raynsford rushed outside to his squad car and opened the door. He motioned for Bondurant to get out. Once Bondurant stood outside, Raynsford arrested him and dug out a Miranda card from his shirt pocket to read him his rights again. Bondurant remained motionless until Raynsford pulled his hands behind his back to snap on handcuffs.

Then his breath quickened and he shouted, "Sandra did this! Sandra killed Carri!"

# PART II

# Chapter Three

Sandra Underhill lay sprawled on her cot in the Georgetown County Jail in a gloomy, windowless room. It had been 15 months since the police had pried her 6-week-old daughter, Angelina, from her arms, slapped handcuffs on her, and ushered her out to their squad car.

Her husband, Robert, had called the police; he gave them a current picture of her and told them exactly what time she'd be home. When they arrested her on February 9, 1990, he only stood and watched.

That bitter memory stayed with her as she eyed the room she shared with two other women. They each had their own individual cell that held a bunk, a desk, and a stainless steel commode and mirror, but their communal shower made the room steam like a sauna when someone used it. Underhill felt smothered. Once released from this 15-year sentence, she vowed to never violate her parole.

Although she yearned to be free, all her life she had managed to put herself under someone's thumb, and she wondered why.

* * *

In late fall, 1967, 4-year-old Sandra looked up at the red, livid face of her angry mother, Elaina.

"Damn it, Sandra, get out! Our bedroom is off limits to you. I don't expect to have to tell you one more time."

"But, Mama. I'm hungry," she cried. Instantly Sandra felt the burning sting of her mother's open hand against her cheek.

"I'll teach her a lesson," her stepfather, Kirby Lackner, warned. He rushed out of bed and crossed the floor of the small room in two steps, grabbing the panicked child and flipping her to the floor. Then he beat her bottom savagely and cuffed the back of her head. "You heard your mother. Get!"

Sobbing and immobilized with fear, Sandra stared through her tears at the two people who had brought her so much pain. But her stepfather would have no more of her presence. He picked her up by her left wrist, and dragged her just high enough so her small feet barely brushed the floor. He hurried to open the front door, then threw her out.

Sandra felt the splinters from the wooden porch pierce her bottom. She heard the loud click of the lock as she found herself outside, bruised, and alone.

Tears of self-pity formed in Sandra Underhill's eyes as she reflected on the perpetual beatings and the revolving door of her mother's husbands. It was hard to think of her life in any kind of order, because when she looked back, there had been no order. Underhill had been raised by a mother who lacked any conscience or capacity to give her the love and approval she craved.

In 1973, her mother married Harry Forsell. Underhill knew that Harry adored his new wife, now pregnant with his child, but she didn't know it would change her life. Underhill couldn't suppress her surprise after she and her sisters had completed their school year at the end of May, when their mother gathered them together.

"Hurry and sit down! Damn it, everybody, I said sit down. I have something very important to tell you." Referring to her recent bouts of morning sickness she said, "You know I haven't been feeling well. I must tell you. I'm dying."

Sandra and the other children gasped and began crying. True, their mother had beat them, but she was their mother, nevertheless, and they felt dependent on her.

Elaina pointed a stubby finger at her four daughters and said, "There's only one thing to do. Each of you *must* return to your father."

Elaina ignored her daughters' tears and pleadings, and the girls obediently made phone calls to their respective dads. Sandra went to her bedroom to fold her meager belongings, and tears fell on her secondhand clothes. She shook her head, realizing that she and her sisters were being thrown away like so much rubbish. She still felt worthless when her father, Leroy George Coburn, arrived.

Ten-year-old Sandra and her sister, Charlotte, 12, shuffled off to Coburn's car. Ensign Coburn had been in the United States Navy for 18 years and was currently stationed at Pensacola, Florida. He had also been stationed in Florida when Sandra was born on January 15, 1963.

Coburn looked rugged and handsome with his reddish-blond beard and mustache. Sandra knew him well from visiting for a month each summer since her parents had divorced nine years before.

Their father drove them to Florida, where they already had close friendships with Coburn's daughters from his second marriage, 8-year-old Lynn and 6-year-old Susie. His new wife, a tender-hearted woman named Willa Coburn, warmly hugged Sandra and Charlotte.

That summer, on August 25, 1973, a typically hot, sultry Florida day, Leroy Coburn said, "Everybody grab your bathing suits and get in the car. Mom's made a picnic lunch. We're going to the beach!"

He took them to the Pensacola beach on the Gulf of Mexico. They piled out of the car and his daughter, Lynn, eagerly rushed to the waves. Suddenly she became caught in the undertow.

A look of panic froze on Lynn's face as the frightened girl glanced back at the distant shore. Sandra screamed, "Dad, go get Lynn! She's way out there!"

Coburn jumped into the surf and reached Lynn, already hysterical as waves crashed over her. Then from sheer fright, she clawed wildly and kicked at her father. One foot hit Coburn's chin, knocking him backwards and forcing him to gulp salty water.

Seeing the commotion, a man in a boat headed toward Lynn and her father. The family clapped and happily watched the man pull Lynn into his boat. But at the same time, a much larger boat approached at great speed and churned towering waves over Coburn. The man in the first boat looked around, but seeing no one else, turned his craft with Lynn safely on board and headed for shore.

Sandra gasped, watching her exhausted father fight the ocean. Then in horror she saw him sink under the water. She and his family screamed in terror, 50 feet away on shore, and waved their arms to attract the boat's captain. Coburn's head bobbed up one last time, and the frantic family yelled louder. But their cries for help were muffled on the crowded beach, and they could do nothing but watch in hysteria as Coburn drowned.

Because of Leroy Coburn's death, only three months after the girls went to live with him, they were forced to return to their "dying" mother.

Sandra and Charlotte plodded back into the small house, and their mother screamed, "You damn girls have ruined my life!"

"How?" they both asked.

"Hell, by being born," she said.

That welcome brought Sandra back to the reality of living with her tyrannical mother. She did whatever her mother demanded in order to find the tranquility that obedience afforded. By the time Sandra turned 14, she cooked and cleaned for the entire family.

In early February, 1977, she burst into the house. "I've been invited to the school's Valentine dance. This will be my first date!"

"That's out of the question," Elaina said. "You have too much to do around here to go to some silly dance."

"I work hard both here and at school. I get all A's and B's. Why can't I go?"

Her mother simply shook her head. Finally, after two weeks of Sandra's pleading, Elaina relented and allowed her to accept the invitation.

With no money for a new dress, Sandra rummaged through her mother's clothes. She found an old dress her mother no longer wore that had been shoved back in a dark closet. First she washed it in the bathtub, the only place her family laundered clothes. Then, adeptly maneuvering a needle and thread, Sandra shortened the skirt and narrowed the sides to fit her trim figure.

On the night of the dance, Sandra looked at her reflection in her bedroom mirror and feared she would be embarrassed in her matronly, gray print dress. But she brushed her long, thick, naturally wavy hair and felt better about herself. Sandra was unaware that she had a pretty face because her mother constantly maligned her looks. It was a paradox, for Sandra and her mother looked very much alike, except that her mother lacked Sandra's thick hair and had resorted to wearing wigs.

Elaina demanded that Sandra be home by eleven, even though the dance didn't end until midnight.

At the dance later, Sandra felt awkward and out of place. The other girls knew all the latest steps and wore colorful taffeta dresses. Eventually, the party atmosphere worked its magic and she enjoyed being in the company of people her own age. As her curfew approached, she had trouble convincing her date to leave more than an hour before the dance ended. Finally at 11:20 P.M. Sandra hurried back inside her house.

* * *

Harry Forsell and her mother were waiting. Her mother sat frowning, and her voice became hoarse with rage. "You were with that young man, weren't you, Sandra?"

"What?" Her mother's meaning puzzled Sandra.

"You've had sex with him."

"No, ma'am. I have not. I've never had sex."

"I don't believe you," her mother hissed and immediately rushed her into the bathroom where she stripped her naked to check.

"We didn't have sex," Sandra insisted. "Ask the kids we were with. We were never alone all evening." Sandra couldn't smell the pungent alcohol that frequently scented her mother's words, so she became more appalled that her mother was cold sober and treating her like this. Finally, after Sandra passed inspection, her mother let her dress. She took Sandra back to the living room where Forsell stood with a pair of shears.

Sandra looked at the sharp blades in his hand and felt a tremor move through her body. "I was only twenty minutes late," she said in a small, frightened voice.

"Shut up," her mother ordered. "We know how to deal with you."

Sandra looked again at the scissors, and saw that Forsell also held the clippers they used on the dog. As he came closer she couldn't smell any fumes on his breath either. Her surrealistic nightmare grew when she realized these people were not intoxicated but, nevertheless, displayed the emotions of drunken sadists.

"We can tie you into that chair or you can sit there while we shave your head," he threatened.

Sandra's hands flew up in a futile attempt to protect her hair. "Oh, my God, no! Not my hair!"

"We gave you your choice," her mother told her.

Forsell shoved the shears closer to her face in a threatening gesture. "Well?"

Numbly, Sandra sat as her mother grabbed the scissors

from Forsell and snipped off a section of hair above her ear. Eighteen inches of brown waves fell to the floor. Then she cut the remaining beautiful length from her hair. Sandra sat sobbing. Her hands covered her face so she wouldn't see the jagged clumps fall to the floor. Then her mother picked up the electric clippers and shaved a trench across her head, exposing the pink scalp underneath.

Although Sandra sat like a petrified stone, her mind raced. What could she do to these people? How could she kill her mother? Maybe she could sneak into her room at night with a knife and find that place between her shoulderblades where a sharp stab would cause sudden death. She had seen that on TV. Or maybe she could get hold of some rat poison the other tenants used to kill the armies of rodents that roamed the decrepit complex. A little of that in her mother's coffee would surely work. Those thoughts gave Sandra solace as the clippers tugged and burned her skin. Within 15 minutes, her head shined bald and her long brown tresses lay on the floor, circling her like a fallen halo.

Sandra's sole asset, her only source of confidence, had been stolen from her. Realizing she had but one recourse, Sandra decided to run away from home.

Elvia, Sandra Underhill's cellmate, interrupted her recollections by pointing to a classified ad in the *Fort Worth Star-Telegram*. Underhill had never seen the personals before, but she became excited as she read: "I have a most unusual offer to make to an ambitious, clean-cut woman, in her mid 20s to 30s. The primary criteria is that this person would like to obtain a college degree. The degree, spending money, credit cards and an automobile will be gifts from me. Working is not necessary."

Underhill had stumbled down a bumpy road all of her life. Now she envisioned the ad as a means to an education and a chance to be someone. The man who composed it had to be her knight in shining armor, she thought as she eagerly continued studying his prerequisites: "This woman must have a spirit, personality and better than average looks. I am a divorced white male, own my own business, mid-40s, better than average looking, sportsman, fun and kind."

Yes, he had to be kind, she thought, none other than a saint would make such an offer. And Sandra Underhill had spirit. Her spirit, frequently reaching to the point of impulsiveness, had often led her into trouble. She grabbed whatever came along that promised instant happiness. But frequently during her 27 years, the promises had proven empty.

Although Underhill tried not to be impressed with the man's listing of his beautiful home, luxury cars, and all the other enticements, she was, even though those were things she had never dreamed of having. She returned to the ad: "The woman will not be just a loving comrade, but a very good friend. Send recent picture, resumé and brief personal history to I.D. #28100."

Underhill tossed the newspaper aside, swung her legs over her cot, and immediately reached for the locked box all inmates have under their beds. She pulled out a ruled yellow tablet, and moved to the fold-down metal table to write her response to I.D. #28100. Always frank and open, she told him about being in jail and that she would soon be transferred to the state prison at Gatesville, Texas. She confided that she hadn't graduated from high school but had worked hard to earn her General Education Diploma. She shared that she had always longed for a college education, but with her background, she never imagined it possible.

Five pages later, she signed her name and slipped the yellow sheets into a plain white envelope, wondering what the man must be like who would write such an ad.

# Chapter Four

On the first Monday of February, 1991, a cold wind whirled through Fort Worth, Texas, as Warren Miles Bondurant left his office to drive to the post office. He fastened the top button of his cashmere sports coat to ward off the biting chill. He had never read the personal columns before, let alone advertised in them, but since he had placed an ad in the *Star-Telegram* a week ago, his daily routine of visiting the post office had taken on an increasingly exciting allure.

The wealthy Texan hoped the ad would give him a generous selection of women other than the greedy socialites he had dated and sometimes married. Bondurant wanted to rid himself of their overly high expectations and demanding, outlandish tastes. He wanted a woman who would truly appreciate what he had to offer. Now he had difficulty whittling down the large number of responses that had more than met his expectations. He grew increasingly astounded at the quality and beauty of the women.

Bondurant slipped his key into the post office box and tugged at the bundle of envelopes stuffed inside, while an intermingled whiff of perfume teased his nostrils. He hurried to his yellow Mercedes and excitedly drove home to rummage through the day's cache.

For a man who should have been happy owning his own business and having three healthy, grown children, he wasn't. He hoped his two married daughters loved him, but his son treated him with such indifference that a tenseness existed between the two. He often regretted divorcing Marian, his first wife and the mother of his three children. She was attractive and fashionable. They had married in 1965, two years after he had graduated from Texas Christian University with a degree in business. Before college, he had spent three years in the army and then dabbled in the oil fields of New Mexico and Utah.

But in the 1980s his business soared, making him $40,000 a month, and with that kind of money he could attract a much younger woman than Marian, his wife of 18 years. So he dropped her like a worn-out suit and chased after Phyllis, a doctor's daughter from a prominent family. That marriage lasted only two years.

Splashing Macallan scotch over a collection of ice cubes, he flipped on his CD player and Frank Sinatra warbled "My Way" through his house. He sat comfortably in his favorite leather chair and rested his reading glasses on his nose before reaching for the stack of envelopes.

The first response came from a woman named Vickie Willis. Willis had been a high school cheerleader, and at 25 still looked like one. Willis stated that her collegiate hopes were dashed by her father's untimely death shortly before her high school graduation. A possibility, he thought as he laid her letter aside.

The next letter was from a Patrice Barnard and had been printed on a computer. Barnard had already enrolled in a university and now wanted Bondurant to finance her education. He gazed at her picture and raised his eyebrows in approval, admiring the young blonde's aristocratic features.

"Nah," he said, dismissing her. She looked too much like his third wife, Kimberly. He had bought Kimberly a gorgeous two-story house facing River Crest Country Club. Then he saw the beautiful woman's cold, calculating side. She had invented one demand after another. Finally, when she said, "I'm the only woman at the club without a canary yellow diamond so you had better start shopping," he knew he wanted out. But it had cost him. Kimberly hired the best divorce lawyer in Forth Worth and sued him for a million dollars. Bondurant skillfully maneuvered around that by declaring personal bankruptcy. Thanks to Texas's generous bankruptcy laws, he kept many of his assets.

After that he went on a rampage and dated many different women, prompting his friend, Assistant Chief of Police Steve Noonkester, to say, "Miles, I think you've run the gambit with every eligible woman in Tarrant County."

He knew Noonkester was right, but the last woman in his life, Teresa Corbett, stayed with him for three years. He had given her a college education, a car, and clothes, yet she showed no gratitude.

One day he decided to get even, and when he held the beautiful woman close to him he said, "Teresa, you have the sexiest body. Let me take some pictures so I can always keep that image with me." He proceeded to take several nude photographs of her. Then he had copies made and threatened to mail them to her family if she didn't behave. One day he came home to find she had fled with everything he had bought her.

He reached for the next envelope and a photograph slid out, revealing a moon-shaped face that no doubt rested on an equally moon-shaped body. Bondurant didn't bother to read the letter. He had spent hours every week in the gym to keep his 6′3″ frame at a trim 200 pounds, and didn't want to waste that physique on anyone who had let herself go.

He continued sorting through the day's 17 letters like a pageant judge choosing Miss America. The eager women included all their positive assets, asserting that they were "intelligent, well-traveled, gourmet cooks," et cetera, until their identities melted together.

One of the last letters had a distinction all its own. For one thing, it was much thicker than the rest. That intrigued him. Then he noticed the return address: Georgetown County Jail, and shook his head in disbelief. But, curious, he pulled out the cluster of pages and began reading. The cheap writing paper looked far different than the other women's stationery, but the printing was neat and stylized. He read the five sheets in only minutes, then found himself reading them again. He discovered that the woman had a witty and clever way with words. When she wrote "look," she had made eyes out of the Os. She drew smily faces, hearts, and tears. Although she had not included a photograph, she did include word pictures. She said she had pretty feet. Her hair was long. Then she drew pictures poking fun at herself. Frequently, Bondurant laughed out loud. He thought she sounded sincere for aspiring to clean up her life and make something of herself, saying she knew a college education would be the key. He remembered his own children having problems when they were younger and it sounded like this woman had experienced some of their difficulties.

Placing the other letters on the coffee table, he took out his Bondurant Corporation letterhead to draft his reply to Sandra Underhill. He complimented her forthrightness in telling him about her prison sentence, and described truthfulness as a virtue he held high. After reading about her life, Bondurant knew she truly needed him. It had been a long time since he felt needed, and that gave him a sense of importance. The other women in his life had given him only vacant stares when his gifts had fallen short of their expectations. Surely, he'd have no such problem with this woman. He included his phone number and an invitation for Sandra to call.

# Chapter Five

Sandra Underhill read Miles Bondurant's letter with such eagerness she thought she'd burst. Years ago when she had been a shy, abused 14-year-old, she'd vowed to change her timid ways. Now her exuberance for life allowed her to make friends easily, even with the prison guards.

She took pride in her record at Georgetown. After being there three weeks, the jail allowed her to submit an application to be a trustee. The jail administration interviewed her and a week later granted her the privileged designation, permitting her to wear the bright orange trustee uniform. Other inmates had to dress in navy, black, and brown and were locked in for the majority of time. Her new status allowed her the comparatively unrestricted quarters she shared with the two other trustees on her floor, Elvia and Kitty. She ran to them now and displayed Bondurant's letter for their screaming approval.

Amid awed exclamations, Kitty gushed, "Look, he wants you to call him."

"And I will, right after dinner," Underhill said.

At Georgetown, everyone ate dinner in their cells except

for the trustees. They pushed food carts down a maze of aisles and slid trays through slots in inmates' doors. Underhill relished the separate trustee laws. Prison officials never locked them in at night, allowing them to roam the halls at will. And their telephone privileges were as generous as those of a teenager with a private line.

Underhill quickly finished eating dinner, then dashed for the phones where only collect calls could be placed. Her hands, wet from perspiration, made it difficult to dial Bondurant's number. Impatiently, she waited for the operator to connect them, and then felt her throat tighten when the operator said, "Go ahead."

"Hello?" Underhill said, stuttering with nervous excitement.

"Sandra?" he asked. His voice was resonant and warm.

"Yes. Thanks for asking me to call." She liked the way he said her name. It sounded distinctive coming from his deep, mature voice.

"I don't know what you look like since you didn't send a picture," he said.

"I didn't have any here. No camera either. But I don't think you'll be disappointed."

Bondurant gave an approving "all right," then asked, "Are you short or tall?"

Underhill thought for a second. Knowing he was 6′3″, he probably preferred tall women, but she was only five feet. "Well, I'm not exactly tall." She giggled, "Rather, I'm exactly short."

"Well, that's all right. He paused, then asked, "Why are you in prison?"

"I got busted for drugs in Georgetown," she said without embarrassment. "The police caught me going five miles an hour at three in the morning. They pulled me over and wanted me to recite the alphabet. I guess I said my ABCs a little too fast." She laughed nervously. "It was my first offense, so the judge gave me probation, but I left town the next day without permission and that's a violation."

When the police arrested Sandra Underhill in St. Louis,

a judge asked her if she was still doing drugs, and she said no. After testing her, they found out she had lied and charged her with aggravated perjury.

"Didn't you have a lawyer?" Bondurant asked.

"Only someone appointed by the court. I served time in the county jail there before Texas extradited me. Everyone has to do some time in the state where the offense occurred."

Underhill wondered what Miles Bondurant thought of the accounting of her lawless past. To her, it seemed like people in his shoes never got into trouble.

He asked, "How much longer will you be in prison?"

"I've been here two months. I'll have another few weeks here, then seven or eight months at Gatesville. Originally, they sentenced me to fifteen years, but I'll probably serve a total of two."

"They'll just write off thirteen years?"

"Yeah, unless I goof up on parole and do something to get sent back to prison."

"What's the first thing you want to do when you get out?"

Underhill chuckled. "I want to take a bubble bath. Then have some Oreo cookies and milk."

"You're not like the women I'm used to," Bondurant said, his voice warmly complimentary.

"What are you used to?"

"Snooty women. I've given them maids and mansions, and they still wanted more."

"Maids and mansions," Underhill repeated in amazement. "You're gonna think this is odd, but my life in prison has sometimes been better than on the outside. Actually, prison isn't so bad. I have a job, a bed to sleep on, and nobody beats me."

"Beats you? Who beat you, Sandra?"

"Lots of people. I've been a regular whipping post. Started off with my mother and her husbands."

"Husbands?"

"She was married five times. Guess that's why I took the

beatings from my first husband. I didn't want to be like my mother. I only wanted to be married once."

Her first husband, Lonnie, had started her on methamphetamine when she was 17 and kept her on it regularly.

"I thought drugs were colossal," Underhill admitted. "For the first time, I could blot out all the bad things that had happened to me."

"I certainly hope you're off drugs," he said with a parental edge.

"Even if I could get them in jail, I wouldn't have the money. I'm clean now, and I won't go back because they really messed me up. They were fun in the beginning, but I think drugs turned Lonnie into a sicko, because he wanted me to have sex with other men in front of him. It turned him on. When I wouldn't, he'd break my arm or mess up my face until you couldn't recognize me. Twice he broke my nose. Once he slammed the car door on my foot. Broke all my toes."

"Oh, my God," Bondurant said, "what do you look like now?"

She laughed. "Don't worry, I'm fine. I did have to go to the hospital several times, but I never snitched because I was afraid of him. Besides, with all the nurses and doctors looking at me, I just couldn't admit that my own husband had done these things, so I'd tell them that someone broke into our house and attacked me."

"How did you stop the abuse?"

"One day I realized that my life had gone out of control just like my mother's. I knew I had to leave."

Despite Sandra Underhill's soap opera story, every word about her deprived life unwittingly corraled Bondurant. How little, he thought, it would take to make her happy, and how appreciative she would be. Here was someone he could transform. The thought excited him. He would make a lady out of Sandra Underhill.

* * *

That first call initiated a succession of nightly calls. Sometimes Underhill called him immediately after dinner and they would still be talking when the sun peeked over the guards' watch towers the next morning. On those occasions, Underhill had to run on her adrenaline the next day. Bondurant's monthly telephone bill climbed in excess of $3,000, but he encouraged her to continue calling; to keep open his lifeline to her.

Then the inevitable happened. Bondurant pressed Underhill to let him visit her in jail.

Sandra Underhill panicked. She believed in first impressions and she wanted to make a good one. But in jail she had no makeup and no way to fix her hair other than washing and combing it. Her orange prison jumpsuit, made of heavy, roughly woven cotton with "TRUSTEE" emblazoned on the back made her look fat. She had already shaved off a few pounds from what she had told Bondurant she weighed.

"Wait until I get to Gatesville," she pleaded. "You can come see me every weekend."

Bondurant sounded perplexed but agreed to wait until she moved.

A week after that phone call, Underhill tried to place her evening call, and couldn't get a dial tone on one of the phones designated for prisoners. Frustrated, she went to the guard who she frequently talked into buying her Big Mac's and then smuggling them back into jail.

"No phones tonight, Sandra. We're about to pull chain."

Underhill understood the prison vernacular for transferring inmates to the state prison. All contacts with the outside world were halted so transfers could be made under a blanket of secrecy in an effort to avoid escapes.

A guard woke Underhill at two the next morning and

told her to pack her belongings. She'd be making the 100-mile drive to Gatesville within an hour.

Another guard ushered her into a holding tank while the staff completed her paperwork. As she sat, she saw a guard coming toward her, clanging handcuffs and shackles. She watched as the guard bracketed cuffs on each of her wrists, then snapped them shut. The guard picked up metal bands that were similar but larger than her handcuffs and clamped them around her ankles. The bands were connected with 15 inches of heavy chain that allowed her to take only short steps. After the guard fastened everything, Sandra felt uncomfortable and humiliated.

The prison had sent one squad car and two policemen because only Sandra Underhill and one other woman were traveling tonight. Their car headed north on Highway 35, a four-lane, well-traveled interstate. Then at Temple it veered northwest onto a more narrow, asphalt road, where the flat, farm-dotted prairie gave way to gently rolling hills.

Underhill's nerves began to twitch when they reached Gatesville. The foursome turned north onto the prison road and she became uncontrollably nervous. Shaking all over, her handcuffs clinked together, and the chain rattled between her feet. She had seen movies involving prisons, but didn't realize how frightening being taken to one could actually be.

As the entourage approached the prison, the cluster of buildings appeared like an armed camp. Six of the seven units were reserved for women—one held maximum security and death row.

The sun had not yet lit the sky, but roaming spotlights zoomed in and out from the guard towers and flooded the grounds. Underhill expected high brick walls, but instead found tall, heavy metal fences topped with coiled, jagged razor wire that loomed even more terrifying and foreboding.

Gatesville would be a much more difficult experience for her. Once inside, a guard locked her in solitary confinement. She would stay there for 30 days so the prison could run medical and psychological tests. After that, another guard led her to a big dormitory called "the barn," constructed of concrete blocks and cement floors. It housed 100 caged inmates. A catwalk stretched above the open cells overlooking sleeping quarters, showers, and commodes. On it both male and female guards paced back and forth every minute of the day and night. Underhill only had to look up through the steam of her shower to meet the guards' eyes. The sole thought keeping her sane was that Gatesville would be the last of her incarceration.

A new experience awaited Sandra. She met the "men of the camp"—women who looked like handsome men, wore their hair shortly cropped and fought over "wives." Once the lesbians learned that Underhill wasn't interested, they left her alone, but she found crossing their path to be a skittish experience. One of the "wives" told her: "Honey, we weren't lesbians before we got put in the slammer. But I said to myself, face it. You're doin' life. Do you never want to have the closeness of another human being? It's tough the first few times. Almost makes you sick to have some woman feelin' your body. But you get used to it. You have to when it's all you got."

# Chapter Six

Sandra Underhill hadn't felt so high since her last line of coke. Although she had been clean for almost two years, she experienced the same rush knowing Miles Bondurant would arrive today. It had taken two months of processing prison forms to add his name to her visitor's list. By now, she had poured out her heart to him and they had shared many intimate secrets. Knowing she would meet him today made it impossible for her to relax.

Underhill spent extra time on her makeup, which she had purchased from the prison commissary. Bondurant had sent her $200 when she transferred to Gatesville, and with careful planning she thought that money should last over the next few months.

Smoothing down her white cotton pants and shirt that had been laundered every week, but never ironed, Underhill checked her reflection for the tenth time in her stainless steel mirror. She frowned at the obvious orange patch over her heart that held her Texas Correction Department number—508547. She thought it made her look so marked, so criminal. Finally, the time came for her to leave her cell for the visitor's room, and her very first visitor at Gatesville.

She hurried to the large rectangular room with soiled walls that at one time were off-white. The room smelled musty and its small windows covered with double layers of heavy metal mesh allowed scant light to filter through. Two concentric rows of chairs, divided by a metal screen, circled the room. The inmates sat on the inside row while guards ushered visitors to the outer circle. Guards on raised platforms overlooked all the inmates and their guests.

She plopped down on one of the yellow, plastic-covered chairs and kept eyeing the door, expectantly waiting for a tall, trim man. It was a guessing game since she had never seen his picture either.

As Underhill waited, she knew Miles Bondurant was being made to remove everything from his pockets, then a male guard would pat him down. She had been subjected to the same search, and afterwards she'd be strip-searched.

Not knowing what to do with her hands, Underhill continuously rubbed them on the pants of her uniform. Finally, the door opened and a guard directed a visitor to her. The man wore a straw hat with a floral band, a sports shirt, and walking shorts. He looked like he was on vacation.

When he stood in front of her, she smiled and asked, "Miles?"

He nodded and also smiled.

She studied his face, taking inventory of his features. His nose could be a little smaller, but all in all she thought him a nice-looking man. Thank goodness he wasn't gorgeous. Her lack of self-esteem convinced her she couldn't attract a real hunk. And besides, looks weren't all that important when this was the man who would rescue her.

He pulled out a chair directly in front of her and planted himself on it. His eyes grazed her face, her long hair, and her body hidden under the prison uniform, then he said, "Hello."

Sandra knew that voice. Warm and wise and familiar,

like an old friend. She knew him on the inside. It was the outside she had to get acquainted with.

Miles Bondurant clasped his large hands together in his lap. "My dear, you're different than I expected," he said without chivalry.

"What do you mean?" Nervously Underhill moistened her dry lips, feeling she had failed the first test.

"Nothing, honey." He tried to cover his remark. "Just different."

Words of endearment had flowed from his lips ever since their second phone call, and he had invited Sandra to do the same. But she liked his name, and preferred calling him Miles.

After they had discussed his long drive, and how green the cotton fields were outside the prison, an awkward silence penetrated their conversation. Underhill noticed that Bondurant continued looking around the visitor's room.

"I imagine pulling a few strings could get you out of this place," he told her.

"I have to serve my time," she said.

"There's more than one way to do things. I'll see what I can do," he said, with cocky arrogance.

Sandra felt intimidated by the mover and shaker in front of her. While he talked of getting her out, she worried if she'd ever see him again.

After more discussion of her release, a guard shouted, "Time's up," interrupting their conversation.

Underhill winced. "The past two hours were the quickest of my life."

Bondurant nodded and said, "Next week, honey?"

"Yes," she said, "next week," hoping he meant it.

Bondurant did come the next week and told Sandra he wanted to help set her free. "I got to thinking about a friend of my dad's, Del Hobbs. He has been on the parole board for years. So I gave Del a call. He told me to write the prison directly and guarantee them that I would give you a job and a place to live." Bondurant grinned broadly. "They had to buy my story. I told them I had known your father for years, and on his death bed he made me promise to take care of you. We'll be hearing from them," he said with a wink.

Underhill laughed at his concocted story while he seemed to be enjoying his game. She would let him take credit for her prison release, but she knew she would only be paroled after serving her required time—one month for each of the 15 years of her sentence. Seven months had been added because of the time required for extraditing her to Texas and her wait in the Georgetown jail.

In June, two weeks after Bondurant's letter, the prison administration summoned her to their office. She walked in and found a woman sitting behind a gray metal desk. The woman asked Sandra Underhill about her relationship with Miles Bondurant.

"I think he's serious about helping me, ma'am. Sure seems like he can afford all he's promised. You know, school, a place to live."

"Since he's guaranteed you a place to stay, you'll not have to go to a halfway house, but you'll be on parole for the rest of your sentence." She flipped through the manila file on her desk. "That would be roughly twelve more years, until 2004."

"Yes, ma'am."

Underhill went back to her cell and donned her black rubber work boots and returned to her prison maintenance job. But now with her release in sight, she worked more enthusiastically as she repaired door hinges, painted walls, and performed many other construction-type tasks thanks to the training she'd received from her second husband, Robert Underhill.

Sandra flushed with excitement when she tore open the envelope with "Texas Board of Pardons and Paroles" printed in the corner. She read that she would be released from prison in three weeks. Shooting her fist into the air and waving the letter, her yelps of celebration brought five other inmates running to see what had caused the commotion.

She would be assigned to a parole officer in Fort Worth, and according to the state's timeline, she'd be out by mid-August.

Underhill called Bondurant that night exuding her excitement.

"Doesn't surprise me," he told her. "When I wrote the parole board I knew they'd move fast on this. Believe me, doll, I make things happen."

# Chapter Seven

On August 14, 1991, Sandra Underhill dressed in a pair of purple cotton pants and a lavender and white polka dot shirt, one of the outfits made in the prison garment factory for newly released convicts. Although not what she would have chosen, the lightweight clothes were a pleasant departure from her coarse uniform.

It was past noon by the time all the paperwork had been processed. Prison officials handed Underhill a $200 check, then she boarded a bus that would transport her through the gates to freedom. Friends and relatives were never allowed to enter the prison walls to pick up inmates; reunions occured only after the prisoner had been released to the outside.

Underhill chose a bus seat several rows back from other just-released inmates. She had had enough of being crammed in with other people. Once they left the barbed wire and steel prison fences, she looked out the window on scenes she had been denied for months. The expansive fields and green trees delighted her and cars full of people wearing colorful clothes instead of uniforms fascinated her.

The bus motored them to a bank in Gatesville where they cashed their checks. Then they were dropped at a rickety gas station that doubled as the bus depot. They were now out of prison hands, and the driver gave them welcome news—a K-Mart could be found four blocks down the road.

At the store, Underhill selected jeans, t-shirts, and cigarettes. Then she spotted bikini panties trimmed with lace, and happily chose three pair to replace her plain cotton prison underpants, which were several sizes too large. Apparently K-Mart was familiar with accommodating ex-prisoners, because on her way out she found a barrel containing many garments she readily identified as prison-made. As she threw in her unwanted apparel, she thought it symbolic of throwing away her past life and beginning anew.

Bondurant had checked in and already paid for his room at Gatesville's Best Western Motel because they couldn't be sure of Sandra's arrival time.

Underhill hurried to the motel and knocked on the door to Room 14, the number given her by the desk clerk. As she stood waiting for her new life to begin, she prayed that the butterflies in her stomach would settle down.

Bondurant opened the door and they fell into an embrace, made all the more tender because it marked the first time they had touched. Sandra felt the warmth of his hands as he hugged her. Then he squeezed her shoulders and looked at her seductively.

"Let's get out of here, sweetie." He reached for her purchases and straightened his hat. Then he proudly escorted her to his Mercedes sports coupe where they sat on the cushioned leather seats. Bondurant inserted his key into the ignition and removed his hat.

At that moment Sandra Underhill looked up, astonished to see his balding pate. When she had first heard his handsome, strong, Texan voice on the phone, she had envisioned her knight in shining armor to have dark, abundant hair. Not wanting to upset him, she said nothing about his thinning locks, and reached for her cigarettes.

"You smoke?" Bondurant asked, frowning.

"Yeah. Isn't that okay?"

"Not in my car," he said with authority. Then in an attempt to soften his words he said more quietly, "No one ever smokes in my car." Slowly Bondurant guided his coupe to the side of the highway and nodded toward the door. Underhill could smoke, but she'd have to do it outside.

After she finished her cigarette, she fluffed her hair to rid it of any tobacco fumes, then returned to the plush comfort.

They chatted amicably about the school Sandra would attend and the computer courses she'd take.

"Even though this is the first time we've been alone, I feel that I know you so well," she said. Then more tentatively she added, "I think I've fallen in love with you."

Bondurant smiled. "Well, I'm ready for a relationship," he said with a smile.

Prison had given Underhill a lot of time to dream, and a large part of her dream involved Miles, making her realize that thinning hair wasn't all that important.

"I'm glad you like children," she said.

"Sure. Raised three."

"I can't wait to see mine."

Bondurant's back stiffened. "Children? Honey, you never told me about children." His grip tightened on the steering wheel.

"Miles, I certainly did." Her face turned red as her mind dashed back to the time she told him about her children during a late-night phone call.

"Well, that's right, you mentioned a two-year-old, Angelina. You told me your ex-husband had done a good job of raising her and you didn't think it would be right to take her away from him. Don't you recall saying you'd be just like a stranger to her?"

"Yes, she's with Robert. Angelina was so hard to leave. I'll never forget her little pink face and dark curls. But at the time I had a fifteen-year sentence ahead of me and thought I'd never see her again. So that's why I let Robert raise her.

"But I'm talking about Nicole and Joshua from my first marriage. You remember," she reminisced. "They're the ones in a foster home that I can now pick up and raise. I have full custody."

Bondurant stared straight ahead. Puzzled, he asked, "Why are they in a foster home?"

Underhill took a deep breath. "You're really going to think this sounds bad, but I had just left Lonnie and went to Georgetown. I got clean and sober and started going to church. The only job I could get at the time was driving a snow cone van.

"Every day I took the children to a baby-sitter from noon until dark. Now before I tell you this, you've got to believe that I would *never* abuse a child. But one day after I dropped off the kids, the sitter called Child Protective Services and swore that I took Nicole to her that morning with a cigarette burn on the back of her leg. I almost died to be accused of something like that. The sitter said she didn't smoke when I knew full well she did. But CPS picked up the kids and kept them for nine months. Can you imagine?"

"When there was no proof?"

"Isn't that awful? Then at my hearing, the baby-sitter wouldn't show her face. So all the charges were dropped and the state returned my children. Please know that as God is my witness, I never did what that baby-sitter said."

"That sure sounds unfair."

"Unfair . . . that's my middle name."

"Couldn't you have sued the state for not investigating the abuse any better than that?"

"I hired a lawyer and went to a lot of court hearings, but my money ran out before they decided anything."

"So you just accepted all that?"

"What else could I do? Anyway, the second time the state took my children—"

"The *second* time?"

"Yeah, I was drunk. This is so embarrassing, but that's the night Robert left me and went to St. Louis. I just couldn't take it, so I started drinking. I had the kids with me in a grocery store and someone saw me stumbling around and had the store call CPS."

Bondurant frowned. "I certainly hope you've learned to be more responsible."

"I have, because the next morning I woke up in jail not remembering a thing. It put me in shock to learn that CPS sent Nicole and Joshua back to foster care. Believe me, I'm clean now and that's how I'm going to stay. I can't wait to see the kids."

Bondurant shook his head. "You did *not* tell me about more children." He hit the steering wheel in disgust.

Sandra said, "I remember telling you what a good father you'd make. You're a better man than Robert Underhill and he didn't mind raising another man's children."

"Robert Underhill," Bondurant scoffed. "The one who broke your arms and feet?"

"No. You're thinking of Lonnie. Robert was a real macho guy and hit me a couple times when I spoke my mind, but after I'd leave for a few days, he'd be nicer."

When Sandra met Robert Underhill, he had a serious drinking problem. But by the time she went to jail, he had sobered up, formed his own construction company and begun putting his life together.

They drifted down the highway in silence for several minutes before Bondurant suggested stopping for dinner at Bubba's Barbecue, on the outskirts of Fort Worth.

At dinner Sandra Underhill licked barbecue sauce from her fingers and thought how deliciously it compared to the bland prison food she had eaten for two years. She almost pinched herself to make sure she wasn't dreaming.

They drove into Fort Worth. As Bondurant approached

his home, Sandra noticed that the houses were getting larger and the lawns were lushly green. He turned onto Collinwood Avenue and drove a few blocks, then stopped. "This is it," he announced.

Underhill looked up at the pretty, two-story brick duplex. Its mansard roof nestled under large oak trees. "My gosh! *This* is where you live?"

Bondurant opened his front door and Sandra couldn't remember seeing a more stunning home. She stepped into the travertine marble entry, then walked on an Oriental rug in the living room. As far as she could see, parquet flooring stretched throughout the downstairs. She craned her neck to look up at the soaring beamed ceiling, then reached out and felt the nubby tweed of two club chairs in front of a sit-down wet bar.

At first she couldn't find words. Then she said, "Miles, it's beautiful. I just love it!"

He smiled and led her around the house commenting, "I decorated this all by myself, sweetie. Picked out that sofa over there, these chairs here—in fact, all the furniture. I chose every painting, every accessory. Six months ago they featured this place in *GQ*."

*"GQ?"*

*"Gentlemen's Quarterly*. It's a magazine about the best in clothes, homes, et cetera."

"Wow." Underhill looked awestruck.

Beaming at her praise, Bondurant headed to the refrigerator in the bar and selected a bottle of Dom Perignon.

"Miles, I can't drink. It's a parole violation."

"Nah, doll, this can't hurt. It's just a bottle of bubbly to celebrate your freedom."

He popped the cork and filled two Waterford champagne flutes with golden sparkle. Picking up the glasses with great ceremony, he gave one to Sandra, then clinking the rim of her crystal, he toasted, "To your new beginning, honey. May we always be happy." He downed his in one gulp.

Underhill let the rim of her glass touch her lips knowing she was about to violate her parole. The fresh memory of prison made her hesitate. Just a sip, she told herself, and let the bubbles break over her tongue. It tasted cold, exciting, and memorable. Soon she passed her glass for a refill.

They sat in the club chairs. "Remember what you wanted to do when you got out?"

"Take a bubble bath," she said, and laughed.

"Right. Everything's all ready. The bathroom's off the master bedroom and there's some bubble bath on the counter. I bought it for you yesterday."

"You did?" She couldn't believe how thoughtful he was.

Even though the exact words had not been spoken, Sandra assumed she'd be sharing Miles' bed and stood to go upstairs. Then she realized there were two cantilevered staircases underneath a balcony that overlooked the living room. "How do I get there?"

Bondurant laughed. "Here, doll. Go up these stairs," he said, pointing, "then turn to the left. The other stairs lead to two guest rooms. The third guest room is down here in the front of the house."

Sandra kissed him, then ran up the stairs and stepped into a huge bedroom, larger than anything she had remembered seeing in the movies. She stared at the king-size bed that faced a sitting area, then reached out to touch the silk of a peach sofa facing two coordinating chairs. The cushions were mounded with down and she couldn't resist plopping in the middle of the sofa. It felt like a cloud.

Then she entered the Texas-sized master bath. Nothing could have prepared her for the experience. A huge Jacuzzi, banked with tropical plants, sparkled under a multitude of overhead can lights. A shimmering silk gown and robe hung from a tall cabinet. She stroked the delicate material and smiled with delight. Skipping to the counter, she grabbed the bubble bath then turned on the hot water. Surely heaven couldn't equal this.

* * *

Bondurant let an hour go by before he called up to her. "Your Oreo cookies and milk are ready."

Sandra Underhill ran down the stairs in the new robe and gown. "You remembered the cookies too?" she said with a touch of awe in her voice.

When she reached him she smiled broadly and threw her arms around him. "You are too wonderful. You are so good to me. And my new robe and gown," she said, pirouetting, "I just can't believe it. I'm so lucky."

He basked in the glow of her praise.

Later, when she picked up the last of the cookie crumbs and finished her milk, Bondurant gazed at her and purred invitingly, "Hey, doll, it's bedtime."

Sandra smiled and extended her hand. They walked up the stairs together. As soon as they reached the grand bedroom, Sandra slowly slipped off her robe while Miles pulled back the spread. He turned around and swallowed hard as she slid the straps of her gown from her shoulders. With Sandra standing naked beside him, he grinned an awkward grin and undressed before turning off the lights.

Once in bed Sandra crept over to his side and hugged him with both arms. She planted a long, lingering kiss on his lips and soon felt the warmth of his large hands on her back. "Miles, I'm so happy. You are a dream come true."

Before he could say anything, she kissed him again, and slithered her body over his. She had not had sex for two years and eagerly anticipated the fireworks as she felt him growing beneath her. Every visit Miles had made to the prison seemed like foreplay; she couldn't touch him and she had fiercely wanted to. Now as she thrust her hips toward him, she yearned to release all the pent-up, passionate desire she had accumulated since first hearing his voice on the telephone.

Sandra's sensual movements intensified as Miles entered her, and the big bed bolted. Her erotic gyrations increased in both frequency and intensity, and she soon groaned with joy as she abandoned herself to the whirl of sensations. Then all fell silent. She waited a few moments before reaching out for him again.

"Oh, God, no!" Bondurant said in a strained voice. "Not now. Get away. You're too rambunctious. Too aggressive. I don't like that kind of sex."

*Bang!* Sandra's self-esteem evaporated. She thought men liked women showing them that kind of heat. She felt her lower lip pucker and tears burn her eyes. For two years she had waited, only to be pushed away. Was she an animal? Or had all of his society girlfriends been colder?

She lay there in the unfamiliar room wondering if something was wrong with her. She could hear Miles' breathing, but knew she couldn't touch him. She glanced at a slice of moonlight as it eased its way through an opening between the heavy drapes and watched the digital clock as one minute slid into another.

Her mind drifted back to her introduction to sex—she had been raped. Her mother had asked her to help her older sister and her husband move their things from a trailer to a small house. Sandra agreed because she loved Charlotte and enjoyed being with her. But when she arrived at the trailer, she learned that Charlotte had to work and wouldn't be there. Disappointed, but still wanting to help, Sandra pitched in and began loading dishes and linens into boxes. Then her brother-in-law, Jason Cockerill, called to her.

"Sandra, come look, I found a mouse building a nest."

Sandra hated mice but had to see what Cockerill had discovered. Tall and dark, he had puckered fish lips that repulsed her and she couldn't understand what her sister saw in him. She walked into the trailer's small bedroom and noticed him kneeling on the floor staring at something by the side of the bed. She bent down to look also. That's when her tall, muscular brother-in-law pulled her down and held his fist on her throat so she couldn't scream.

"You try to get away, and I'll beat your face in," he hissed through clenched teeth.

Sandra struggled, but he threw her on the bed and like a madman ripped off her jeans, shirt, and underwear. She cried out in pain as he tortured her virgin body. He only laughed.

Bruised and sore afterwards, Sandra had trouble walking. She picked up the phone and called her mother. "Hurry, come get me," she said quickly as Cockerill stood listening. She could not wait to tell her mother about her tragic experience. Her mother would be outraged, and probably insist that Charlotte leave the monster she had married.

Once in her mother's car, Sandra poured out the details of her attack. Her mother frowned as she listened and shook her head.

"Sandra, you must promise me. Never, never tell your sister. That would just kill her."

Sandra reeled in shock at her mother's words. She stared horrified at the woman who had failed her so badly. But receiving no sympathy for her plight, Sandra felt forced to keep her misery a secret.

The next year, her sister moved from the small house to a larger one in town.

"Sandra," her mother called. "Charlotte needs your help. She's moving again."

Not believing her mother's sanity this time, Sandra screamed, "You know what happened last year!"

"Sandra! I told you to keep your mouth shut about that. Now you be a good sister and help Charlotte. Jason probably won't even be there."

Thinking she would be spending the afternoon with her sister, Sandra went. But again, Charlotte had to work and Sandra found herself with Cockerill—alone. It was like playing a broken, dysfunctional record all over again. However, Sandra would be smarter this time. No way would she allow him to catch her in any cramped area where she couldn't escape.

Midway through the afternoon in the open space of the living room, the huge man came up to small, petite Sandra and simply picked her up by her feet. Holding her upside down, he peeled away her jeans and panties, then he bent his head and opened his mouth.

Sandra lay quietly, inches from the man she loved. She began to feel suffocated by the room's darkness and the overpowering feeling of rejection. Maybe she wouldn't be able to escape her background after all.

# Chapter Eight

Cowboys in pickup trucks with shotguns racked in rear windows epitomize Lubbock, Texas. Lubbock, sitting on the wind-blown prairies of west Texas, is where Warren Miles Bondurant was born on September 20, 1934, 12 minutes after his twin sister, Mary, whose shy, studious personality was the antithesis of her brother's.

Bondurant's father, D. K. Drury "Bondy" Bondurant, made his fortune selling insurance. But in 1941 when Bondurant was 7, his father filed for divorce. In a place the size of Lubbock just prior to World War II, divorce was rare and small-town gossip alone drove the prominent businessman out of town, especially when he immediately took on a new wife named Flossie and left his first wife to raise his four children. Bondurant's older brother and sister were teenagers and they pitched in to help their mother. Young Bondurant felt bewildered that his father had deserted the family, but it was something he would later do himself.

His mother, Jacqueline Bondurant, came from a pioneer family. Her grandparents were the first innkeepers in west Texas and now out of necessity, Jacqueline, an attractive honey-blonde, drew from that innovative heritage and became an interior decorator.

Bondurant's father didn't mind selling his profitable insurance business—the largest insurance company in Lubbock—because he moved to Fort Worth and quickly formed another one there. An intelligent man, he cut a dashing figure with his tall, athletic frame and dark hair.

By the time Miles Bondurant was old enough to attend Lubbock High School, the other "Westerners" as the students were called, were aware he had become an expert hunter, a precise marksman, and a gun specialist *extraordinaire.* Later, after he enrolled at Texas Christian University in Forth Worth, he had turned into a raging party animal. When he returned on school breaks to visit Lubbock, he outdrank his friends and frequently caused fights at parties, prompting a one-time friend to smack him on his head with a breadboard in order to quiet him.

Lubbock taught its sons not to flaunt their money, considering it downright tacky. The men preferred to hide behind blue jeans, boots, and starched white shirts. Bondurant proved an exception. After he moved to Fort Worth and built his data processing business, he developed a need to demonstrate his success. He did nothing to conceal his love of expensive clothes, cars, and homes.

In parallel thinking, Bondurant saw Sandra Underhill's appearance as a direct reflection on himself, and two weeks after her release from prison, he convinced her that he knew best about her looks. He drove her to Neiman Marcus and ushered her into the hair salon of the most fashionable store in Fort Worth.

He told the hairdresser to cut her hair real short. He wanted a sophisticated look that wouldn't need to be long enough to curl.

Sandra looked bewildered.

"I can't do that to this woman," the hairdresser said.

"Too drastic. Just too much change all of a sudden when her hair's this long. We'd shock her for sure."

Bondurant said, "Baby, you'll be a doll with short hair. Tell the man to cut it."

Underhill meekly told the hairdresser that she was sure Miles knew what he was doing, but the hairdresser shook his head as he started snipping away at her locks.

Sandra looked in the mirror and a feeling of sadness engulfed her—the same feeling she'd had at 14 when her mother had shaved her head.

Next, Bondurant whisked her to the Elizabeth Arden counter for a makeover. "Get rid of all that dark stuff she puts on her eyes," he told the consultant, who occupied herself with pulling soft corals and pinks from her demonstration makeup.

The consultant meticulously rubbed rich creams into Underhill's skin, teaching her skin care and makeup application as she worked. When the consultant finished, she handed Sandra a mirror. Underhill scowled, barely recognizing the woman with short hair and a pale face.

But nothing could hide her amazement when she saw Bondurant go to the Clinque counter. The consultant greeted him with a familiar smile and said, "Hello, Mr. Bondurant. What can we help you with today?"

"I need some base. Honeyed beige."

Underhill's eyes became huge. She remembered seeing Miles rub something on his face that came in a little bottle, but she had assumed it was an expensive aftershave and paid scant attention to it.

"Are you getting good results from the skin bleach?" the consultant asked.

"It's great. Takes care of those dark spots and this base covers anything that doesn't completely bleach out."

After they left the counter, Underhill said, "That's makeup you put on your face?"

"Sure. Lots of guys do. It blends the color of my skin and makes me look healthy."

Still in shock, she allowed Bondurant to transport her

upstairs to Couture. Before long, she stood viewing herself in full pleated pants and a smartly cut blazer, realizing Bondurant had performed a complete transformation. Then her mind went back to his makeup and she had to smile; now she knew that appearance was everything to the man.

The first month Sandra Underhill lived with Miles Bondurant, she displayed an unquestioned obedience which pleased him immensely. When he complained that his cleaning lady wanted a raise, she suggested he fire the woman and she would clean his house. For all of that cooperation, Bondurant decided she deserved a present.

The following week he told her, "Get into the car. I have a surprise for you."

No amount of questions and pleadings would cause him to divulge his surprise. He drove out to a Fort Worth suburb, Willow Bend, and stopped in front of a white frame house.

Underhill accompanied him to the door, where a woman greeted them and invited them inside. There Sandra saw three pens of yipping Shih Tzu puppies. Bondurant had apparently paid for a puppy and she only had to choose.

Sandra clapped her hands like a child. She had never had a pet of her own. Looking at the pens full of squirming, fluffy balls, she knew it would be a difficult choice. After spending 30 minutes going from pen to pen, she stopped in front of one and watched a puppy that had sequestered itself into a corner, separated from its yelping siblings. Underhill reached out and picked up the puppy she could identify with, and the sandy-white concoction licked and tickled her.

"This is the one," she giggled.

Bondurant scratched the dog behind her ears. "How about naming her Sand Pebbles Bondurant?"

"I like that. How do you like your new name?" she asked, nuzzling the dog. "Let's call her Pebbles."

* * *

Each night Bondurant sipped his scotch with Pebbles nestled by his leg. He'd lean back and tell Sandra how he had maneuvered into the Fort Worth civic scene. He pointed to one of the plaques on his wall, commemorating his 25-five year membership in the downtown Rotary Club. That had been a year ago.

Other nights he told her about his work with the Arthritis Foundation. Another plaque thanked him for serving two terms as its president. "When you make a lot of money in a community, doll, you need to give something back. That's why I donate all this time."

He nodded toward a wooden plaque acknowledging his donations for two decades to Texas Christian University's Athletic Department. Describing his achievements was one of his favorite hobbies. Then he sat back in his leather chair, sipped his scotch, and enjoyed his self-massaged ego.

Sandra Underhill's favorite subject was her children, but after living with Bondurant for three months, she still hadn't convinced him to let them share his home. She received periodic reports and photos from their foster parents, giving her a constant reminder of Nicole, who was 8, and Joshua, who had just celebrated his seventh birthday. Sandra looked at the pictures, and realized how beautiful her children were. Having lost Angelina, she desperately wanted to keep these two.

Bondurant artfully dismissed her pleadings to have her children, and turned a deaf ear to how much she loved and missed them. He spoke to her in the same persuasive manner that had landed him lucrative business contracts. Patiently he'd began, "Well, darlin', what do you think?" He'd look at her with his heavy, hooded eyes that made him appear both tired and serious at the same time, and say in a deep voice, "Don't you think the children might be better off where they are?"

Then one night after she had pestered him, he asked, "Exactly, Sandra, what do *you* have to offer these children?"

Underhill looked around the den of the spacious home with its three extra bedrooms and realized what he meant. It wasn't hers. She had come to him without one worldly possession and she still had nothing. Up until now she had felt right at home. They had their nightly drinks together, she slept with him, cooked his meals, and spent every minute of each weekend together. But suddenly she felt like a house guest.

"Think about it, honey. You told me yourself. These nice foster parents have wanted to adopt the children for several years. You said they were the same folks who had been the children's first foster parents when they were babies. Wouldn't it be a shame to take the kids away from these two stable people who love them so much? *I'd* sure hate to do that to the little tikes."

As he waited for her answer, Underhill began thinking of herself as a monster for trying to separate her children from their loving foster parents. She had been attracted to Miles' sensible approach to life. She wondered if her many mistakes over the years could be attributed to her mule-like habit of refusing to take advice. Maybe it was time to listen to someone she respected. Finally, after many tears, she agreed to let her children be adopted.

When Sandra Underhill called the foster parents to tell them, they were thrilled. She felt destitute. It was comparable to cutting off her arm. Then she talked with Nicole and Joshua—they no longer called her "Mom." Maybe she already had been separated from them too long.

Sandra Underhill and Miles Bondurant walked into the dark, paneled courtroom and saw her children sitting by their foster parents, like merchandise to be traded. Sandra crept over to them, wondering what they thought of a mother who would soon tell them goodbye forever. She threw her arms around Nicole first, then Joshua, tightly embracing them both, while they tentatively hugged her back.

Looking into their faces, she said, "You know I love you. Have always loved you." She fought the tears that lingered in her eyes. "I won't ever forget you."

Nicole self-consciously reached for her foster mother's hand, staring at Sandra as if she were a stranger. Joshua sat close to his foster father. Unable to choke out another word, Sandra went back to sit with Bondurant.

When the judge asked, "Are we setting up annual visitations?"

Bondurant spoke up. "Your Honor, I feel, or rather we feel that would be too disruptive to their young lives. Let them continue to be the tight little family they are."

Obedient as Pebbles, Sandra agreed. But the entire picture felt achingly familiar to her as she stood in front of the judge affirming her intention to put up for adoption her own flesh and blood. She hung her head and began crying softly. Why did she keep losing the people she loved?

# Chapter Nine

Two weeks after Sandra Underhill lost her children, Miles Bondurant put down his drink and sat up in his chair. "What do you mean your father's coming to visit? Sandra, am I losing my mind? Or are you? You distinctly told me that your father drowned when you were ten."

"That's what I thought," she admitted. "But when I turned sixteen my mother told me the truth. She had been married to Leroy Coburn when I was born but the Navy sent him away for months at a time. During one of those times, she had a fling for a couple weeks with a man named Donald Horn. He's got to be my dad because Leroy had sea duty for three months when my mom got pregnant."

Bondurant shook his head.

"When I was in jail in St. Louis, I thought maybe I'd die without ever meeting my biological father. So I called him."

"Oh sure, bet he was real glad to hear from his daughter, the jailbird."

"No, he and his wife were just great. They visited me immediately and treated me like family. He's a wonderful person—been at the same job for forty-five years. He's coming through town now because he's a champion bowler and flies all over the country to tournaments.

"And the most amazing thing, Miles, and you'll have trouble believing this, but—"

"What makes you think all the rest has been easy to swallow?"

Ignoring him, she said, "This is the best part. He has a daughter who named her first three children—Nicole, Joshua, and Angelina. Isn't that incredible?"

He looked at Underhill as she ticked off the names of her three lost children. "Sweetheart, I want you to have my children."

Hearing the word "children," Sandra's breath caught in her throat. "And we'll get married?" she asked.

"You mean we'd have to do that too?" he laughed.

She couldn't think of anything more wonderful than being married to Miles and having his children. With the security he had to offer, she'd never lose another child.

Three months after Underhill's prison release, Bondurant's strategy for her transformation moved steadily forward. He took her to expensive restaurants where he'd lean over and whisper which fork to use. Constantly he reminded her to keep her voice down. He insisted that she have weekly manicures and became pleased when her once cracked and split nails were now long, slender, and professionally polished. Her facials at Neiman's made her skin prettier and gave her an inner glow.

Following Bondurant's overall plan, Underhill jumped into the red Mercedes that fall to attend the Northwest Branch of Tarrant County Junior College. She took electronic typing, and WordPerfect 5.1. Her esteem soared with her grades. The junior college qualified as a college just as Bondurant's ad had promised, however, Sandra had qualified for the Job Partnership Training Act, so he didn't have to pay a penny for her education.

After Underhill finished her first semester, she told him she wanted to visit her mother.

"The one who beat you and shaved your head?" He looked at her incredulously.

"I feel guilty. Haven't seen her in over three years. Besides, I can tell her I've completed a semester of college. That should make her happy."

Bondurant shook his head.

Underhill understood his reaction. "I guess I always want to think there's a place called 'home.' A place I can return to periodically and find security."

"And just how many times do you have to get kicked in the teeth before you realize there's no such place?"

"I've gotta go. It will eat me up until I do." For one rare instance, she discounted his objections, took advantage of the school break, and talked him into paying her airplane fare to Illinois.

Having lived in Miles Bondurant's lovely home, Sandra Underhill found her mother's public housing unit in Granite City, Illinois, all the more a contrast. She sat down on a frayed, dirty chair and felt herself sink into worn-out springs. A half-eaten sandwich sat on the table beside her. She glanced around and realized her mother still had an aversion to cleaning or throwing anything away.

"Sandra, what a beautiful outfit," her mother, Elaina, exclaimed as soon as she saw her. "Tell me, who is this new friend of yours?"

Sandra told her mother about answering Bondurant's ad, and Elaina's eyes gleamed between heavy folds Sandra had not remembered seeing before. Elaina had blossomed to 190 pounds, which stretched her skin taut on her 5-foot frame.

"I must come meet him."

Underhill tensed. The image of her uncultured mother rubbing elbows with the condescending Bondurant gave her a sharp pain between her eyes. Sandra enjoyed being with her sisters, especially since Charlotte had divorced her husband. But after a few days of her family, she happily flew back to Forth Worth.

Underhill returned to Bondurant's stunning announcement. On her first night back, he raised his wineglass as if to make a toast, and said, "Even though you've just completed one semester of school, I want you to join my company as vice president of operations."

Sandra smiled broadly and enthusiastically agreed. The title was impressive; the accompanying salary less so. He would pay her only $150 a month, a miserly wage she never questioned as she consented to take the job that was, in reality, a data entry operator.

The following week, he chose the dress Underhill wore when he drove her to the Bondurant Corporation, housed in a one-story red and yellow brick building on Chapel Avenue. His business involved entering clients' accounts receivables into a computer, printing out statements and mailing them each month.

Bondurant introduced her to his other two employees: the president, Charles Arnspinger, who actually ran the company, and Francis Amman, an older woman, who unbeknownst to her, Underhill would replace as soon as Amman taught her her job.

Bondurant proudly showed off his company. "I started from scratch," he boasted. "Built this company from the ground up when I was only thirty-five."

Arnspinger nodded. "And in twenty-two years you've landed contracts with lots of important customers. I came along ten years later," he said to Underhill.

Bondurant and Sandra walked into his private office.

"Why did Charles say that you've been in business twenty-two years?"

"I have. Started in 1969."

Puzzled, she said, "But your ad said you were in your mid-forties."

"Oh, that." His face reddened. "It was a misprint. I'm really fifty-seven."

No sooner had she begun working for Bondurant than she noticed the daily inquiries from creditors seeking payment on their overdue accounts. When she had sufficiently learned her job, Arnspinger fired Amman. But soon Bondurant and Arnspinger talked of chapter eleven—business bankruptcy.

Bondurant called Underhill into his office and handed her a check. "Here, sweetie, do me a favor and go cash this. Of course, bring the dough back here," he said, pointing to his chest.

She looked down at the $950 check made out to her. Obediently, she went to the company's bank and cashed it, then gave Bondurant the stack of bills. He took her out for lunch and stopped at a different bank.

When he got back in the car, she asked, "What's this all about?"

"I opened another account to put that money in. The balance sheet needs to show a bigger loss if the judge's going to let me file bankruptcy. The court won't know anything about the account at this bank."

Underhill continued cashing checks for him that would total several thousand dollars.

# Chapter Ten

Each night Miles Bondurant poured Scotch over clear ice cubes, and mixed a vodka and tonic for Sandra Underhill. One night after she had lived with him for six months and after he had mellowed into an alcoholic warmth, he took her hand and said, "Darlin' you know I love you. I want us to get married."

"Oh, Miles. That would be wonderful! When?" Underhill became giddy with the possibility of marrying such a person. But when she brought up the subject a few nights later, he had trouble remembering what she was talking about.

Their nightly drinking bouts began taking their toll. Sandra sipped her first vodka and tonic, and giggled as Bondurant teased Pebbles. With her second drink, she'd put on a CD and invite him to dance. By the time she had finished her third, her voice became deep and accusing. "I don't understand you. You asked me to marry you, then you keep putting it off."

Bondurant, just as inebriated, would raise his voice and yell, "Why would I want to marry an ex-con?"

Underhill picked up a book from the table and hurled

it at him. He ducked and laughed at her, egging her on.

"You make me so mad!" Her frenzy continued as she threw more items and spoke irrationally. After more drinks, she dropped to the couch, her head hit the cushioned arm, and she passed out.

The next morning, she found herself in bed, not knowing how she got there, and vowed to refuse more than one drink an evening.

"I don't know why it affects you like that," he said, looking down at her in bed as she held her head. "I just get more mellow with each drink."

One night Underhill decided to dress comfortably in a sweat suit and caught Bondurant staring at her. In an alcoholic haze he said, "In that outfit, you look just like white trash."

She was appalled at his words, but he told her that trash was what she came from and he guessed that's what she'd always be.

She felt like someone had yanked a ladder out from underneath her. He hadn't hit her as her two husbands had, but he slapped her with his words and somehow that hurt more. She ran crying from the den into the living room. Pebbles followed after her. Underhill fell to the floor and reached for the dog, then buried her face in her knees. Memories of all the men she had ever known marched through her mind. Why couldn't she find someone nice?

Bondurant stumbled into the living room calling to her. Sandra's reaction to adversity was always silence. She said nothing and only cried.

He stood watching and tried to get her attention, but when he received no response he said, "Sandra, you're crazy."

* * *

Underhill's frequent emotional outbursts began to gnaw on Bondurant; in fact, the latest argument proved to be a turning point. Although he didn't want to rid himself of her altogether, he felt that his home life had become less serene with her around.

The next day he told her, "I need some time to myself, sugar. So I've rented a nice furnished apartment for you at the Taj Mahal. I'll pay your rent and all your other expenses." Then, as an additional enticement, he added, "And I'll let you drive my Mercedes sedan."

Underhill's eyes watered. "But I thought we were going to get married. Have children and all that."

"We are. We just need some time apart right now."

She had no more to say about her move than a child being sent off to live with relatives. She wondered at the extra expense, recalling how Bondurant had complained about the cost of having his house cleaned. Soon she learned that she'd still be cleaning his house, as well as working in his office.

Underhill had started to gather Pebbles' dish and food when Bondurant put out his hand.

"You're leaving, Sandra. Pebbles stays here."

Six months of living in the apartment and cleaning Bondurant's home made Underhill yearn for a house. He complied by leasing her a small place on Dexter Street that he grabbed for a steal since the place had fallen apart. Sandra broke off several manicured nails painting and polishing until the home shone like new. Bondurant filled it with $7,500 worth of furniture from Montgomery Ward and threw in a couple of end tables that his mother had left him.

Now Underhill had her set schedule. She worked for Bondurant every day and went home alone at night. On the weekends she returned to clean his house and sleep with him. She had finally learned the quiet, less demonstrative sex that he enjoyed. But spending every weeknight by herself left her feeling abandoned. She wanted companionship.

By now Sandra Underhill resented Bondurant and yearned to be with people she *was* good enough for. Unfortunately, the more decrepit her companions, the more highly she regarded herself. Despite that inclination, she should have known trouble when she saw it.

Early in 1992, she had met Joe Davila when they each had apartments at the Taj Mahal and she still remembered the young man with the tangled blond mane. Now, on a cold December night of that same year, he lived in his truck on a street not far from Underhill's little house. Sandra couldn't mask her surprise because they both had had comparable apartments just a few months earlier. She had noticed Davila shivering under blankets, and with naïve compassion invited him in to get warm. As the evening grew later and the weather turned colder, she didn't have the heart to toss him out. She said softly, "I've got a separate bedroom, Joe, you can spend the night there." Davila stayed, but not in the separate bedroom.

Davila didn't mind letting Underhill pay the bills with the money she received from Bondurant. He also tried to entice her into an idea very close to his heart. "Remember how fuckin' great you felt on coke?" he said with his arms wrapped around her. "Nothing in the world's a problem when you're smoking or shooting that shit."

Thanks to Davila's constant reminders, it didn't take long before Sandra began thinking about drugs. She had been clean for almost four years, but the more she thought about drugs, the more she wanted them.

Previously, Underhill's husbands had purchased her narcotics, so now Davila had to educate her about procuring them. "Hell, don't worry about finding a dealer. He'll find you. All you have to do is take Horne Street south past Camp Bowie. You'll know Como when you see it. There'll be some fuckin' pawn shops. The damn windows will have bars on them. Some buildings will be boarded up—'course most of them are crack houses. Get my drift?"

She nodded.

"And, for God's sake, don't haggle price. It's fuckin' set. Now this is important. The guy will stick his hand into your car with the rocks, but he won't let go until you put the cash in his other hand. You grab, he takes, and you roll up your window and get the hell out of there."

Still Underhill felt hesitant about getting back into drugs until an episode at work the following month. She walked into the office and took off her jacket.

Bondurant frowned at her. "Is that blouse something left over from prison?"

Sandra clutched a lapel, and said, "I bought this at K-Mart. Thought you liked it."

"It's all faded. It looks like you got it from Goodwill."

Underhill threw the statements she held on her desk and headed for the restroom. She slammed the door shut and lit a cigarette. *Damn him. I can't do anything right.* She inhaled deeply, feeling the nicotine relax her, then she furiously exhaled. She stood in a white fog thinking Miles was impossible to please. Why even try?

That night, she hopped into Bondurant's sedan armed with Davila's directions, and drove to the Como area of Forth Worth, one of the toughest, most dangerous sections of the city. Underhill had no knowledge of the area prior to meeting Davila, but she felt confident that his instructions would lead her to the best drug dealers who would sell her almost pure cocaine. The dealers had no trouble spotting Underhill in the bright red Mercedes, and soon milled around her to peddle their wares.

She rolled down her window. Four dealers shoved their hands inside. She panicked, but managed to make eye contact with one and nodded. She grabbed his plastic bag of crack with one hand while she released her money from the other. At that moment, the passenger side door opened. She turned her head to see a black man with dreadlocks and a crazed stare had jumped into the seat beside her. Taking one look, Underhill jumped out. She left the car in the middle of Horne Street with the keys still in it. And ran.

# Chapter Eleven

The police called Miles Bondurant at 3 A.M. to tell him they had found his car on Horne Street. They said the stereo and speakers were gone and the sunroof no longer worked.

Bondurant's shoulders sagged. Not knowing his car was missing, all he could think was, what had Sandra done now?

The police went on to explain that it also had been used in a burglary the night before.

He fell back in his bed and covered his face with his hands. After only a few minutes he heard someone pounding on his front door. He stormed downstairs.

"Miles! *Miles!*"

Sandra's panting voice sounded desperate. He pulled open the door and saw her standing there looking pathetic and tired. Even though it was a cold January night, her short wet hair stuck to her forehead.

"I ran. I ran all the way here."

"From where?"

"Como. Went to buy drugs. Haven't done any in years. Then this guy . . . this guy . . . jumps in the car. I left it."

"You left my car in *Como?*" Bondurant screamed at her.

"Had to—I was so scared."

She fell toward him but he pushed her away. He had no desire to give her comfort. Now it was early 1993, less than 18 months since he had written the prison trying to get her released. He rubbed his aching head and wondered what the hell had he gotten himself into.

The next day, Bondurant climbed into his sports coupe to go look at his sedan. He had called Foreign Motors, the shop he always used, and had them pick up his car from the city pound where the police had towed it.

When the service attendant showed Bondurant his abused vehicle, his temperature rose.

He bent down and looked through the windshield, remembering that the police said the radio and speakers were yanked out. He also found the dashboard cracked where the stereo had been.

Bondurant gritted his teeth and stared at the ragged open spaces. The thousands he had invested to maintain his car flashed through his mind.

The serviceman slapped the top of the car. "See how bent up the sunroof is? That will have to be replaced along with the motor. We've got the estimate ready." He looked down at his clipboard. "It'll run $4,690.35 to put it back in shape."

Bondurant placed his hands on his hips and stared at the damage. He'd call his insurance company and pay the deductible. Underhill, on the other hand, would have hell to pay.

Before surveying his damaged car, Bondurant had dropped Underhill off at her house on Dexter Street, but apparently roared away before noticing Davila's beat-up heap sitting on the street in front.

Now Underhill couldn't push Bondurant's angry face

out of her mind. From the looks he had given her, she knew she'd no longer be driving his sedan. She assumed she'd still work for him, but how did he expect her to get there?

In her depression, the only thing that had a chance of making her happy lay inside the plastic bag buried in her purse. And Davila was there to help.

She pulled out the cocaine and waived it in the air. Davila's eyes twinkled.

"Way to go, girl," he said, smiling. "I love that shit. Hold on a sec. I've got a pipe in my truck. It'll only take a fuckin' minute to get it."

After Davila left, Underhill made sure none of her precious cache had fallen into the bottom of her purse and while checking, she noticed her driver's license was missing.

When Davila came back, she asked, "Have you seen my driver's license?"

"What the hell would I want with your license? It's got your picture on it. Do I look like some fuckin' dame?"

She looked at his long blond hair, but decided not to answer.

Davila expertly stuffed steel wool and cocaine into the glass pipe and lit it.

"Hot damn. The rock's beginning to melt." He grinned. "Won't be long before we're in some fuckin' dreamland." He put his arm around her and guided her toward the living room.

When smoke filtered from the pipe, he held it out to her. "Here, you go first. It's your shit."

Underhill took the pipe and inhaled deeply. She smiled and shut her eyes as she exhaled. Davila took his first drag. Then, trading the pipe back and forth, they forgot all about Bondurant and the wrecked car as they cuddled on the sofa in front of the fireplace. Their euphoria lasted almost an hour.

* * *

The next Monday, Underhill put drops in her bloodshot eyes and brushed her limp, lifeless hair away from her face. Davila had dropped her off at the office, then went home to spend the rest of the day in bed.

She discovered a drastic change in her efficiency as she made one error after another. Before drugs, her hands literally flew over the keyboard and she prided herself on being productive. Now her rate had slowed considerably so she vowed to confine her pipe dreams to evenings in hopes of hiding her newly resurrected habit.

She continued to smoke crack and work for Bondurant, but Davila began calling her at the office countless times a day.

Bondurant couldn't help but notice all the phone calls Underhill received. He waited until she had left for lunch one day then pulled out a voice-activated recorder he had bought from Radio Shack and crawled under her knee space to attach it. Now whenever Davila called, Bondurant had proof.

At the end of the week, Bondurant drove her home without looking at her or saying a word.

When he steered down her street they passed a man in a dark blue Chevrolet sedan. Underhill thought nothing of it until after Bondurant left. The doorbell rang and she saw the man standing at her front door. She knew he had to be a professional messenger when he handed her a letter. She quickly opened it and read, "Your services are no longer needed at the Bondurant Corporation."

Underhill leaned against her doorjamb wondering why Bondurant had to be so dramatic. Then it hit her. For the first time since leaving prison she had lost her financial support.

* * *

Dunkin' Donuts didn't cover Sandra Underhill's rent and living expenses as fully as Bondurant had, but selling donuts was the only job she could find on such short notice.

Three days into the next month, Underhill couldn't pay her rent and immediately received an eviction notice. She crumpled up the letter and sat down to contemplate her options. Davila and drugs had drained her reserves. There was only one person to call.

"Okay," Bondurant said, his voice harsh with irritation, "I'll rent a U-Haul and get your furniture. We can put it in storage."

When Underhill told Davila of her conversation with Bondurant, Davila tried to talk her out of going back to him. But she remained adamant, knowing Davila just didn't want to lose his meal ticket. The next day, Davila returned to living in his truck.

Underhill moved back into Bondurant's house, 10 months after first being ejected to the Taj Mahal.

Before she had walked any farther than the entry, Bondurant said, "There will be no hard drugs in this house, young lady."

"I promise. They make me feel rotten. And I'll keep my job at Dunkin' Donuts and help pay for some of the damage I've done."

He shook his head.

"But it makes me feel independent to have my own money."

"Absolutely not. You'll quit that stupid job."

Their relationship became even more erratic—turning on and off like a light switch, but when she lived with him, he expected sex. She complied, hoping the physical closeness would give their relationship some stability.

But over the next few months, the hirings and firings continued with pendulum predictability. Time and time again, Bondurant tossed her out of his house and business, only to invite her back again. He didn't need much of an excuse—one time he evicted her for playing the radio too loud while she ironed. He enjoyed showing her who was boss.

A prominent business associate of Bondurant's later described him as "quiet, sociable, and one of the nicest guys I know—when he's not drinking." Liquor acted like poison to Bondurant, but nightly he continued to poison himself.

He sat in his favorite chair that had molded to the contour of his body. Now whenever Underhill did anything objectionable—such as raising her voice, not wearing makeup, or donning her comfortable warm-ups—he'd call her "white trash." He seemed to enjoy her reaction.

Having taken the verbal abuse for months, she warned him, *"Don't* you *ever* call me that again."

Like a little boy told to stay away from the cookie jar, he looked at her and said, "Sandra, you're white trash."

Abruptly she jumped up and slapped his face with her open hand. His mouth gaped in shock and he dropped his drink. Scotch spilled over his pants and chair.

She thought he might cry.

Then he collected himself and whined, "I never thought you'd hit someone who wore glasses."

Underhill bit her lower lip to stifle a grin. But with what she had just done, she knew she'd soon be leaving. Only she couldn't have dreamed where she would go.

Bondurant picked up the phone, dialed 911, and asked for the police.

Furious, she ran and grabbed the phone. In their tussle, the receiver fell and hit the glass tabletop by his chair. Glass splinters crashed to the floor. Defiantly, he picked up the phone and dialed 911 again. This time he told the police to hurry; he had a crazy woman in his house.

Underhill's temper turned white and she didn't want to stay in the same room with the man. Her normal response of silence was her worst personality trait because for long periods of time she'd take all the injustice, the ridicule, and the frequently deserved blame, and shove it deep down inside her until it bubbled and boiled, and came exploding out over everything around her.

Now she flew up the stairs only to slip and come crashing down on the hard parquet floor. She landed on her knee and split it open. Blood splattered everywhere.

Bondurant laughed as she lay sprawled on the hard floor. Her fury grew as she struggled to stand up. A copper bell sat on a table by the stairs. Underhill picked it up and threw it at him, scoring a direct hit on his cheek. Now they were both bleeding, but his scratches couldn't compare with her damaged knee.

When the police officer walked in, Bondurant told him, "This woman tried to kill me. I'm afraid of her."

The policeman looked at Bondurant, who held a Kleenex to his face, and then at Underhill, whose knee kept bleeding through the paper towels she had covering it.

"Ma'am, did you strike this gentleman?"

"Yes, but—"

"If you check her record," Bondurant informed the policeman, "you'll see she's an ex-con."

Those words were magic. The officer clamped handcuffs on Underhill and drove her to the downtown station. Bondurant watched her go. His face showed no regret, only a smug grin.

# Chapter Twelve

With Sandra Underhill's hands locked together, the policeman opened the door for her at the Tarrant County Jail. A circular counter stood in the center of the large entry with police standing inside, busily processing people in and out.

An officer pointed to an X taped on the floor and told Underhill to stand on it. He handed her a number to hold to her chest, then a flash of light temporarily blinded her.

They marched her to another station and a different officer said, "Miss, put your hands on the electronic scanner."

Underhill extended her hands, pleased with technology that wouldn't leave her covered with ink.

As she limped from station to station, the police saw Underhill's bloody knee. One female sergeant bent down to examine the wound and said, "You better get a stitch in that, miss, or you're gonna have a bad scar."

The staff sent her to John Peter Smith Hospital in handcuffs and embarrassment. The doctor gave her a sharp jab of Novacaine and five stitches to join the gaping skin of her left knee, then she returned to jail.

A guard led her to a holding tank where she saw no place to sleep. The cell held only a narrow wooden bench and a toilet. Underhill sat down on the bench while trying to keep her leg extended. She watched prostitutes come and go like a burlesque show. One was dressed in slacks and a sweater, while some wore fishnet hose with satin short-shorts. Breasts bulged from low-cut, tight blouses. The girls sat popping their gum and calling Sandra "honey," wanting to know what had happened to her. She couldn't tell them. She hadn't figured it out herself.

By nine the next morning, Underhill still had not been charged, and her knee throbbed. When a jailer came to her cell, she planned to ask her for a painkiller. She changed her mind when the large woman unlocked the metal door and said, "Looks like you're gettin' out of here, miss. Underhill cringed in pain when she stood up. Then she limped into the entry and found Bondurant.

"I decided not to press charges," he told her.

Underhill looked surprised, then quietly limped to his car.

He straightened his tall frame and raised his chin as if to exaggerate the 15-inch difference in their heights. "Well, honey," he said, "did you learn your lesson?"

Even though she had spent the night in jail, Bondurant wanted more revenge. "I rented you a duplex on Mercedes," he told her.

Underhill felt like a pet Bondurant kept on a leash. He'd give her so much slack, then pull her back or cut her loose, depending on his whim.

The furniture Bondurant had bought her became a pawn. She needed it for the duplex. He acquiesced, but then the next day maliciously sent furniture movers to retrieve the newly delivered goods. She never knew what to expect as he alternated between generosity or penny-pinching.

Underhill, astonished to see movers at her front door, quickly called 911, and told the operator to send police.

When the police arrived, the movers could produce no proof that they had a right to her furniture.

The officer sent them on their way and told her, "Don't worry, ma'am. I'm going to go talk with Mr. Bondurant and tell him to stop harassing you."

A few months later, Bondurant didn't need Underhill in his office and laid her off again. In only two weeks she was broke. To raise money, she called an auctioneer who bought all of the disputed furniture for $150. Once and for all, she put an end to the tug-of-war.

Bondurant poured himself another Scotch. Pacing the floor as he digested the news of the furniture sale and fumed about how Sandra had done it again. Unwilling to buy her more furniture, he realized if he asked her to move back they'd have to sit down and discuss their relationship.

He drank two more Scotches to build his resolve, then called her. "We need to talk about whether we're going to get back together or forget this whole thing."

"I'll be waiting for you," she told him.

Thirty minutes later they were in his den and he said, "I'll get us a drink."

After several more Scotches, Bondurant said, "Honey, I have to admit how lonely I am here without you. Pebbles isn't a great conversationalist."

She laughed.

"And when you're all dolled up, you're a great-looking lady. It sure makes a guy feel good to have somebody so young around."

Underhill smiled and said, "I'd like to try and make things work out, too." Sandra, always ready to try again, had spent eight years with her first husband who beat her weekly, and had believed him every time he promised to change.

They continued drinking and around midnight they still hadn't started to fight, so they stumbled upstairs together. Sandra knew they would have quiet sex because he allowed no talking, and as usual there would be no deviation from the missionary position.

The next morning he tried to sit up. "Oh my God, my head." His arms had trouble supporting him. "I feel like an eighteen-wheeler rolled over me."

Underhill began stirring. "I think I'm gonna throw up. I drank too much."

They both realized they needed to change their habits if they were to mend their broken relationship. Bondurant knew about a class at All Saints Hospital for nicotine addiction. The hospital also had a gym to keep them physically fit, and they decided to give it a try.

Soon they were attending classes at the hospital and using the same willpower to control their drinking.

By the spring of 1993, their tangled and flawed relationship had suddenly improved. With a more sober mind, Bondurant became a nicer person, Underhill less emotional.

They drove around Fort Worth in his Mercedes sports car, and Bondurant pointed out the plush homes he'd once owned. He showed her the two-story white stucco Mediterranean he had mentioned buying Kimberly. In Westover Hills, Underhill ogled at his stone mansion that held forty rooms and nestled under towering oaks and majestic Italian cypress. On Bryce Street, a marker on the entrance gate certified that the three-story, red brick Victorian had been constructed in 1893 by a former Fort Worth mayor. Each house increased her appreciation of him. She thought he had to be very intelligent to be so successful.

While they drove, they dutifully followed what she assumed rich people did—they drank flavored water. Sandra would have preferred a Coke.

Bondurant's countless marriage proposals echoed hollow because Underhill had heard them so many times. Then on April 20, 1993, Bondurant took her out for dinner and asked her to marry him. He opened a black velvet box and exposed a beautiful engagement ring. Sandra stared at the three-carat, pear-shaped stone with baguettes on each side. All three gems stood high in a yellow gold mounting. The dream she had dreamed in prison was finally coming true. Her mouth opened in shock and soon her mind saw children and security, and she began smiling.

Later that night, Underhill moved her hand to watch the stone's facets reflect in the dining room chandelier. Bondurant said, "Sweetie, you can have this ring, but remember, you need to keep your hair short."

She nodded.

"Then make sure you have those manicures. And I want you to only wear really sharp-looking clothes."

"Whatever you say, Miles. It's your money."

"Okay. Also, honey, I want you to remember your voice. Keep it down. Sometimes you sound like dynamite exploding."

Sandra whispered, "I will."

"Now this is important, you are never to see Joe Davila again."

Underhill looked surprised to hear Davila's name. "I haven't seen Joe in months. I don't even know where he is."

"Well, make sure you don't. And the last thing, you have to quit smoking."

Underhill had lapsed back into her decade-long habit. She found quitting drinking to be a minor problem, but she needed her cigarettes. She looked at him, then at the ring. She wanted it more for all the things it symbolized, rather than its sparkle, but he had asked too much. "But you're back to smoking, too."

"I'm going to quit again."

She glanced back to the ring, weighing her options. "Okay, I'll try," she told him, but her voice lacked conviction.

* * *

The aroma of halibut filets crackling and hissing under the broiler drew Bondurant into the kitchen.

"Smell's wonderful, doll."

"We're ready to eat. Go into the dining room. Table's all set."

"The dining room? What's the occasion?"

"I'll tell you later." Sandra smiled coyly but she insisted on waiting until they were seated.

Once at the table, he asked, "Well, what is it?"

She looked at him, beaming. "I think I'm pregnant."

"Really? I'll go get a pregnancy test as soon as we finish dinner." Many times before Underhill had thought she was pregnant. Whenever she'd make the announcement, Bondurant rushed to the drugstore and picked up a home pregnancy test, and always looked upset when it proved negative.

Tonight when he returned, she ran off to the bathroom to take the test. When she came back into the den, she shrieked, "It's positive!"

"Oh my God." His shock directly contrasted to her elation and assured her that the tests were to ascertain she was *not* pregnant.

Hearing about the pregnancy made Bondurant resume drinking. The next night, after having time to digest her announcement and gulp down several Scotches, he told her in no uncertain terms, "I want you to get an abortion!"

# Chapter Thirteen

A week later, Sandra Underhill had not forgiven Miles Bondurant for demanding an abortion. Two weeks later, her pregnancy remained an issue they hadn't resolved. He grew increasingly hostile, especially when he had been drinking. His abortion demand turned into an ultimatum.

He told her that she wouldn't know how to raise a child properly since she was just white trash.

"You made me get rid of my last two children," she told him. "I'm not going to lose this one."

"For all I know, that's probably not even *my* child. I bet it's Joe's."

At that moment, Underhill held a half-full coffee pot. Her anger soared and she threw the pot across the room, staining the kitchen wallpaper with long brown streaks. "I haven't seen Joe in months," she screamed. "It's *your* child and you know it!"

A month later, Underhill still hadn't erased his reaction to her pregnancy and began asking herself why he acted so upset. He appeared to be planning for the future when he gave her that expensive engagement ring. Even for someone as inconsistent as Bondurant, his reaction to her pregnancy seemed bizarre. She knew her pregnancy was genuine; she thought she'd check out the ring.

The following week, she walked into a jewelry store and asked the man behind the counter to tell her about the ring.

In only seconds he said it was a cubic zircon worth about $300.

By mid-September of 1993, Underhill was four months pregnant. After Bondurant had witnessed her determination against an abortion, he finally accepted her pregnancy because he didn't want her raising his child by herself.

Then a week later, she overheard his frequent phone calls with his family, obviously planning something. After asking him several times, he finally told her, "The family's just planning a little dinner for my birthday next week. That's all."

"Great! Where are we going? Mannings? That's your favorite."

"Darlin', I'm sorry. It just wouldn't be appropriate. Actually, the kids are putting this together and you're not on the guest list. It's their call. Anyway, you know you wouldn't have a good time. You don't like being with those people."

Although hurt, she had to admit he was right. "Those people," she knew, always looked down at her so she didn't enjoy being around them. And now that her pregnancy had started to show, it would probably embarrass him to take her.

On his birthday, September 20, he dressed in a new dark suit, crisp white shirt, and a burgundy and blue striped tie. Underhill watched him get ready, feeling more depressed as she saw him dash around the bedroom in an upbeat mood. He smoothed down his thin hair and sprayed it one last time.

He left and she heard the garage door close, locking

her in. Now she sensed that she lived in another kind of prison. She sat down on the living room floor feeling depressed.

Mental pictures of Bondurant's family and friends floated through her mind. She imagined them at the restaurant talking about proper subjects in soft, low, correct voices, and always choosing the right fork, and never slurping their velvety soups.

She hadn't been happy for weeks. Whenever a special occasion arrived, Bondurant always spent it with his family. She wanted out, but she hadn't the means to go anywhere. She felt stranded and let herself wallow in self-pity for an hour, then remembered that when she was sad, activity always boosted her spirits. She decided to clean house, and she also decided to fix herself a vodka and tonic.

She had dusted the downstairs, then pulled out the vacuum. Starting in the living room, she worked her way out to the hall. She opened the door to the hall closet which housed the hot water heater and began vacuuming the floor. As she did, her driver's license dropped to her feet. Not believing her eyes, she stared at it for a few moments, then picked it up realizing Bondurant had taken it. Damn him. She remembered missing it right after she drove his car to Como.

She looked up to see where it came from and found a packet stuffed between the hot water heater and the wall. She grabbed the bundle and discovered a phone bill that itemized her many calls to her mom and sisters. She wondered if he had saved it for blackmail to show how much she cost him. She also found a zip-lock bag that looked inviting. She opened it and recognized some of Bondurant's jewelry—two watches and several rings. She read the name on the prettiest watch—Cartier. It looked expensive. She remembered seeing his Rolex on him when he left earlier.

Underhill had difficulty accepting the contrast between her phony engagement ring and Bondurant's hidden, expensive jewelry. When she had confronted him about the ring, he said, "I should give an ex-addict a real diamond she could pawn for drugs?"

His words had stung her, and her anger grew over his leaving her alone on his birthday. Now that he had hidden his jewelry, she knew he obviously didn't trust her. She looked at the bag of jewelry and her hands began to shake with excitement. That jewelry could be her ticket to freedom—something she could pawn to finance her flight. Also, her current depression had spiraled to such a depth that only drugs could wind her back up. The jewelry could also buy her that.

Running up the stairs to their bedroom, Underhill didn't consider right or wrong. She grabbed two suitcases and filled them with all the "proper" clothes Bondurant had bought her. Then she threw in his bag of jewelry, ran back downstairs, and walked out the front door. For a brief moment, she considered taking one of his cars as well, but decided against it and started off on foot.

Underhill headed down Camp Bowie Boulevard. She had known a woman from an apartment complex about eight blocks away on Seventh Street where Bondurant had exiled her once for a week. They had hit it off, so she hoped the woman still remembered her. Hurriedly, she walked down the street with a bag in each hand. A car slowed down as it neared her.

"Hey, you need a ride?"

Underhill looked over at the young man with greasy long hair and a drooping handlebar mustache. A small Hispanic woman sat next to him. They had "addict" written all over them but by now she felt as desperate as they appeared to be. "Yeah, I could use a ride."

"Where are you going?"

"Around Seventh Street. But I need to go to the drugstore first." She didn't want to tell two total strangers that she planned to buy hypodermic needles. Underhill had been drinking for almost two hours and her befuddled brain thought she could buy drugs and still plan a trip to Illinois. The fact that she was pregnant had totally left her.

"We can take you to the store. And we know about a party. Wanna come?"

"Sure," Underhill said, and handed her suitcases to the man.

After she bought needles, the man drove her to his apartment, which coincidentally was in the Taj Mahal Apartments where she had once lived, although she hadn't remembered seeing these people there.

She told her new friends that she wanted to buy cocaine and asked if they could get her some.

They smiled broadly, assuring her they'd be more than happy to help. Once inside their apartment, they started making phone calls. Ten minutes later, a dealer walked in to make the trade and Underhill exchanged the Cartier watch for one gram of powdered cocaine worth about $120.

Her two friends shared the bounty and it quickly disappeared into their veins. Whenever Underhill did drugs it was like taking a fast sled downhill. She couldn't stop. Two hours later, she bought a second $120 gram with the balance of the jewelry. She had no idea the Cartier watch alone retailed for $17,000.

Bondurant drove home from his dinner party and walked in from the garage.

"Sandra?" he said, entering the den where he expected to see her watching television. He walked to the stairs and called her name. Still nothing. He rushed through the house looking for her, then checked the side and front yards. His puzzled thoughts turned to annoyance as he pondered where she could have gone. He went upstairs to change his suit and when he opened the closet door he saw the empty hangers where Sandra's clothes had hung. Then he realized her absence could be permanent.

He paced the room trying to imagine what could have happened to her. The name Joe Davila came to mind. But Davila was a moocher, and his interest lay in what Underhill could do for him. She had no money. Then Bondurant froze, thinking how she could have come across some.

His heart beat rapidly as he flew down the stairs, ran to the hall closet, and jerked open the door. Quickly checking behind the hot water heater, he stared at the empty crevice where his jewelry had been.

"Damn," he yelled, slamming the door shut. He'd been certain she didn't know about his hiding place. But left alone, maybe she started searching for whatever she could find. One thing was for sure, with all he had to worry about, he wouldn't get much sleep tonight.

The phone rang at ten the next morning and Sandra Underhill's strained voice pierced his aching head.

"Where in the hell are you?" he asked.

"At the Taj Mahal. I'm with some friends."

"You get over here right now!"

She hung up the phone knowing better than to argue. The euphoria that had floated her through the evening had evaporated with the phone call, and she immediately left the apartment and her two companions who had crashed into a drugged sleep.

She started walking toward Bondurant's house—a good two miles away. An hour later, a very tired Underhill strolled into his house, dragging her two suitcases.

"Okay, where is it?"

"Where's what?"

"You know goddamn well what I'm talking about. Where's my jewelry?"

"I won't lie to you. I took it. But you had my driver's license in there and—"

"To hell with your driver's license. Have you any idea how much that jewelry was worth?"

She shook her head.

"Probably over $30,000. One watch alone cost a fortune."

She swallowed hard. "I don't feel so good."

"I don't give a damn how you feel. I want that jewelry back. And I want it back now."

"Miles, I'm sorry. I shouldn't have taken it, but I was so upset that you'd go out and leave me alone on your birthday. I didn't know the jewelry cost that much. But take my word for it. It's gone."

Bondurant shoved his hands in his pockets and stared at Underhill as he paced across the parquet floor.

"I'm going to call the police."

She sucked in a deep breath. Her involvement in any felony theft would revoke her parole and put her right back in prison. She thought of running, but with all the jewelry gone, she had no way to leave. "Miles, please," she begged, "you know what they'll do to me."

"Guess you should have thought about that earlier," he said with a haughty smirk. "You've screwed up royally this time, young lady. You've got to learn to take responsibility for your actions." He went to the phone and punched in 911.

As they waited for the officer to arrive, Bondurant said, "Look at you. You're a mess. You got back into drugs, didn't you?"

Her gaze fell downward. "Yeah. Mainlined some coke."

Bondurant shook his head. His silent disgust lingering in the room yelled louder than his words.

Within 30 minutes, the front doorbell chimed. He opened it and greeted the police officer.

Underhill tried not to look as nervous as she felt. She hadn't eaten since lunch the day before and her stomach heaved from the drugs and her hunger.

"Sandra," Bondurant called. "Sergeant Wilheidt needs you to make a statement. I've told him the truth."

"What did you say?"

"I said you took my jewelry."

"That's not true," she said, defiantly frowning at the young policeman.

The confused officer looked at Bondurant, then back at Underhill.

"I need a written statement from both of you."

"Fine," she said, and filled out a burglary report stating she knew about the jewelry but had no idea who took it.

After the policeman left, Bondurant turned to Underhill and raised his chin. "You may stay here until you find a place to live. But you had better make it quick."

Sandra Underhill's parole had mandated that she attend Alcoholics Anonymous every week and Bondurant had driven her to and from the meetings, but he had discouraged her from making friends with "those kind of people."

Now he needed help from "those kind of people." He decided not to trust Sandra to make departure arrangements, so he called Jenny Campbell, Sandra's AA sponsor, who had been addicted to hard drugs herself but had been clean for 12 years. He felt relieved to hear Campbell's soft, caring voice. He told her, "Sandra stole my jewelry and used it for drugs. I think she needs to get into some program where she can get cleaned up once and for all. Do you know of any?"

"The best place around here is Pinestreet Rehab. But there's a long waiting list. It's a live-in facility for four to six weeks. Very concentrated. She'll have classes in self-esteem where she'd hopefully learn to stop abusing herself." Campbell sighed, "Let me see what I can do."

Campbell would soon complete her certification for substance abuse counseling. With her contacts, Bondurant hoped to pull some strings.

"In the meantime," Campbell offered, "I want Sandra to live with me. I know all the signs to look for. Believe me, over here she'll stay sober."

# Chapter Fourteen

Thanks to Jenny Campbell's arm-twisting, only nine days after Sandra Underhill moved in with her, Pinestreet Rehabilitation called with an opening. Underhill wanted to go because she knew she needed help, having sunk to the lowest depth of her life the night she traded Bondurant's jewelry for drugs.

The loss of his trinkets didn't worry her. But by injecting cocaine into her veins, she'd also injected cocaine into the bloodstream of her 4½-month fetus, and knew she could produce a child with congenital defects or drug withdrawal seizures.

Jenny Campbell drove Underhill to the secret location of Pinestreet on October 4, 1993. A building packed with addictive people would be easy prey to drug dealers, but as an additional safeguard, a high metal fence had been erected around the entire rehab. The women neared the two-story building that looked like an office building or motel. Many buildings in the surrounding neighborhood had boards over windows and doors, making the entire area resemble Como.

Campbell dropped her at the rehab's front door and wished her luck.

An employee directed Underhill to the main classroom, a large upstairs room that looked cozy with carpeted floors and burlap-covered walls. She walked to one wall of floor-to-ceiling windows and peered down on a courtyard, and smiled when she saw clients down there smoking.

An instructor showed Underhill to her bedroom. She explained that most of the 25 bedrooms were on the second floor; a hall separated the men's and women's rooms. Only those most trustworthy could sleep in the two unsupervised downstairs bedrooms.

Underhill strolled into class the first day and smiled at her fellow classmates, the 45 men and women she hoped would like her once they knew her. From outward appearances, the crowd looked anything but homogenous. Earrings pierced many men's ears and some women wore them in their noses and lips. A few men had long flowing hair but some people were also dressed in conservative business attire.

The classmates' common bond was their addiction, which they now were forced to confront.

The morning session began with each client rising, giving only his or her first name, and saying, "I am an alcoholic and a drug addict." But when one woman declared her addiction, her voice boomed louder than the others and she had a boldness about her that seemed to smother the room.

Before Underhill left the classroom, the same woman approached her and said, "What do you think about our crummy little bedrooms? Aren't they the pits?"

Underhill looked at the woman whose dark blond hair had been cut so short, it looked like a bowl had been used to guide the clipping shears, but the top remained longer.

Her aggressive manner made it difficult to notice that she had beautiful smooth skin, a perfectly turned up nose, and probably wasn't older than 20.

Underhill shrugged, trying to ignore her question because in her opinion the little bedrooms were adequate.

When class convened the second day, the loud voice was absent.

"Where's Carri Coppinger?" the instructor asked.

A petite brunette raised her hand. "I'm her roommate and she was still sleeping when I left."

The instructor nodded to an assistant. "Go get Carri, please."

Fifteen minutes later, the class heard Coppinger's voice thundering from the hall before they saw her. She addressed the young woman who had been sent to deliver her. "It was so noisy last night. I couldn't get to sleep until two. No wonder I had so damn much trouble getting up. Missed breakfast, too." Coppinger entered the classroom wearing baggy jeans and an extra-large t-shirt that hung around her ample body. In contrast to her refined facial features, she had broad shoulders and large breasts, and when she walked into the room she strutted like a man.

In comparison, the woman made Underhill feel quiet and shy. She didn't need that kind of intimidation and made a mental note to avoid Coppinger. Someone with her attitude would be bad company and a bad influence.

The center distributed yellow forms for clients to daily register their feelings and hopefully their progress. Underhill looked at the first line: "Your goal at Pinestreet?" Thinking about all of the erratic behavior that had marred her life, she wrote: "To stay more level-headed and not make quick, unwise decisions."

Everyone had been assigned the project of making a line graph of their life. Underhill's reflected all peaks and valleys. She began her graph by plummeting toward a valley in 1975 and noted, "Mother gave me away." Also in 1975, her father drowned and her grandmother died. She reached bottom in 1977 when her brother-in-law raped her. Then sharply rising to a peak, she ran away from home the same year. The pinnacle came in 1978—"First shot of dope." The year 1982 showed a slight dip when she married Lonnie, but the line rose upward with the births of Nicole in 1984 and Joshua in 1985.

Spiraling downward again, she considered her 1986 divorce from her abusive husband to be extremely negative, and only worse getting busted and having her children taken away. She began an upswing with her second marriage, hitting the high point in 1990—the birth of Angelina—but that abruptly turned downward when she went to prison and lost her daughter.

By the end of the first week, Sandra Underhill had come to love her Pinestreet sponsor, Brenda, because of her genuine interest and never-ending patience. After Brenda had listened to Sandra at length during their weekly counseling session, she said, "Sandra, every other word is 'Miles,' do you realize that?"

Underhill looked surprised and shook her head.

"To tell you the truth, I think you're addicted to the man. That's every bit as damaging as the other addictions you have."

"How do I stop thinking about him? It's the same way with all my hang-ups—Miles, drugs, and beer. I still have the cravings."

"Actually the cravings are the disease," Brenda told her. "Use replacement therapy. What do you enjoy that is less harmful than drugs, alcohol, and Miles?"

"Ding Dongs and cigarettes."

Brenda laughed. "Okay. If you can get someone to bring you those two vices, I think you'd be less frustrated. It's too hard to give up everything at once.

"And by the way, Sandra, I've heard good reports on you from your instructor. You've never been disciplined and all your homework is complete and on time, so I've nominated you to have one of the downstairs bedrooms."

Underhill stared back in amazement. She pointed to her chest and said, "Me?"

"Yes, you," Brenda laughed. "You've only been here a week, but I think you deserve it. The rooms are much larger."

The news delighted Underhill. Then she went back to thinking about Ding Dongs. Because of her abrupt departure from Bondurant's home, she knew he wouldn't want to visit, let alone bring her anything. She took a deep breath and called Joe Davila.

Davila sounded amused to hear her voice. "Hey, girl. What cha doin'?"

"I'm at Pinestreet blowing off all that candy I got hooked on. I wondered if you could do me a favor?"

"Depends. What do you need?"

"We can have visitors every Sunday afternoon from two-thirty to four. Could you bring me a carton of cigarettes and some Ding Dongs?"

Davila laughed. "Shit, I can do that. And for all the nice stuff you've given me, I'll even fuckin' pay for them."

After Davila appeared the following Sunday with the requested items, Underhill began putting him on her daily yellow sheet under, "People I can trust." Her list was remarkably short.

Frequently, Sandra Underhill found Carri Coppinger staring at her. It made her uncomfortable and she tried to avoid the woman.

One day at lunch, Underhill sat with two friends at a table for four. Coppinger spied the vacant seat and pushed her tray onto their table. It wouldn't have been Coppinger's mode to ask if the seat were taken. "That morning session was sure shit, wasn't it?"

The women ignored her, but that didn't seem to bother Coppinger. Underhill knew what she meant because their sessions dredged up painful history over lifetimes of problems that everyone wanted to forget. But they also learned about each other. In the daily classroom discussions, Carri Coppinger had no problem telling everyone she was a lesbian.

Coppinger looked across the table at Underhill. "Great looking shirt," she told her and her eyes lingered over the bustline.

Embarrassed by Coppinger's stare, Underhill quickly finished her lunch and left. The second week, she spent her time trying to avoid the woman. At one point when Coppinger continued shadowing her, Underhill turned around and bellowed, "You know, I really don't think it's cool to be gay." Undaunted, Coppinger pursued her even more, treasuring Sandra like a distant trophy because she found her so difficult to win.

"Positive affirmations" is a process in which the students stood on top of their chair seats to say 10 good things about themselves. The room held no desks, only chairs, and they were in a circle so everyone faced each other. Sandra Underhill found affirmations very difficult after a lifetime of being told she was worthless.

Underhill dreaded her turn and visibly shook when she climbed on top of her chair. Looking down at her shoes, she began, "I'm a good person." The class members had to lean forward to hear her quiet voice. "I can do what I need to do today. I'm special." She paused to think of something, anything, that was constructive.

Her instructor sat in a chair identical to the students'. She let a few silent moments go by, then prompted. "Do you trust people, Sandra?"

"Not many, ma'am. I find it hard to trust. I've had two husbands. One beat me. The other turned me over to the police. My current boyfriend kicked me out of his house. No, ma'am, I've learned not to trust people."

"Sometimes, we need to trust. There *are* good people out there."

"I've never found any. Do you remember when my mother shaved my head and I ran away from home?"

The instructor and students nodded in unison. Her story had riveted them.

"I left home three months after the shaving. Had to wait 'cause I was as bald as a cantaloupe. I wore a scarf around my head and was too embarrassed to go to school. In fact, I ended up dropping out. Anyway, when I left Illinois, I went to live with my father's second wife who lived in Florida, but I ran out of money in Pascagoula, Mississippi. So I got a job as a waitress at a roadside steak house. My hair had barely grown an inch and a half and I had to lie about my age since I was only fourteen.

"For a year I worked hard, didn't have any friends, and went back to my cheap little apartment every night. Then one day, I confided in another waitress. I told her my age and went through my whole life story because I thought we were friends. She reported me to the restaurant management who checked my background. They found that my mother had a missing persons report out on me. So the police put me in a girls' home, and my mom let me sit there for six weeks before she came to pick me up. That's my experience with trusting people."

The class fell silent. Then the instructor said, "Sandra, would you be interested in doing a special project? Something that would teach you to put trust in another person?"

"I don't think I could."

"Here's what I have in mind. For one entire day, from the time you get up, until you go to bed, we'll blindfold you. We'll have someone be your guide. You'll have to trust that person for the entire day. Would you be willing?"

Underhill looked pained. But her classmates enthusiastically urged her on. Timidly, she said, "Okay. I guess so."

"We'll need a helper. Do we have a volunteer?"

Immediately Carri Coppinger's hand shot up. Sandra almost fainted.

* * *

Early the next morning, Coppinger knocked at Underhill's door with a brown scarf the instructor had loaned her for the blindfold. She securely tied it around Sandra's eyes.

"Comfy?" she asked.

Sandra nodded.

Coppinger put her arm snugly around Underhill's waist and escorted her out of the room for breakfast and into the cafeteria where they ate all of their meals. Underhill didn't see people looking at her, but she could feel everyone's eyes. She winced at Coppinger's loud voice as she asked what she wanted for breakfast. Sandra realized Carri had complete control of her and she found it frightening. All morning she wanted to jerk off the blindfold and declare herself incapable of learning to trust.

In class, Underhill sat next to Coppinger who continually whispered in her ear. After a couple hours, Underhill became accustomed to Coppinger's hand on her arm or back, guiding her to their next destination. But as the day progressed with someone so verbal at her ear, Sandra heard constant chatter, especially Coppinger telling her how pretty she was. At other times Carri said, "That sure sounds like a jerk you lived with. But then I haven't met a man who's worth a plug nickel."

Lunch and dinner required the same assistance as breakfast, except now Coppinger gave elaborate descriptions of the food.

"I wouldn't choose the Jell-O, Sandra. It's shaking. Looks awfully scared."

Sandra found herself laughing at Carri, and was surprised to be enjoying her company.

But having endured the entire day without sight, Underhill felt relieved when she could finally remove the blindfold and go to bed. Coppinger gave her a goodbye hug that lasted too long. But Underhill began to think that, as a friend, Coppinger was fun to be around.

A week later, Underhill walked into her room and found a note on her bed. She unfolded the sheet of paper and found stick figures of two women, broad smiles on their faces with their arms outstretched to each other. Carri had drawn little hearts floating above the women's heads. Sandra saw a different side of her.

> "In the years before we met
> The friends I had were few.
> I never dreamt that I would find,
> A friend as dear as you."

The notes continued, and each one became friendlier than its predecessor. Underhill began answering. With Coppinger so caring and attentive, it was hard not to like her. Then Carri turned up the heat:

> "My love for you grows everyday,
> It's like a seed within my heart,
> Growing slowly in little spurts,
> Like a flower new in spring."

In the middle of the night of the third week, Underhill woke, sensing the presence of another person in her room. She opened her eyes thinking her roommate had gotten out of bed, but instead was shocked to see Carri standing over her. "What are *you* doing here?" Sandra asked. "You could get us in a whole bunch of trouble."

In the dim glow of the streetlight outside her bedroom window, Underhill saw Coppinger's smile. "I just wanted to see you."

Then quietly she turned and went back upstairs. Underhill lay there, unable to sleep. She kept thinking how she had first perceived Coppinger as overbearing, but now realized she was just a little girl, needful and searching for a friend. Then as she thought about her treatment at the hands of men, she wondered if maybe a woman would be better.

The incident lingered in her mind the next morning as she headed to class. They were acting out "families" today. After the group had heard her life story, they always chose her to play the role of the "lost child" who had to stay in the background acting shy, quiet, and withdrawn. Sandra knew the role. Carri felt her pain and sent her another note:

> "All your life you've been neglected,
> Ripped apart from your own self.
> All the years of pain and suffering,
> Have left you alone and bereft."

Coppinger's understanding comforted Underhill. It was difficult to ignore someone who treated her so sympathetically. But it would be a week before she could drift off to sleep without thinking Coppinger would come visiting again.

Underhill's days at Pinestreet were stuffed with activities. Class lasted most of the day and they had homework to do every evening. They used the gym for their weekly volleyball matches. Other times, buses transported the students to Narcotics Anonymous lectures where they heard personal testimonies of other ex-addicts reciting how they rid themselves of drugs. Underhill found their success stories inspiring. The center also took them to AA and NA dances, roller skating, and picnics in the park. All the activities added to her resolve not to do drugs.

Soon Coppinger followed Underhill's example and made it to class on time and showed a more positive attitude. Sandra didn't know if Carri just wanted to be near her, or if she actually wanted to work the program. Coppinger's addictions had been alcohol and marijuana. Rarely would she take hard drugs.

In class discussions, Coppinger talked about her lifestyle, saying, "You people just don't understand how I feel. I've always been attracted to women. I'm the 'male' of the relationship because I enjoy taking care of women. I didn't choose to be gay."

Derisive murmurs from the class made Coppinger all the more adamant. "Listen class, we don't have a choice in our sexual orientation. It's how we're born."

As Sandra Underhill's 30 days neared an end, she begged her counselor to let her stay two more weeks. The administration happily granted her request, especially when they knew Carri Coppinger would be leaving. Twice Sandra and Carri had been counseled individually against having a relationship because the Pinestreet administration saw it as possibly inhibiting their recovery.

Coppinger cried when she heard that Underhill had decided to stay, and told her, "I can't wait to get out but I don't want to leave without you. I'm clean now and nothing is going to make me try booze or grass again. Sandra, you're the same way. Leave with me."

"No. I like it here. I feel so much better about myself. I just want a couple more weeks."

Coppinger hugged her, and went off to her room to pack. She left a couple hours later, but before she walked out the door, she handed Sandra another note:

"The good times; the bad times,
I don't know what to do.
What will life be like,
Without the likes of you?"

"Don't forget me." Coppinger said as she headed for the Pinestreet bus that would take her home.

After Coppinger left, Underhill had little chance to forget her. The after-care program required Carri to be at Pinestreet three nights a week. Underhill knew what time to stand by the entry so she could see Coppinger walk in. Clients could have no contact with outsiders, but Carri would mouth "I love you" through the glass partitions, then walk away.

Underhill eagerly listened for mail call and looked forward to receiving Coppinger's notes. Then just before Underhill ended her stay at Pinestreet, Coppinger's note read, "I want to know you better—physically."

# Chapter Fifteen

After Jenny Campbell attended Sandra Underhill's graduation from Pinestreet on a brisk November 17, 1993, she took her home to her comfortable, but modest, brick and frame three-bedroom home. Underhill had received no invitation to live with Bondurant.

Unable to find a job in her sixth month of pregnancy, her sole financial support consisted of food stamps. She felt like a burden to Campbell who reassured her that she was like the sister she never had.

Underhill had only been at Campbell's an hour when Carri Coppinger drove up. She had come by on her way to her job as a certified nurse's aide at a nursing home in Arlington. Underhill had never known anyone as intense as Carri. Coppinger acted either extremely happy, her shrill voice telling raucous jokes and she laughing loudest of all; or she would be despondent, pensive, and withdrawn, and Underhill would have to coax her to talk. Sandra wrestled over what to do about her moody friend, and now realized she'd soon have to make a decision about a sexual relationship.

Coppinger walked in and sat down, continually grinning at Underhill. If Campbell questioned Coppinger's interest in Underhill, she didn't show it, but Underhill flushed with all the attention.

Before she left, Coppinger said, "Save some time for me tomorrow. We'll go for a ride."

Sandra knew what Carri had in mind and found herself nervously fascinated.

The next day, Underhill sat in Coppinger's truck. Carri said, "Did you read all my notes?"

Sandra nodded.

"What do you think?" Coppinger said, taking her hand.

Underhill pulled away. "You've become my best friend. You're always there for me. And I love being with you. But I'm still not sure it's for me."

"Okay, I won't push." Coppinger let a few minutes go by. "What about all the crap the men in your life have handed you? They've been nothing but users and abusers. They're jerks."

"That's for sure. Broke my bones. Took my children."

"Besides, a woman is more caring and patient," Coppinger said. Then she looked lovingly at Sandra, "And a woman knows what another woman likes. You know, in bed."

Underhill was surprised to feel a flutter of sexual arousal deep within her as Coppinger's gentle coaxing began to find its mark.

"Got a surprise for you," Coppinger said, and handed Underhill a brightly wrapped box and told her to open it.

Sandra tore off the paper and found a matching beaded necklace and bracelet. "Cool," she said, holding the beads to her neck and trying to see herself in the truck's rearview mirror.

"Made them myself."

"I can't believe it." Underhill said, and hurriedly fastened the pieces around her neck and wrist.

"Yeah. Thought about you all the time I was stringing those beads. I really care about you, Sandra. I'd never do anything to hurt you. Please say you'll at least try to be more than a friend?"

Sandra's smile crinkled her eyes, but she felt concern over crossing the line. Once crossed, could she step back without being labeled a lesbian?

Underhill realized Coppinger was courting her and began to see her in a different light. Coppinger's aggressiveness made her seem manly—a very attractive, caring man. She never wore makeup, her hair was cropped shorter than some men's, and she always wore blue jeans and masculine tailored shirts.

Feeling like an inexperienced teenager, Underhill said, "I wouldn't have the first idea . . . you know . . . of what to do."

"Oh, don't worry about that. I'll show you. In fact, I'll tell you." She looked over at Sandra, her eyes twinkling. "Just imagine that you and I are driving around, kinda like now. We're just enjoying the music and each other's company. Say we drive out to the lake and park in a dark, vacant place overlooking the water. For a while, we sit there in silence, feeling the energy intensifying between us." Coppinger glanced at her to gauge her reaction, then looked back at the street. "You reach across and touch my hand, then squeeze it tightly." Coppinger took Underhill's hand, and this time Sandra didn't pull away.

Coppinger continued, "My body is already reacting to your touch, and shivers with total excitement. I reach across and pull your face to mine . . ." She stretched for Sandra's face and kissed her cheek while she did her best to watch the road. She put both hands back on the wheel and said, "As we kiss, my hands begin to slowly explore your body. I find your breasts and gently squeeze your nipples."

"Carri!"

Coppinger smiled broadly. "You begin to breathe heavily and slide your hand up the back of my neck and pull my hair. I begin to squeeze your nipples harder and move my hand to your crotch. I feel your warmth and press my lips harder against yours. I untuck your shirt and circle your nipples with my tongue and begin to bite them."

Perspiration broke out on Underhill's forehead.

"Don't worry. I won't hurt you. Then you start unbuttoning my jeans and slide your hand down inside my pants. You feel my warmth and *total* wetness." She looked at Sandra and took a deep breath. "Okay, man. I can't do this any more. Jesus! I don't know what this does to you, but I'm going to have to take a shower. And with the massager, of course." She laughed her hearty laugh.

Underhill laughed too. "Oh, God, Carri. I see what you mean, and I have to admit you have me *very* curious."

A smile of victory glazed Coppinger's face. "Let's go to my place."

Sandra nodded.

Coppinger drove out to Arlington, the suburb that sat half-way between Dallas and Fort Worth. She pulled up in front of a large two-story home that had been transformed into a rooming house. Once inside, she introduced Sandra to a lesbian who lived on the first floor. "Not my type," Coppinger whispered after they passed the woman and climbed the stairs to Carri's second-floor room.

Now Underhill took the initiative. "You're right, Carri. Show me what it's like to be treated kindly, patiently, and gently. I know all about the other," she said, putting her arm around Coppinger.

They walked into Carri's room and Sandra lit a cigarette. Then she slipped off her shoes.

Coppinger patted the bed. "Come over here. I'll give you a back rub."

"I love back rubs," Underhill murmured and stretched out on the bed. Carri's strong hands caressed Sandra's short body and Sandra smiled with delight. Then she found herself growing eager to experience the intimate contact Coppinger had described. Soon the back rub lost its boundaries, and the women began to enjoy the warmth of each other's body.

Underhill and Coppinger sat propped up in bed on pillows, Sandra smoking a cigarette and watching *Wheel of Fortune,* Carri grinning, happy, and content. Only smudges of Underhill's makeup remained.

"I wuv you, Sandra," Carri said as she massaged the back of Sandra's neck.

Sandra smiled. "I didn't totally dislike that," she said coyly. "Making love to you was very exciting."

"Just wait. You'll love it more each time."

Underhill took a deep drag on her cigarette and thought about what Coppinger had just said. Until Carri came along, Underhill had never considered any sexual option other than with men, but now she was surprised at how she enjoyed all the stroking and caressing. "When did you first realize you were gay?" she asked.

"I can't remember being any other way. A neighbor sexually abused me when I was 4. My mom's convinced—I mean, she knows for *sure* that at that moment in my life, I got all messed up sexually. I have no idea why, but it makes her feel better. You know, like my being gay isn't her fault."

"What do you think?"

"Of course it's not her fault. How could my family have made me gay? When I was in the second grade, all of the children sat on the floor listening to the teacher read stories, but I would lie down and try to look up her skirt. Isn't that an early and clear indication?"

After Coppinger had graduated from high school and rented her own apartment, she finally found the courage to tell her family. She walked into her parent's strict, religiously conservative home one day and happily announced, "I figured out why I'm different—I'm gay."

The family was horrified. If they had suspected her sexual orientation, they had swept it under the rug, hoping it would remain there. Her shocked mother told her she'd burn in hell for being a lesbian.

Ever since Coppinger had been a little girl, she had been religious and couldn't imagine that a compassionate God would condemn her now. She had remembered her parent's God as the great avenger—shooting lightning rods at people.

As they watched TV, Underhill said, "Have you ever had sex with a man?"

"Oh, sure. A few times. I've tried. Really tried. But frankly, I hate their hard, hairy bodies. It makes me sick to have sex with a man." Coppinger shivered.

Underhill laughed. "Why do you think women meet your needs?"

Coppinger blew out her cheeks. "What a great question! I guess since I don't like men, I've always looked to women to make me feel worthwhile. And touching is more important to most women. There's something comforting about a woman's touch that a man just doesn't have. But going way back, I guess I look to women because my abusers were men."

"Abusers? You had more than one?"

"Yeah, I've been abused at the YMCA." Coppinger had always been very athletic and swam for the school team for seven years. She worked out at the Y and didn't have any friends there. An older man, hired to clean the pool, noticed her and got into the water, waiting until she was alone. He came over and rubbed her body, then took her hand and made her feel him. Coppinger had a sick little thought that sex showed people she cared. She was probably 8 or 9 and real skinny, but around then she had started to put on weight and grow breasts.

She didn't tell her parents because they would have made her stop swimming. That type of man always seemed to find her, making her feel safe only at school and church.

"I didn't have a close relationship with my mother," Coppinger said. "She worked hours as an interior decorator. Then too, I was adopted . . ."

Underhill rolled her eyes. "Oh, come on, Carri. I wasn't adopted and my mom hardly ever worked. Talk about relationships. You know what she did to me."

"I know." Coppinger took a deep breath. "My AA counselor tells me I've got to start looking inside when I'm trying to find someone to make me feel worthwhile. I've always been searching for the perfect mother, friend, lover, whatever, to make me feel whole."

"But it sounds like religion helped you feel better."

"Yeah. I'm always talking to God. He's one of my best friends. If it wasn't for God and AA, I don't know what would have happened to me."

Coppinger reached into her nightstand drawer. "Here's a poem I wrote a couple years ago." She handed it to Underhill.

"Life is so unmanageable
  Unmanageable by me.
God is the only answer,
  The answer I'm blind to see.
If I could just remember,
  God has seen me through the storm,
And always brought the sunlight
  With His love to keep me warm."

Underhill smiled and nodded. "That's very good. What made you write it?"

"I was just thinking about God one day. He helped me feel secure when I was a kid. Guess I'm still trying to find that same reassurance to hold onto. I've got to find it somewhere."

# Chapter Sixteen

Sandra Underhill felt deceitful when she thought of Miles Bondurant and her sexual encounters with Carri Coppinger. She had found the first lesbian liaison erotic. Maybe she enjoyed its novelty, but as their lovemaking continued, the novelty wore off. Now she didn't want to return Coppinger's gentle, physical affection because it seemed so unnatural. Sandra would find it very difficult to tell her.

Underhill had been out of Pinestreet for two weeks, and whenever she talked with Bondurant, she couldn't help but bubble enthusiastically about Coppinger. He sounded bored to the point of irritation, causing her to wonder if he had guessed about their lesbian relationship.

One night when he picked her up from an AA meeting, she introduced him to Carri. He took one look at her short hair, listened to her thundering voice, and told Sandra to hurry up and get in his car.

Once Underhill sat next to him, he said, "So that's the lesbian you've been seeing. She *is* gay, isn't she?"

For two days Bondurant thought about his meeting Coppinger, and shuddered at the experience. The woman stayed on his mind, and now he realized how close she and Sandra had become. From past experience, telling Sandra to stay away from Coppinger would probably backfire on him. He phoned Sandra at Jenny Campbell's house and softened his voice until it barely whispered.

"Are you all right?" Underhill asked.

"Got some really bad news today." He paused.

"Well, what is it?" she asked anxiously.

"Lou Gehrig's disease. It's serious. People usually die quickly."

"Oh, my gosh! I don't know anything about Lou Gehrig's."

Bondurant smiled. "Dr. Rose found it through a blood test. He's sending me down to the M.D. Anderson Cancer Center in Houston for more tests. Honey, I'm afraid Rose isn't too optimistic that he found it in time."

Underhill began to sniffle, then said, "This is awful. What will it do to you?"

"I'll deteriorate. Go down to nothing. Won't be able to take care of myself. I'll be confined to a wheel chair. It's a monstrous thing."

Now she openly cried. "How much time do you have?"

"Hard to say, sweetie. Not long."

She didn't hesitate. She told him, "I'll move back. I'll take care of you. I won't let you be alone, ever."

Bondurant smiled broadly.

When Campbell walked in from her counseling job, Underhill told her Bondurant was dying, adding she thought he was full of cancer.

Campbell's voice was heavy with sarcasm, "Full of cancer? Do you honestly believe that? Maybe he's full of shit!"

Underhill's red eyes opened wide, not believing Jenny's reaction. But Campbell didn't argue. She told Sandra to go back and take care of Bondurant, but not to expect his gratitude.

Big and pregnant, Underhill returned to Bondurant's home determined to make his last days comfortable.

A week went by and he hadn't scheduled an appointment at M.D. Anderson.

When she asked him about it, he said, "Rose is taking care of that. Sandra, believe me, I don't need the stress of your questioning me all the time. My doctor would be the first one to tell you that."

The urgency of his situation dissipated and life went on as normal. Bondurant never again discussed his Lou Gehrig's disease.

The following week, Underhill received a call from Coppinger, who worked part time during the day caring for an elderly lady, Ruth McClendon. The woman, crippled with arthritis, needed someone to run errands and drive her to doctor appointments. In mid-December, Coppinger sat with McClendon in a doctor's waiting room while the doctor's schedule ran two hours late. Soon Coppinger had to be at work. She called Sandra and said, "Really need you, girl. I'm in a big-time bind."

Underhill didn't hesitate. She drove Bondurant's sedan to the medical office and took Carri's place beside McClendon. Gratefully, Coppinger went on.

At 6 P.M. Underhill returned home. When she walked in, Bondurant flew into a rage. "And where have you been?"

"Carri had to go to work, so I filled in with Mrs. McClendon."

He stood in the middle of the room with his hands on his hips. "Well, isn't that nice. I had no idea if you'd run off to Como again, or you had a wreck on the freeway. You could have told me."

"I'm sorry. I didn't think it was that late."

"The point is, Sandra, you just didn't think. You get around Carri and you forget about me."

Bondurant's wrath seemed to feed on itself, and he became angrier the longer he spoke. Finally he shouted, "If that goddamn lesbian means more to you than I do, you can just leave."

His outburst of jealousy gave her no options. She had only lived with him for two weeks, but he wanted her out that day, seven months pregnant, and only a week before Christmas.

Coppinger felt responsible for Underhill's plight and suggested they find an apartment. The only one they could afford was a tiny one-bedroom with a kitchen hidden in a closet. It had adequate furniture, but the rent ran a good $25 more than Coppinger paid in the rooming house.

Coppinger grinned as they looked at the apartment. "Hell, we're bigger than the cockroaches. Let's take it."

Underhill agreed and smiled at her friend. She had come to truly love Carri. She had never found anyone so trusting and kind, or so generous and fun to be with.

Coppinger hugged her after they made their decision, and as usual, her hug lingered.

"Please don't do that."

Carri's hurt expression begged Sandra for an explanation.

"You are my dearest friend, but now the size of my body . . ." Underhill said, looking down at her protruding stomach. "It makes intimacy so embarrassing. Don't look at me like that, Carri—if I were dating a man, I wouldn't have sex this far along in my pregnancy."

Underhill didn't know if it was the tone in her voice or the look she gave Carri, but the inference was that from now on their relationship would be strictly platonic.

Coppinger took the change hard. But because of her love for Sandra, she agreed to continue being friends.

Two days later, McClendon fired Coppinger for ignoring her the week she hunted apartments with Underhill. Her firing shoved her into a deep depression. She became almost immobilized knowing that they didn't have enough money to live on.

However, Underhill had an idea and asked Coppinger to drive her to the Ridglea Presbyterian Church on Camp Bowie Boulevard. To Underhill, it was big and impressive and she thought it would probably be wealthy.

Although enormously pregnant, she forced her body out of Coppinger's truck and down the big step to the pavement. She was so short, she looked like she was having twins, and her appearance pleaded for sympathy.

Underhill waddled down the hall of the church offices until she found an assistant minister sitting at his desk. She told the young man that she needed $180 for half of the rent on an apartment. One look at the blooming mother-to-be and he said the church would think about it. A week later they handed over the money. Once the baby was born, Underhill would be eligible for state aid. Her mother had taught her well.

Underhill had groaned and tossed for almost two hours at Harris Methodist Hospital. She had begun labor at an AA-sponsored dance and Coppinger had rushed her to the hospital, then called Bondurant. Finally, he nonchalantly sauntered into the labor room, and she felt relieved to know he cared enough to show up.

Coppinger and a nurse hovered over Underhill as she screamed in pain.

Bondurant sighed, "Come on, Sandra, it can't be *that* bad."

The women shot him disgusted looks, and Sandra would have given anything at that moment for Bondurant to be having the child.

When Coppinger left to find the coffee machine, he leaned toward Sandra. "I can't believe it. You're here with your gay girlfriend. Even the *Bible* says 'A man with a man, a woman with a woman, is an abomination.' "

At that moment, a pain grabbed Underhill.

Bondurant said, "Okay, I'll be nice."

It was past noon when the orderlies rushed Sandra Underhill to the delivery room and Bondurant and Coppinger followed.

Underhill had never taken so long to have a baby, but she never had one that weighed 8 pounds, 7 ounces. Cody Lee Miles Bondurant was born at 2:15 P.M.

Dr. Don Smith, whom Bondurant knew from TCU, suggested that he go clean off his new son.

Bondurant stiffened as though he had been struck. "You want *me* to clean off all that muck?"

Coppinger didn't hesitate. Fascinated with the entire process, she eagerly went to the shivering infant to give him his first bath.

As soon as the doctor left the room, Bondurant rushed into the hall after him.

An orderly returned Underhill to her room, and a nurse who overheard Bondurant's conversation with the doctor spoke to the new mother.

"I don't care if that man is the father of your son. He's definitely someone you should stay away from." At that moment the nurse was paged, leaving Sandra to wonder what she meant.

After living with the new baby for two weeks, the women realized they needed a larger place and found a two-bedroom duplex on Byers Street. They could afford it only because of its run-down, dirty condition. Before they could move in, the duplex had to be completely cleaned and painted.

Bondurant acquiesced to letting the women and Cody stay with him for two weeks while they scoured the duplex. He hovered over Cody and happily baby-sat each evening as the women worked at the duplex.

While they were at Bondurant's house, Underhill noticed that whenever Coppinger walked into a room, Bondurant would either leave or refuse to talk with Coppinger. Only two days after they had moved in, he abruptly went upstairs with his dinner plate and stayed there for the remainder of the evening, drinking Scotch and watching TV.

During that visit, Underhill thought she detected a difference in Bondurant. Although his friends might never have believed it, she had witnessed him smoking marijuana a couple times a week ever since she had known him. She wondered if the dope had been killing his brain cells all these years. She had heard pot did that.

Bondurant's treatment of Coppinger caused Underhill to work harder and faster on the duplex so they could get out of his house. When their move-in date arrived on April 1st, they left with undisguised glee.

Bondurant visited the duplex and lingered over Cody. One night after he left, Underhill said, "I'm worried. Miles is acting so possessive around Cody, especially in the last two days since the DNA results arrived and showed he's the father."

"Cody looks just like Miles," Carri said. "He had to know he was his all along."

"Yeah. But the DNA proved it. I'm actually afraid he might try to take him from me. He put a lot of weight on the DNA—wouldn't let the doctor write 'Bondurant' on Cody's birth certificate until the test came back."

"You know what he tried to get the doctor to do in the hospital?" Coppinger asked.

"What? That's when the nurses told me to stay away from him."

"Miles asked the doctor to go back to the delivery room for a blood sample from the umbilical cord to run a DNA test. The doctor said no because he didn't want to ask for your permission after all you'd been through."

"Damn him! I'm scared. He only wants Cody. He certainly doesn't love me." She looked at Coppinger. "I'm probably more worried because I've lost my other children, but I can't lose Cody too. Miles keeps saying I'm a rotten mother. If he took the parental custody to court, you know how his background would compare to mine."

Underhill folded her arms over her chest. "There's only one thing to do. We've got to get out of Texas."

Coppinger looked excited. "Where are we going?"

"We could drive your truck to Illinois and stay at my mother's house until we decide what to do." They had only lived in the duplex a little over a month, but Underhill wanted to leave that night.

Coppinger eagerly stood up to start packing while Underhill wrote a note to tape on the door: "Miles, take anything you want. We're not coming back."

# Chapter Seventeen

When Carri Coppinger and Sandra Underhill entered the public housing unit of Sandra's mother, Elaina, in Granite City the first week in May, it seemed more decrepit than ever. Mental pictures of Carri's mother with her flair for interior design flashed through Sandra's mind. She cringed thinking Carri would see how Elaina lived.

The tile floors had been so abused that random pieces had come loose, revealing the black adhesive underneath. Food that children had dropped stuck to the mastic, forcing her to watch her step.

Underhill's mother now raised three of her daughter Allyson's children, who was too nervous to cope with all four of her boisterous youngsters. Underhill noticed that since her mother had grown older, she didn't have the energy to discipline her grandchildren. Elaina's shrill voice reverberated throughout the house, but her yelling was ineffective as the children continued their mischief, knowing their grandmother wouldn't leave her TV game shows long enough to punish them.

The three bedrooms upstairs were already full, so Sandra and Carri slept on two sofas in the living room.

* * *

After the two women had been in Granite City 10 days, Bondurant called. Elaina turned toward Underhill and mouthed, "It's Miles."

As she walked toward the phone, Coppinger reached out to stop her. "Don't talk to him," she whispered. "You know he'll only throw you out if you go back."

She straightened. "Mom, tell him he can only talk to you."

Elaina looked surprised but gave Bondurant the message. After listening to him for a few minutes, she said, "Sandra, he says he misses Cody and thinks it's awful when a father can't see his own child."

Underhill said, "Tell him he can come see Cody, but I'm definitely not interested in going back to Fort Worth."

Elaina relayed the message, frowned, and hung up. "Oh, my God, he sounds furious."

"Bet he was," Coppinger said. "He realizes he's lost control of Sandra. That would devastate him."

Carri Coppinger took in the situation in which she found herself, and immediately went out and landed a job. She found work at a nursing home that paid a meager salary, but it would cover her half of her truck payment; her mother paid the other half. She gave the balance to Elaina, who had enough trouble paying her bills without three more mouths to feed.

Three weeks on her job, Coppinger walked out the front door toward her truck. She took a right and walked down the block of broken concrete sidewalk and cluttered front yards, but when she reached the corner, her truck wasn't there. She glanced across the street, then turned and hurried to the other end of the block, thinking she might have been confused about which corner. A mist began drizzling as she arrived at the second corner. Still no truck.

Damp and heartbroken, she hurried back to Elaina's

house. With the expense of refurbishing the Fort Worth duplex, she had been unable to make last month's truck payment, and without immediately notifying her mother about the move, her mother's check had arrived too late to make this month's payment on time. Coppinger knew from her contract, that three missed payments and Ford would pick up the truck. She called the company and said, "Y'all, I can't find my truck. I parked it right near where I'm staying." She gave the information Ford requested, and waited while they fed it into their computer.

"Miss Coppinger," the woman began apologetically, "we repossessed your truck. You were two months late with your payment, and we were informed that you took it out of state and didn't plan on making any more payments."

"Who on earth told you that, and how did you know where to find it?"

"A gentleman in Forth Worth was kind enough to give us the information."

Coppinger slumped to a lumpy couch in the living room. Her depression began to grow. The truck wasn't her only problem; missing her weekly probation meetings also bothered her. Her crime, involving a friend named Tony Rapolo, had been one of naïve cooperation. She remembered Rapolo's anxious face when he explained he couldn't get to the bank in time to cash three checks. She knew she'd pass that bank on the way home so she offered to help. She presented his checks for payment and in minutes the bank called the police. She could still feel her embarrassment at learning the checks were hot, and that Rapolo had helped himself to other people's mailboxes.

Now she had her probation officer to worry about, and a revocation meant jail.

Bondurant smiled as he opened his front door for Maggie Rhiner, Sandra's parole officer. The attractive woman, in her mid-30s, had supervised Underhill for over two years. She had readily accepted Bondurant's invitation because she fondly remembered him from the previous year, when he gave her a Shih Tzu puppy. Since Bondurant wouldn't let Underhill take Pebbles with her on her many moves, he had bought her another puppy, but one of the apartments he had exiled her to allowed no pets, so she had had to give up the dog.

"How's Jezebel doing?" Bondurant asked.

"She's wonderful. Growing like a weed."

"Those little dogs don't make very big weeds."

They both laughed.

"Sit down," Bondurant said after leading her into the living room. "I'm glad you could come. There's a few things I wanted to discuss with you. I don't think you know that Sandra moved to Illinois."

Rhiner looked shocked. "Illinois? She never once discussed it with me. That's a serious parole violation."

"I know," Bondurant said. "That's just typical of her. I can imagine how she puts on her best behavior when she meets with you. I thought it only fair to let you know about the *real* Sandra."

Rhiner's eyes never left Bondurant's. "There's more?"

"Sandra's fully aware that drugs and alcohol aren't allowed while she's on parole. But, frankly, she drinks like a fish. Not only that, she's on drugs." He spoke slowly and fixed his eyes on Rhiner. "Hard drugs."

The woman gasped, and took out a yellow ruled tablet. "How often does she do drugs?"

Bondurant smiled to himself as the woman bought his story. "Fairly often. She gets downright crazy. But actually the worst part is when she's drunk. You should see how she devastates this place. See that armoire?" he said, pointing.

She turned around, then nodded.

"That used to be filled with beautiful hand-painted Haviland dishes. She smashed every piece."

Bondurant wanted to laugh when he heard Rhiner cluck her tongue against the roof of her mouth and listened to her pen scratch the tablet.

"I'll have to spend more time checking up on Sandra,"

she said. "I thought she was doing so well last year when you gave me Jezebel."

He leaned toward her. "Now what I'm going to tell you is even more serious. I don't know what repercussions this could have for Sandra. But one night she tried to kill me. I was just sitting here watching television and she snuck up and started slapping the holy bejeepers out of me. Just really coming down hard with her hand and fist. Then she threatened me with a carving knife."

Rhiner shook her head. "A carving knife? That's terrible. What did you do?"

"I called 911. Got the police out here to take her away. She was arrested and spent the night in jail. But I guess I'm just too kind-hearted. I went down the next day and got her released. I didn't press charges."

"Mr. Bondurant, the things you've told me are grounds for parole revocation. And this business of Sandra being arrested is something that can't be disputed. It's automatic revocation for not reporting an arrest even if it later gets dismissed."

Wide-eyed, Bondurant said, "Is that right?"

On June 10, Sandra Underhill received a registered letter from Bondurant containing a notarized statement signed by Joe Davila. Davila swore that Underhill told him she took $30,000 worth of jewelry from Bondurant to buy cocaine. A note at the bottom in Davila's hand read: "Every man has the right to be with his son."

She was positive money had crossed hands to get Davila that involved. According to his letter, Bondurant threatened to turn Davila's statement over to the Fort Worth Police if Underhill didn't return Cody to Texas. His letter warned, "If you choose not to do this, there will be an arrest warrant issued for you and you will be a wanted person. Should you run, I will see to it that Cody is permanently mine while you are in prison. You'll never see him again." He even threatened to put her profile on the

*America's Most Wanted* television show, and contact her parole officer so she would be sent back to prison. He wrote, "I don't care if you're a lesbian or not, but you're going to be one in Fort Worth [jail] or Gatesville [prison].

"I know where everyone lives, everyone, almost from the minute you open this letter you'll be watched. *YOU HAVE THREE (3) DAYS.*" As a postscript he added, "I've done my homework this time, and there's more. Don't underestimate me when it comes to Cody."

Underhill felt Bondurant's vise tightening around her throat and didn't want to involve Coppinger in her problems.

"Go home to your family in Chattanooga," she urged. "Miles will make your life miserable."

"I won't go to Chattanooga unless you go with me." Coppinger called her parents but learned they would only pay her fare to Tennessee. Sandra was not welcome.

"That's okay," Underhill told her, "they probably think we're still having a relationship."

"That settles it," Coppinger said. "I'll only go where you go."

Underhill took Bondurant's letter to a lawyer and asked if he could do what he threatened. When the lawyer learned of her parole status, he suggested she not take any chances and comply with Bondurant's requests.

On June 13, the last day of the time limit, Bondurant arrived in a Lincoln Town Car that he had rented to transport Sandra and Cody back to Fort Worth.

Unhappy to see him, Underhill went out to his car to talk. She had left Cody with her mother, not wanting Bondurant to have an opportunity to be with the boy until he agreed to her demands. "I won't go without Carri," she boldly told him.

Bondurant shook his head. "I don't want that lesbian around."

"I can't leave Carri stranded in a strange town. If you

ever want to see your son again, you'll not only take Carri back to Fort Worth, you'll also help her with her probation problem. I know you called Ford Motors. That's why Carri's in trouble in the first place."

"You're asking too much."

"It's not too much for you. I know your silver tongue. Just talk to her probation officer and explain everything."

Bondurant threatened, cajoled, and pleaded, but Underhill held her ground. Finally he agreed to buy a bus ticket to Fort Worth for Coppinger, as well as talk to her probation officer. In return, Underhill consented to pack up Cody and accompany Bondurant to Forth Worth.

Bondurant softened when he saw Cody and a few miles later was making faces and clowning with the baby.

Underhill smiled. Miles had always been such a paradox. He'd go to great lengths to cause her problems, then he'd go to even greater lengths to solve them.

The first night they drove as far as Joplin, Missouri, where Bondurant rented one motel room. Underhill knew where he expected her to sleep. She climbed into bed and curled up on the edge of the mattress, but soon he crawled to her and began stroking her body with his big, familiar hands. She lay dormant until he started arousing the sensual feeling she once had for him. She turned to face him and he tugged at her nightgown. Within minutes he straddled her, whispering how happy he was to have her back.

# Chapter Eighteen

When Miles Bondurant and Sandra Underhill arrived in Fort Worth the next evening, they found the light blinking on their answering machine. A message from Carri Coppinger said: "Hi guys. I'm over here at AA. Got in yesterday since the bus took me straight through. I'll wait for you here."

They piled back into the car and picked up Coppinger. Bondurant treated everyone to dinner at their favorite Mexican restaurant and willingly took his turn holding Cody when the baby became cranky.

Underhill's surprise showed in her face. She was also pleased to witness Bondurant treating Coppinger politely.

He turned to Underhill. "You know I mentioned on the way home that I'd like you to go back to work for me?

She nodded.

Bondurant had planned to have Underhill go to the office and Coppinger would stay home and take care of Cody. Hearing his plans, Carri looked concerned. Underhill told Bondurant that Carri was manic-depressive and took Lithium to keep even-tempered. But even on the drug, certain things triggered a nervous reaction, such as Cody's crying.

"I'm sorry," Coppinger apologized.

"It's not your fault," Underhill assured her. Turning to Bondurant, she said, "We can work it out. I can take Cody's porta-crib to the office and keep his formula in the little refrigerator you keep drinks in. Babies sleep a lot at four months. I'm sure it could work out just fine."

Coppinger said, "I'm going to try to get my job back at the nursing home. But I bet they're really pissed at me for taking off like I did."

"Okay, sugar," he said to Underhill. "Whatever you work out is fine. We could really use your help."

From completely ignoring Carri Coppinger a couple of months ago when the women lived with him while refurbishing the duplex, Bondurant now sat with Coppinger in the evenings and talked and laughed. The two of them would pass a joint back and forth and enjoy a couple of beers. Underhill couldn't have been more astonished, but she had given up trying to figure him out.

She refused to be involved in their "Mary Jane" parties. Marijuana made her tired, cranky, and hungry, feelings she experienced without smoking dope. However, marijuana caused a peculiar transformation in Bondurant. He would grin continually, then drop down on all fours and bark at the dog. Other times he would chase her through the house, tickling her. When he was grass-happy, he never criticized Sandra for anything, and that made her think marijuana wasn't so bad for him.

After Coppinger and Bondurant got stoned, the three of them would watch television until bedtime, then Underhill would slip off with him.

The next week, Coppinger landed a job at another nursing home and had the 3 P.M. to 11 P.M. shift. With the kindness of an older brother, Bondurant dutifully left his office to take her to work and then he'd pick her up at that late evening hour.

On June 27, 1994, Sandra received divorce documents from Robert Underhill. Not surprised, she willingly signed the papers and enclosed a note. Even if Robert was the man who had turned her over to the police and taken away her infant daughter, Angelina, Sandra's reservoir of forgiveness allowed these word:

> "Hello again, old friend,
>
> I appreciate all you have tried to do for me—it couldn't have been an easy task. God bless you. You should have been in my shoes all these years.
>
> We both have always known that you didn't want me as your girlfriend, much less your wife, and you could never possibly love me.
>
> It took all these many years to understand the things you told me like, one day at a time, and my favorite, get a life.
>
> You know, you never once told me you loved me.
>
> Sandra."

Her bittersweet words were combined with guilt from desperately chasing him in the beginning and from using drugs when they lived together. Drugs ultimately were the root of their separation and when she had been spaced out on amphetamines, she knew she hadn't been "an easy task."

On Friday, July 1, Bondurant drove Underhill home from work, and when he pulled inside the garage Sandra couldn't conceal her surprise at seeing two bright blue plastic barrels sitting inside.

"Where'd they come from?"

"I found them out on the road today. Must have dropped off a truck."

"Why did you bring them home?"

"I thought they'd be great for some stereo equipment I have. I've been wanting to clean up the garage and they'd be good storage bins."

Underhill glanced again at the barrels as she carried Cody into the house. She had never heard of storing stereo equipment in plastic barrels.

On Tuesday, July 5, Bondurant walked into the office while Underhill busily penciled in dates on her desk calendar. She gazed at him with a look he had seen once before. "I think I'm pregnant."

"Sandra, sweetie, you're imagining things."

"Miles, there are some things a woman just knows. I'll get a pregnancy test on the way home."

"There's no reason for that. Just wait a week. You'll probably find out you're not."

Not wanting to upset him, Underhill waited four more days, then purchased a test.

Coppinger's probation officer ordered her to come in for an appointment. It was inevitable that he would either hear of her unauthorized trip to Illinois from Bondurant or receive a poor credit report from Ford.

Bondurant accompanied her to her appointment, per his agreement with Underhill in Granite City. Once there, he spoke in his characteristic self-assured manner. "Carri had a family emergency in Granite City, Illinois. With all her concern over family problems, she forgot to take her lithium for a few days. You know how she depends on that drug to keep her even-Steven."

The parole officer nodded.

"So without lithium she wasn't thinking straight, and

forgot to phone for permission. I'm sure you could see how that would happen."

"But what about her truck?" the parole officer asked. "I understand Ford repossessed it."

"Yes, that was another unfortunate mishap. Her mother pays half the payment, and she sent the check to Fort Worth before Carri could tell her she needed it in Illinois. So, actually, it was her mother's delayed check that caused the late payment. Just a real unfortunate string of circumstances." Bondurant shook his head. "Carri has been so upset by all of this. I know she's really sorry."

Coppinger sat nodding as Bondurant's well-oiled words smoothed away her probation officer's objections. The officer smiled and reached to shake Bondurant's hand. "I knew there had to be a reasonable explanation such as the one you just gave me, Mr. Bondurant."

On the drive home, Coppinger said, "Boy, you sure saved my butt. I could have gone to jail for that violation."

"No problem," he said, then took a deep breath, hoping his action would placate Underhill so she wouldn't run off again with his son.

Bondurant pensively watched Underhill as she dipped the little stick into her urine sample. Within seconds a plus mark appeared in the indicator window.

"Well, what do you know. You're pregnant."

She detected no enthusiasm in his voice.

"The children will certainly be close in age," Bondurant said. His pasty color spoke louder than his words.

On Tuesday night, July 12, Bondurant left to pick up Coppinger from her job. Underhill took advantage of the free time and again doused Pebbles with flea dip. Surely she had killed all the pests since she applied the pesticide this three times in the last two weeks. She finished drying the dog just as they walked in from the garage.

Coppinger eagerly went into the living room to watch a special on her favorite show, *Beavis and Butt-head.* Bondurant begged off and yawned as he traipsed upstairs, saying he needed to get some sleep. Underhill had no interest in *Beavis and Butt-head,* but accompanied Coppinger because she hadn't talked with her at any length since they had returned from Illinois a month ago. Carri had seemed mollified to be friends, and although Sandra knew she wanted more, Carri had never again mentioned having a physical relationship.

After enduring the first television episode, Underhill asked, "Isn't Miles a completely different person?"

"Yeah," Coppinger said. "He doesn't seem like the ugly guy he used to be. I can't imagine what's gotten into him. But it's bound to wear off. Once a son of a bitch, always a son of a bitch. Since he can turn on a dime, I'd be on my guard if I were you."

At that moment Underhill sensed they were not alone. She glanced at the second floor landing that overlooked the living room. Suddenly, she saw Bondurant crouched down on his hands and knees, partially hidden by a leafy plant, listening to them.

# Chapter Nineteen

Sandra Underhill woke early the next morning and went to the kitchen with Cody in her arms. A few minutes later, she heard Carri Coppinger come down the stairs. Underhill filled the coffee pot with water and stuck it in the Mr. Coffee.

"Morning," Coppinger yawned, then warmed a bottle for Cody and began feeding him. She intermittently tickled Cody's stomach with her fingers.

Underhill watched. Cody laughed so hard he had trouble keeping the nipple in his toothless mouth. She knew both Coppinger and Cody were having fun, but she didn't want a colicky baby at the office. "That's enough you two," she said, laughing. "I think you're both a couple of little kids."

Underhill had finished her first cup of coffee by the time Bondurant walked into the kitchen. She had not talked with him since she had seen him on the landing last night. Later, when she went to bed, he'd appeared to be asleep. Now, she didn't want to start the day with accusations.

He looked preoccupied anyway. He kept scratching his

arm. Then he scratched his back. "I think the damn dog has fleas."

Underhill shook her head. "He can't. I got rid of them." She slipped four formula-filled bottles into the diaper bag.

Coppinger held up an empty bottle. "The little man's finished," she yawned. She threw a diaper over her shoulder and burped him, then carefully laid him in his infant seat. "I wrote letters until one this morning. I'm so tired, I'm going back to bed."

"Believe me, if I worked as late as you, I wouldn't jump up at seven."

Coppinger yawned again. "It's the only way I get to see you guys before you go to work. Besides, I want to play with my Cody."

Underhill watched her leave, realizing Coppinger genuinely loved Cody. For his baby gift, she had given him the blanket her parents had wrapped her in to bring her home from the adoption agency. Underhill would always cherish that.

Bondurant threw a teaspoon of Metamucil into a tall glass, then poured in orange juice. He would drink that with the mound of vitamins that sat before him while reading the *Fort Worth Star-Telegram.*

Underhill blew steam from her coffee and gazed at him. Something must be on his mind because he looked so preoccupied. They drank the pot of coffee and left all the dishes for Coppinger, who always insisted on cleaning up after them. Underhill grabbed the diaper bag and picked up Cody. "We're leaving," she called up to Carri.

Coppinger padded out from her bedroom to the upstairs landing. "See ya," she called down.

Thirty minutes after they arrived at the office, Bondurant said, "I better get those flea bombs. I can set them off while we're gone."

"Not if they're harmful. Carri's there."

"Yeah, you're right. I'll have to see what the store has. This might take a while."

Underhill rolled her chair to the computer to finish the stack of entries Charles Arnspinger, the officer manager, had given her the day before.

Two hours later she reached for the phone for her morning ritual of calling Coppinger. The phone rang several times causing Sandra to think Carri might have taken Pebbles for a walk. She'd try later.

Around noon Underhill ate the turkey sandwich she'd brought from home, then heated a bottle for Cody. When the baby finished his lunch, she changed his diaper, put him back down and continued calling Coppinger.

The office manager brought her another stack of medical accounts. Underhill would input about 10, then call Coppinger. She grew anxious as her phone calls continued unanswered.

Bondurant walked back into the office. He had stopped for a hamburger and wanted to check on everyone.

"Were you at home?" Underhill asked.

He nodded.

She wanted to ask if Coppinger were there. She would have told him how many times she had called without getting an answer, but hesitated, remembering his previous reactions.

Bondurant hadn't stayed more than 15 minutes when he said, "I've got to run one more errand, then when I get back I want to leave a little early. I've been wanting to get an all-terrain vehicle. Been scoping out dealerships and have narrowed it down to one."

Underhill looked at him and shook her head at his latest unpredictable act. He had never mentioned buying an all-terrain vehicle. But she knew he'd consider a car or truck purchase none of her business, so she turned back to her computer. After more than 10 calls to Coppinger, she had the operator check the line, but found it was not busy nor had any problems been reported for that number.

Soon Bondurant returned and hurried her into leaving.

* * *

The three of them drove past the suburbs to Granbury, south of Fort Worth, and pulled into Hooks Ford. As Bondurant opened his door, he turned to Underhill. "I've had my eye on a Ford Explorer. I'm looking at that white one over there. What do you think, doll?"

"Where would you put it? We only have a two-car garage."

"I'd trade in this one," he said, patting the leather seat of his sedan.

"Your *Mercedes?* I thought you loved it."

"I do. But I could take the Explorer hunting, and with another baby on the way, we need something to put all the paraphernalia in. Come on, sugar, let's take it for a test drive."

Soon Bondurant settled Sandra and Cody in the Ford, driving down a bumpy country road. Underhill's head bounced back and forth and Cody began crying.

"Great, don't you think? We could have a lot of fun with this."

"It's so different from what you're used to." Underhill frowned.

Bondurant stared straight ahead as they drove, taking the two-lane road to the small town of Aledo. A few miles later, he pulled off and parked in front of their favorite place: an old log cabin nestled on a carpet of green velvet, at the edge of a fork of the Brazos River. They sat watching the water. Twice Bondurant looked over at Underhill with a look that said he had something to tell her. He would clear his throat, then return to stare at the water. After 10 minutes, he started the engine and returned the vehicle.

At the dealership, he walked over to the salesman and told him to get the Explorer ready. He's pick it up as soon as he had the insurance and financing arranged, then he handed him a check for the down payment.

* * *

Carrying Cody, Underhill walked into the kitchen from the garage. She noticed the breakfast dishes were still on the counter and table. Ashtrays overflowed with cigarette butts from the night before.

"Carri?" she called.

"Don't do that." Bondurant admonished.

"Don't do what? Carri?" She yelled louder and headed for the stairs.

"Don't call her."

Underhill ignored him and walked up five stairs when Bondurant rushed toward her. "Don't go up there."

"Why? Will you tell me what's going on? You're acting so damn strange. I want to find Carri."

"We need to talk, Sandra." He forcibly pulled her back toward the sofa, but she fought his efforts.

"Cody's crying. I've got to change him. Besides, he's hungry. And I can't find Carri."

Bondurant took hold of her shoulders and shoved her down on the couch.

"Is it about Carri? Miles, did you send her away?" Her eyes were dark, accusing.

"She's not here."

"*Where* is she?"

"Carri and I had an argument this morning. I told her to come into my bedroom. I wanted to lay it on the line, and told her it was time for her to leave."

"You told Carri to go?" The corners of Sandra's mouth turned down.

"Hold on. I just wanted to talk about when she'd be leaving. But instead of discussing anything, she became indignant and went back to her room. I didn't know what to do. She obviously had no intention of listening to me and I needed to get her attention. So . . ." Bondurant paused. "I got a gun. I thought I could scare her into leaving, but it was an accident."

Underhill frowned. "What was an accident?"

"I shot her."

"Oh my God!" She jumped up, screaming. "Where is she? Where did you take her?"

Bondurant looked at the floor.

"What hospital is she in? I've got to go there. She needs me."

"No, she doesn't, Sandra. She's dead!"

# Chapter Twenty

Underhill's hands shook as she grabbed Bondurant's shirt. "No, she can't be dead. You're just saying that to make me mad. Tell me where she is."

"If you don't believe me, go look in her room. Look at the side of her bed by the wall."

She stared at him for a fraction of a second, then almost threw Cody into his arms and dashed to the stairs. Her heart pounded as she climbed to the second floor. She darted to the door of Coppinger's room and stopped. Blood splattered the pale blue wall and dribbled down into a huge congealed puddle on the light beige carpet. Her shrill scream echoed throughout the house.

Underhill backed away from the room and ran down the stairs, her eyes staring and crazed. She flew to Bondurant, shrieking all the while. "What happened to Carri? Where is she?"

He had poured himself a Scotch and had gulped down half of it. "Sandra, I told you she's dead."

"Did you call 911?"

"No, I panicked."

"Where *is* she?"

"I swear on my mother's grave; she's *not* in the house. Now you have to believe me. After all I've done for you. You owe me your loyalties." His face remained calm. "You can't talk to anyone. Don't answer the telephone and don't call out."

Her eyes left his face to stare at the closed door to the hall closet. "Promise, she's not in the house?"

"I said she wasn't, didn't I?"

"I want my friend," she screamed, "I want my Carri." She picked up a pillow from the couch and hurled it across the room. It struck a crystal vase and shards of glass stabbed the oriental rug. Water and flowers soaked the table where the vase had stood.

Bondurant hurriedly fixed her a vodka and tonic. "Here, this will make you feel better."

Underhill quickly drained it, and her rage increased. She whirled out of control and cleared the mantle with one hand. Books and candles flew through the air. "I can't believe you did this to Carri. You know how much I loved her. She was my dearest friend. It's like you killed my sister!"

Underhill ran to the bar and dug ice out of the maker with her bare hand, filled her glass, and poured straight vodka over the cubes. She downed it, then immediately backed into a table, knocking over a porcelain lamp that shattered, looking like confetti fluttering. She showed no mercy for photographs of Bondurant's three older children and smashed them as she dashed through the house, creating a path of destruction wherever she went. All the time Cody bellowed for his dinner.

"Sandra! Get hold of yourself," Bondurant shouted.

Sandra paid no attention.

An hour later, exhausted, she collapsed in one of the club chairs. "Did Carri beg you to help her?" she asked as she looked at Bondurant through wet bangs that hung in her eyes. Her clothes, damp from perspiration and spilled vodka, stuck to her skin. "Miles," she said, raising her voice, "did you try to stop the bleeding?"

"We'll discuss this later."

"Later?" she shrieked. "I want to know *now.* Did you hold her while she died?"

He refused to answer.

His mute stubbornness unleashed another tirade from Underhill, this time with deadly design. She opened the glass doors to the bar and quickly evacuated his Waterford crystal. Then she pulled out bottles of his beloved Scotch and christened the bar's ceramic tile countertop. Her bare feet crunched on mounds of broken glass and left blotches of blood as she limped through the den.

The next morning, Thursday, July 14, Sandra Underhill's head felt like a rock on her pillow. It was so heavy she couldn't raise it, and when she remembered the night before, she didn't want to open her eyes. She kept seeing Coppinger's blood-splattered room down the hall from where she now lay and she couldn't bring herself to get up. She had no idea how she had made it up the stairs last night and into the bedroom.

Bondurant looked over when he felt her stir. "I'm going to call Charles." His voice sounded like gravel. "Neither one of us is in any condition to go to the office today."

He picked up the phone and called his office manager to elaborate their terrible flu symptoms, and told him he hoped they'd be in tomorrow.

Underhill couldn't believe Bondurant's calm voice on the phone. Incredibly, he acted like nothing had happened. Confused thoughts whirled in her head as she dropped back to her pillow and dozed for another hour. She woke to the sound of Bondurant taking a shower. He toweled off, walked back into the bedroom naked, and slid between the sheets.

"Tell me what happened, Miles. How did you kill Carri?"

"I don't want to talk about it," he yelled. "I feel rotten. I won't discuss it right now."

His harsh words woke Cody, whose crib stood only two feet from Underhill. She crawled out of bed and headed downstairs for his bottle. Once in the hall, her eyes cut to Coppinger's room. She saw the dresser, and on the floor next to it sat a plastic container labeled "NOW." The gallon jar had once held an all-purpose household cleaner. She and Carri had filled the empty container with flea dip to spray the dog. She shook her head. Bondurant had tried to clean up the enormous area of Coppinger's blood with flea dip. Underhill dropped to her knees in the hall, stared at the dresser, and sobbed.

Finally Cody's cries prompted her to continue to the kitchen to make another batch of formula. After she returned to their bedroom, she fed and changed Cody, then laid him between herself and Bondurant. "Miles, I made a dozen calls to Carri yesterday. You must have heard the phone."

"Every time. I sat on the couch and listened to it ring over and over."

By two in the afternoon, they still had had nothing to eat. Bondurant kept a stack of menus to several restaurants in town. He had a delivery service, "Meals 2 U," that would pick up the food and deliver it. He sat up in bed reading menus.

"Don't order anything for me. I couldn't think about eating," Underhill said.

"Well, I've got to keep up my strength."

Two more times, she tried to get Bondurant to tell her what happened, but he refused. "Later," was all he said.

When the food arrived, Sandra didn't want to be around it and went out in the hall to sit on the floor across from Carri's room. Now cold sober, she found that Bondurant intimidated her and she didn't want to cry around him.

Underhill tried to keep her senses about herself so she could take care of Cody. She and Bondurant didn't watch

TV. They rarely spoke. Somehow they got through the rest of that day and night, but with fragmented sleep, they woke exhausted Friday morning.

"Sandra." Bondurant nudged her. "We've got to get going. Charles needs to leave the office to go to Central Medical to discuss their accounting. You need to watch the office while he's gone."

Groggily she crawled out of bed and looked at Cody. The child seemed to sense that something was wrong. He had barely cried for two days, only when he needed his bottle or a dry diaper.

Underhill packed the diaper bag and opened the door to the garage. Bondurant hovered immediately behind her. She stepped into the garage and fell silent, quietly scrutinizing the area. Something was wrong. She sniffed the stagnant air that smelled like wet, dirty tennis shoes. Something was terribly wrong.

She walked out a couple more feet, still searching the garage, when she caught sight of the plastic barrels. She hadn't thought about them since Bondurant had driven her home from work two weeks ago. One barrel was so grotesquely swollen that its white lid had mounded and it looked ready to explode. She felt dizzy and nauseated as she turned to Bondurant.

"Do you smell anything?"

He shook his head.

She looked back at the barrel, then to Bondurant. Without saying another word, at that moment she knew. She knew that her best friend in the whole world lay in that bloated barrel. She could almost feel the expression of ungodly shock and horror on her face. Had she followed her first impulse, she would have run to the barrel and hugged it or ripped it open.

Bondurant had intimidated her since the day they had

met, but at no time did he intimidate her more than now. He had to know how she felt, yet his face remained expressionless as he hurried to get in the car.

Revolted and sad, Underhill walked to the car in a fog. Her shock prevented her from crying and her eyes never left the barrel until the garage door closed.

Bondurant had sworn that Coppinger wasn't in the house, but as usual, his words straddled the fine line between truth and lying. She wasn't exactly in the house. All this time, she had been exactly in the garage.

# Chapter Twenty-One

A chill swept through Sandra Underhill as she sat next to Bondurant on the way to work. The image of that bloated barrel was seared into her mind. And the odor. She had never smelled anything like that. Not even the pound of hamburger that had sat for a month in her mother's refrigerator.

July had been as hot as Tabasco—getting into the 90s everyday, and sometimes hitting 100. With temperatures that high outside, Underhill knew the unvented garage would have soared to over 110 degrees. Her stomach bolted when she thought of Coppinger's condition.

She could no longer hold her thoughts. "My God, Miles, did you see the size of that barrel!"

He nodded.

"We need to discuss this," she said. "We can't wait until tonight. The barrel may explode by then."

At first, he sat glacially unresponsive, then said, "All right, but there are two things I want to say. First, I need your loyalty. You have to help me, and you can't ever tell anyone. Second, I think I should kill myself." He paused for effect. "However, I'm not quite ready to do that. And until I am, you've got to cooperate. I need to put my estate in order. I'll go back to the house and dictate my will on tape."

Underhill felt her heart race. The thought of Bondurant committing suicide shattered her. He was the father of her children; her future support. How could she make it without him?

Charles Arnspinger left for his appointment as soon as Bondurant and Underhill arrived at the office. Sandra numbly slumped in her chair.

He offered to go to Whata Burger, and 15 minutes later appeared with two hamburgers. It was the first food she had had since Wednesday—two days ago. They gulped down their lunch, but Bondurant immediately ran to the restroom, and she heard him throwing up violently.

He stumbled back into his private office; his oyster-white face looked pained as he wiped his mouth. He crashed into his tufted leather chair, and rested his head on its high back.

Underhill ran after him, pleading, "What are we going to do?" She curled up in a chair facing his desk.

"This is crazy," she said. "We have to figure out something." Underhill had always considered Bondurant smart and thought he'd call the police and explain what happened. The mindlessness of doing nothing exasperated her.

Bondurant said, "This wouldn't have happened if you hadn't talked me into buying a bus ticket to bring that lesbian back to Fort Worth." He frowned at the memory.

"But I do have a plan," he told her. "First, I'm going to cut out the carpet where her blood is and clean it somehow, or replace it if I have to. Then I'm picking up that Ford Explorer this afternoon to haul off the barrel and bury it."

Underhill couldn't comprehend how calmly he acted. He might as well have been discussing data processing for all the emotion he packed into his words. "Where will you bury it?"

"I have that all worked out. Don't worry about it." His voice became irritated. "Just remember, there's been lots of times I could have filed charges against you, but I didn't.

"I'll need to confess what I've done before I commit suicide. I'll tape a statement and mail it to my Dallas lawyer, Calvin Jacobs."

Bondurant pushed his chair back and stood up. "I'm going home now."

She sat staring at his vacant chair. *If he has this all worked out, why does he have to commit suicide?*

Bondurant quickly drove home. Minutes later, he called Underhill to ask where she kept the air freshener. "By the time you get back here, the garage won't smell. You'll see."

He returned to the office shortly before 5 P.M. "Put that accounting away," he demanded. "We've got to get over to Hooks Ford and Allstate Insurance. Hooks closes at six so we need to make it snappy."

Bondurant rushed the insurance agent through the paperwork, then left for Hooks Ford.

At the dealership, he showed no emotion when he traded his maintained-to-perfection, 1979 vintage Mercedes sedan for the Ford Explorer. Underhill transferred Cody's car seat to their new purchase, and together they lugged everything out of the sedan's trunk and glove compartment and stuffed it into the new truck. Without looking back at the car he had treasured for years, Bondurant turned on the ignition and headed to Forth Worth.

"I'm hungry," Underhill said. "Let's grab something to eat."

"We have to go by the house first."

"Why?"

"Don't ask."

In a stern voice that surprised even herself, she said, "I deserve to know. Someone's been killed. I'm on parole.

You said you were going to bury the barrel, so tell me what you're doing now!"

"If you *must* know," Bondurant said as if she had done something wrong, "I need to go by and let some air seep out. I'll just be a few minutes."

Underhill swallowed hard. "I can't be in the garage."

"All right. You and Cody wait in front. It shouldn't take long." Then with a melancholic gaze he said, "Unless I decide to commit suicide while I'm in there."

Shutting her eyes, she became disturbed with his continued threats.

Bondurant pulled up to the curb and left her and Cody in the Ford. Thirty minutes crawled by. Underhill's anxiety grew as her mind leaped back to his suicide warning. Had he actually done it? Should she venture back into the duplex? And if she did, what would she find?

Finally, Bondurant walked out and motioned for her to get into the driver's seat. He shook noticeably as he directed her to drive to their favorite catfish restaurant, Jack's.

At Jack's they ordered dinner, but they both barely nibbled on their food, then left for the office to pick up a two-wheeled dolly to move the barrel.

Bondurant stuck the orange dolly into the back of his new vehicle, then returned to the driver's seat. "Sandra, once we're home, you take Cody upstairs. I've got to take the barrel to the patio."

When Underhill opened the front door, the stench overpowered her. She tried to escape the fumes by covering her nose and mouth, and held Cody close, but her efforts were useless and she started gagging. "My God, this is terrible. Our baby will be cursed for breathing death. I won't be part of this."

"Take Cody outside as soon as you can," Bondurant told her. "I won't even bother with the dolly."

As Underhill hurried to gather more bottles and diapers, she noticed Bondurant had flopped the barrel on its side,

Formal portrait of Carrington Elizabeth Coppinger taken for her high school graduation in 1989. (*Courtesy Sandra Underhill*)

Warren Miles Bondurant at 16.

In the Fall of 1991, Bondurant bought Pebbles, a Shitzu, for Sandra Underhill. *(Courtesy Sandra Underhill)*

St. Louis County Jail, the first of several in which Sandra Underhill was incarcerated prior to answering Miles Bondurant's personal ad.

Miles Bondurant changed Sandra Underhill's look a few weeks after she moved into his home. *(Courtesy Sandra Underhill)*

Bondurant took Sandra Underhill on a tour of Fort Worth to impress her with the homes he had once owned. This is the 40-room stone mansion in Westover Hills where he had previously lived.

"Fairview" was the 1893 Victorian home Bondurant once owned.

Also on the tour of his previous homes was this Mediterranean home facing the golf course which he had purchased for his third wife, Kimberly.

Carri Coppinger voluntarily entered Pinestreet Rehabilitation shortly after being arrested in July 1993 for non-drug-related charges. (*Courtesy Fort Worth, Texas Police Department*)

Coppinger (*left*) and a pregnant Underhill in November 1993, after their release from Pinestreet Rehabilitation. (*Courtesy Sandra Underhill*)

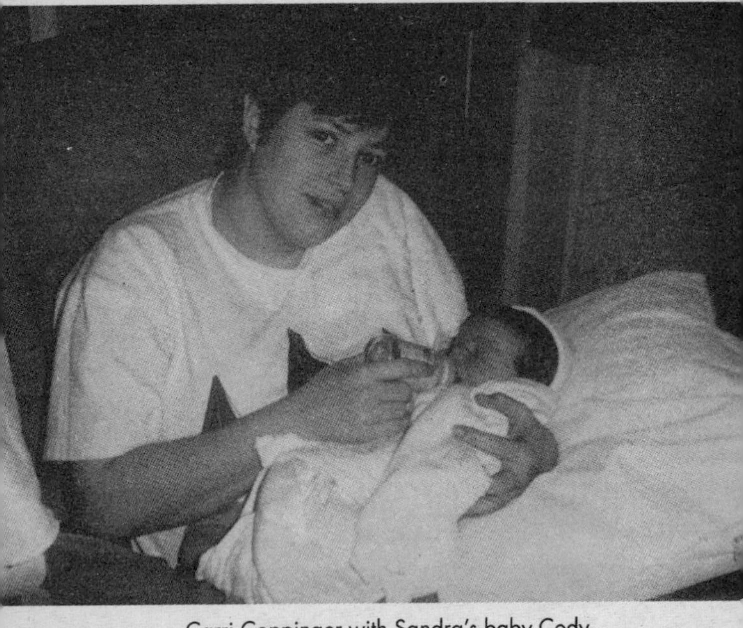

Carri Coppinger with Sandra's baby Cody.
(*Courtesy Sandra Underhill*)

Det. Eddie Neel and Officers Philip Woodward and Edward Raynsford outside Bondurant's Collinwood home.
(*Courtesy Fort Worth, Texas Police Department*)

Bondurant threatened Coppinger with a bat while telling her she had to move out of his home.
(*Courtesy Fort Worth, Texas Police Department*)

The bedroom in Bondurant's duplex where Carri Coppinger was fatally shot. (*Courtesy Fort Worth, Texas Police Department*)

The blue plastic barrel swollen with Coppinger's body inside before the police opened it. (*Courtesy Fort Worth, Texas Police Department*)

The dolly Bondurant bought to use for transporting the barrel. (*Courtesy Fort Worth, Texas Police Department*)

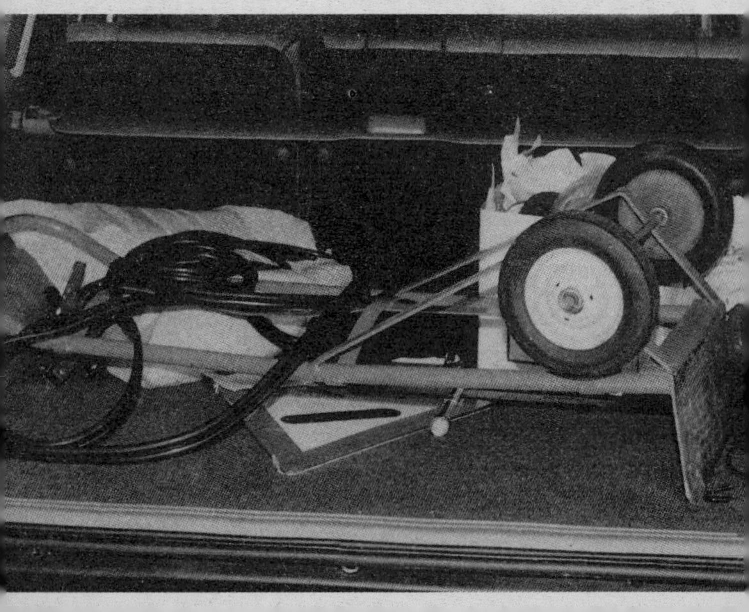

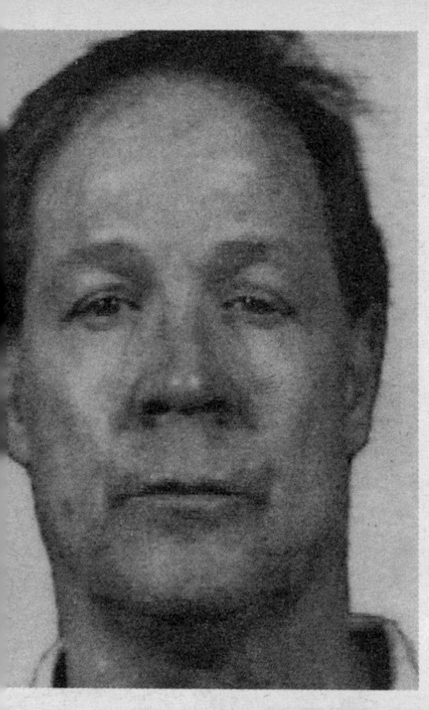

Miles Bondurant was indicted by the grand jury on August 29, 1994 for intentionally causing the death of Carri Coppinger with a deadly weapon. *(Courtesy Fort Worth, Texas Police Department)*

Accused of assaulting Bondurant, Sandra Underhill was arrested on October 3, 1994. The charges were later dropped. *(Courtesy Fort Worth, Texas Police Department)*

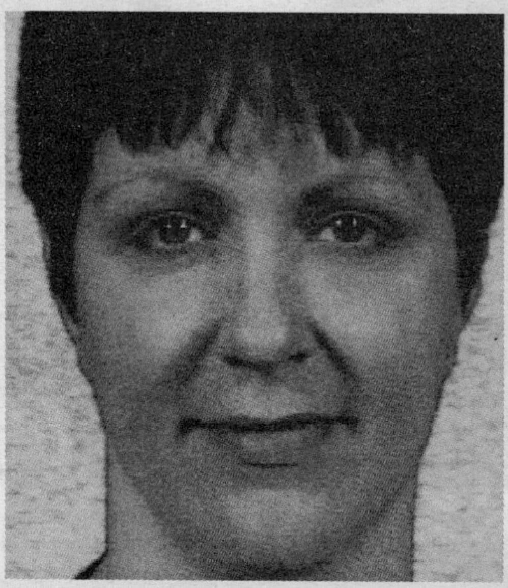

Warren Miles Bondurant on hearing the jury's verdict at his murder trial. (*Courtesy* The Dallas Morning News/*David Woo*)

Sandra Underhill shortly after Bondurant was sent to jail. (*Courtesy Sandra Underhill*)

Detective Eddie Neel, lead homicide investigator. (*Author's collection*)

Dr. Gary Sisler, Tarrant County Assistant Medical Examiner, performed the autopsy on Carri Coppinger.
(*Author's collection*)

Michael D. Parrish, Tarrant County Assistant District Attorney.
(*Author's collection*)

and was entering the opening to the living room where she stood.

His perspiration splattered on the barrel, then dribbled onto the carpet. Every time he rolled the barrel a half rotation, Sandra imagined the thump of Carri's body against the inside of the container.

Pebbles became fascinated and wagged her tail and barked as if Bondurant were rolling a huge ball for her to chase. Trying to avoid the dog, Bondurant almost hit the sofa. He grunted as he struggled to keep the barrel on a straight path toward the patio.

When he jostled the barrel near Underhill, she turned so she didn't have to look, then dashed upstairs. "This is it," she screamed. "My best friend is turning to Jell-O and you have absolutely no idea what you're doing." She ran into the bedroom and grabbed clothes for herself and the baby.

She raced down the stairs still yelling at him. "I can't take this anymore. It's absolutely crazy. You're crazy." She hurried through the front door and out to the Explorer.

Bondurant reddened from the exertion of manipulating the heavy barrel. He aimed for the French doors leading out to his fenced patio, but banged the barrel's edge against the doorjamb. Frantically, he bent over to check the lid. Fortunately, it had remained secure.

He hoped once the barrel stood outside, the odor would stop permeating his home. He also hoped the vacant lot bordering his patio would afford additional fresh air. Finally he shoved the barrel onto the patio's gravel and used all his strength to set it upright.

Obviously shaken, he stumbled outside to the Explorer.

Underhill knew she had to do something. What Miles was doing was so wrong. "I've got to call somebody," she said.

"Don't worry about it. This will all be over tomorrow.

I'll find a place for us to stay tonight, and you'll feel a lot better tomorrow."

She couldn't imagine how she'd feel better tomorrow. They could both be arrested by then, and she could very well be sent back to prison.

He drove by the Residence Inn near the Trinity River and grimaced when he saw a security guard standing by the front door.

"Looks crowded to me."

Bondurant drove a block away to a small grocery store for more baby formula, Cokes, and air freshner, then returned to the Residence Inn.

He walked in and told the registration clerk that he needed a room because he had started painting his house and the fumes were too much for his young son.

Bondurant climbed back in the Explorer and drove to their room. Underhill started carrying in groceries but he cautioned her not to take in the air freshener, he would need that. He waited until she and Cody were settled, then left.

Thirty minutes later he called from the house. He couldn't find the brown extension cord. Later he called to see if she knew where he could find an additional fan.

Soon he returned. This time with Pebbles, more soda, wine, and a change of clothes for himself.

He removed the plastic wrap from two glasses in the bathroom and filled them with wine, offering Sandra one. She shook her head.

"I found another fan in the attic and a heavy duty extension cord. Things are definitely getting better. Just wait until morning."

"You *keep* saying that. How could things ever possibly get better? I'll give you thirty minutes. Then I'm going to call the police."

"Please, Sandra, wait."

"Miles, you've gone crazy. How do you ever expect to get away with this?"

"I'll give you anything you want. Just don't call anybody and I'll make the sky the limit. You'll be a wealthy woman."

Underhill watched Bondurant beg pathetically. Ever since Wednesday night, she had been torn between her dead friend and Miles, who pleaded with her not to turn him in. And now every time she reached for the phone, he placed his big hand over it and pushed it farther from her grasp. She got up and walked to the door. "I'm going to use the phone in the lobby."

With his pleadings failing to get the response he wanted, Bondurant changed tactics. "I'm going to leave now. I'm going to go home and kill myself. Maybe I'll tell the police you killed Carri."

Underhill felt dizzy with the possibility. The police would easily believe an ex-con had killed Carri Coppinger. Now she shook with fear. But his last words chilled her most.

"Or maybe, I'll just kill you."

# Chapter Twenty-Two

Bondurant retreated to his house and hurried through the French doors that led to his patio. His shirt stuck to his body in the clammy night.

Flipping on the patio light, he watched a line of ants cross from the fence and crawl up the barrel, then he slapped at a big roach circling the lid. Cautiously, he unclasped the metal band surrounding the barrel's lid. He held his breath until his lungs burned while more of the hot, noxious gases seeped out. When he finally inhaled, the smell of rotting innards grabbed him.

He realized he had to do something about the horde of insects attracted to the barrel and went in search of repellents. He came back and dusted layers of white powder around the base, then sprayed a repellent mist that covered the barrel's plastic sides until poison ran down in rivulets.

While the barrel breathed, Bondurant went inside to clean the downstairs that Underhill had all but destroyed two nights ago. He vacuumed and squinted in disgust as small slivers of crystal clattered and clinked their way into the vacuum.

Returning to the barrel, he clamped down the lid and tightened his grip on the caulking gun as he sealed the lid with more caulk. The layer he had applied that morning had already crumbled.

He marched back inside and poured a full glass of Macallan Scotch over ice cubes, sat down on his den sofa, and reached for his tape recorder. He took a deep breath and began, "My name is Miles Bondurant . . . Sandra Lee Coburn Underhill is the one who murdered Carri Coppinger. The pistol she did it with is sitting underneath me where I am getting ready to dispose of myself because of the life I have had to live with this person. I never knew three years ago when she got out of TDC [Texas Department of Corrections] on August 26, 1991 [what it would be like]. She has stolen from me. You may talk to Richard Parker, your captain, and he will attest to this.

"She's a dopehead and she's been a dopehead for seventeen years. She's very disturbed mentally. Her whole family is.

"I was a very normal person until I met her. All of a sudden I became a clown, unfortunately. I lived a good life. I'm not sorry for it. I'm sorry it ended this way. I hope that God will forgive me for what I've done."

He pulled out a cigarette and lit it. He snapped his lighter shut, inhaled, and felt the nicotine relax him.

"Sandra killed Carri. The gun is under the couch where I'm sitting. She and Carri had a quarrel. Carri is a lesbian. Sandra is bisexual. I wish that after all is said and done, that you will give her a mental test. I've had a little wine and I'm talking incoherently, and I'm sorry that I do not know what I've done to mess myself around with this person.

"You can probably find Sandra in . . . Granite City, Illinois, living with Elaina Forsell, her mother, in the project homes.

"I wish you would contact my lawyer in Dallas, Calvin Jacobs. I have $175,000 in insurance I want to leave to my three older children. I want Tracy to have the 450 SEL, it says 500 but it's a 450.

"Contact Joe Davila, a decent fellow. He can tell a lot of dumb things about Sandra.

"Sandra is mentally incapable of taking care of the son that I bore with her. This is her fourth child. He's born with a hex having Sandra for a mother. Two of her previous children were taken away. She left two children on the railroad tracks in Round Rock, Texas, and fire ants ate them. She burned another one with a cigarette. Sandra had all of her children taken away.

"Sandra wanted me to bury Carri under the rocks on the patio. Carri's body started to stink very much." He paused for a moment and gazed in the direction of the patio.

"Carri and Sandra had a fight the night before. They had broken up their relationship. They were always lesbian lovers. Sandra shot Carri in her left eye in Carri's bedroom. She had me buy a barrel about a month ago, so evidently she planned . . . to do this . . ."

The door had slammed shut at the Residence Inn after Bondurant left their room. Sandra Underhill sat on the bed as Miles' threat reverberated in her head. *He's going to kill me?* The words seemed foreign and unbelievable until she remembered seeing *two* barrels in the garage, and her heart skipped a beat. *That second barrel was for me! Why didn't I think of that before? And why didn't he just kill me when he killed Carri?* She shook her head, trying to clear her thoughts. She mentally raced back to what had happened just prior to Carri's death. Then she remembered. Miles had learned about her pregnancy. That apparently had been the turning point. He would have easily killed her; he had already killed her friend, but he wouldn't kill his own unborn child.

New concerns surfaced. Could he have left to get the gun he used to kill Carri? Then her mind flicked back to something else Bondurant had said: "I'm going to tell them you killed Carri." Suddenly that became her deepest fear.

She grabbed the phone and called her mother. Without Coppinger's strength to bolster her, Underhill slipped back into being a little girl.

"Mom, you won't believe it. Miles killed Carri. She's dead. What am I going to do?"

"Oh my God! That's awful!"

"It's so terrible."

"Listen," Elaina said, "you need to get off the phone, call the police and tell them what happened, then come home."

Shrouded in a trance, Underhill hung up and tried to call Yellow Cab, but her fingers wouldn't punch the correct digits. After four wrong numbers, she ran to the lobby.

The elderly night clerk, Margaret Templeton, stood behind the desk, her gray hair pinned up in folds. The woman looked startled to see Underhill dart into the lobby.

"Someone may be coming after me with a gun. Please call me a cab," Underhill begged.

"He's coming *here?*" Templeton said, pointing to her desktop.

Underhill nodded.

"Shouldn't we call the police?"

"No, I'm going to my mother's house in Illinois and I'll call the police from there."

Templeton frowned. "What's going on here?"

"I can't say," Underhill stuttered, and felt warm tears roll down her cheeks.

Underhill paced the lobby trying to concoct a believable story as Margaret Templeton stared at her. She could tell the truth, but that seemed the least creditable. Finally she blurted, "Someone killed my friend and put her body in a barrel. He said if I tell anybody, he'll kill me."

Templeton began shaking and asked, "Is it your husband?"

"He's not my husband, but he's my baby's father."

The clerk shook her head and hurried to the front door to motion for the security officer. "John, we need you in here immediately." She turned to Underhill. "He'll protect you while you wait for your cab.

John Wayne Harvey, tall and dark with a muscular build that handsomely filled out his uniform, came in and saw two women. One frightened. One hysterical.

He listened to Underhill who cried and trembled as she retold what happened to Coppinger, but she still insisted on getting a cab and calling the police from Illinois.

"Forget the cab, lady, you need to call the police. Now!"

At 2:20 A.M., Templeton punched in 911 and handed the phone to Underhill.

# PART III

# Chapter Twenty-Three

The police still milled around Bondurant's house, collecting evidence, taking photographs, and sketching the scene.

There's an old Fort Worth Police saying: "If you catch it, you clean it." For Officer Philip Woodward, the first man at the duplex and the one who had opened the barrel, it meant, if you want to be the one who jumps up in front, you're the one who cleans up the rear. In this case he had expected to open the barrel, find a dead animal, report it to animal control, and leave in less than an hour. Instead, he had positioned himself at the crime scene's front door and logged everyone in and out for hours.

He looked at his watch and grimaced. He would miss his 5 A.M. "dinner" break, but he was the only person there who could have eaten anything.

At exactly five, Detective Eddie Neel drove down Collinwood Avenue. He parked his unmarked police car on the crowded street. Although his windows were up, he could smell the decomposing body.

Neel walked into the house to make sure the investigation had begun in earnest, then he went to find Underhill.

Sandra Underhill watched warily as Detective Neel opened the door of his police car for her. In the past, entering a police car usually meant being arrested. But this time the detective treated her respectfully. Had they seen her devastation over losing her best friend? Could this be the one time in her life when being an ex-con didn't automatically mean she was guilty? Or was this their way to get her cooperation before nailing her with the crime? Neel told her he'd personally drive her downtown to police headquarters and stay with her while she made her statement.

As he pulled away from the curb, Neel said, "You can't go back to the house or Residence Inn because they're both crime scenes and the police will be busy investigating them. Do you have a place to stay tonight after you talk with the police? If not, we can arrange for something."

"I'll be fine, thanks. I'll book a room at the Ramada Inn. Miles gave me one of his credit cards this morning."

"Will you be around Fort Worth for the next few weeks?"

Underhill shook her head and thought this could be a stumbling block. "No, I want to go to Illinois to stay with my mom or sister. I'd like to leave tomorrow. Is that okay?" She looked at the detective and worried that he wouldn't let her go.

"Just give us a phone number where you can be reached."

Then Underhill thought of another problem that might keep her in town. "I need to contact my parole officer, Maggie Rhiner."

"Give her a call when you get to Illinois in case she has any questions."

His answers sounded too good to be true.

* * *

The police cars carrying Underhill and Bondurant pulled up at the imposing gray granite police headquarters at the same time. It was 6:12 A.M., and the sun threw a pink glow over the morning sky, but Sandra couldn't imagine the day held any promise.

Neel looked over at the second car and said, "Just a sec. I'm going to have them hold Mr. Bondurant so I can get you sequestered."

Inside, the detective led Underhill to an elevator. On the third floor, they entered a room crowded with cubicles. She followed him through the labyrinth of textured, light beige dividers that were short enough for her to view the entire office at once. She entered the detective's cubicle and propped Cody's infant seat on the desk.

Detective Neel excused himself to run a background check on her. He scanned the computer printout and learned that on February 4, 1993, she had been charged with assault and bodily injury. Then he noticed that Bondurant, who'd brought the charges, dropped them the next day. Neel knew he wasn't dealing with a Vassar graduate, but he thought her story sounded plausible, and she seemed so devastated over losing her friend. Nobody could pretend that amount of emotion.

He glanced over at his open cubicle and saw Underhill attending to Cody. He surmised that somewhere down there was a decent person. She might even be pretty, if she didn't look so drained and nervous as she did right now. In fact, the woman appeared totally in shock.

Neel went back to his cubicle and pulled out a pad of paper. "We're going to need some background information, so let's get started. When did you last see Carri Coppinger alive?"

The thought saddened Sandra. "Wednesday morning," she said as tears filled her eyes.

"I'll get us some coffee," Neel suggested.

Soon he came back with two steaming Styrofoam cups. "The word down the hall is that Bondurant's saying you killed Carri."

Underhill tensed. Was he now going to arrest her? But the detective didn't appear to be accusing her, only providing her with information. He seemed perplexed when she said nothing.

She could hear his words, and knew being accused of Coppinger's murder had been her greatest fear. She realized shock had caused her immobility, and could only shrug her shoulders.

"That's all?" Neel looked surprised.

She forced herself to respond. "When Miles left the hotel tonight, he said he planned to either kill himself, kill me, or say I did it."

Before Neel could reply, one of the other investigators came by. "Bondurant says he'll only talk if we give him a cigarette. He's been asking for fifteen minutes. Shall I give him one?"

Neel looked up. "No."

The investigator said, "You're the boss," and returned to his interrogation.

Underhill organized her thoughts and began recalling hour-by-hour the three most intense days of her life. She missed Carri terribly, but Miles had spent the last three days hammering her about her allegiance to him, so she felt reluctant to say anything that might incriminate him.

Neel rapidly filled a tablet with neat block print as he asked questions and listened to the many layers of Sandra's story. The detective questioned her on small details, and if she couldn't provide them, he'd suspect she was fabricating her tale. He looked ready to pounce on any inconsistency.

"Did you go somewhere for dinner tonight?"

"Yeah. We went to Jack's Catfish."

"What does Jack's look like?"

"Let's see." Underhill squinted. "Before you go inside, there's a liquor store across the street."

"Impossible. It's a dry area; they can't sell liquor."

She rubbed her eyes and felt disoriented. She was so tired. Had she forgotten what businesses surrounded the restaurant? "I distinctly remember a liquor store," she said, but a wave of apprehension swept through her, shaking her confidence.

Neel wrote himself a note. "We'll check it out. But I doubt it. What else did you do since Wednesday?"

"Miles bought a Ford Explorer from Hooks Ford and he had Allstate insure it."

At 8 A.M., the normal business day began and secretaries who had noticed Cody wandered into Neel's cubicle to look at the baby. Soon Underhill had many volunteers to care for her child, providing her freedom to continue answering the detective's endless questions.

At almost 9:30 A.M., they completed their discussion and went across the hall to have a secretary feed the information into a computer. After the printer spat out five single-spaced, legal-sized pages, Underhill read and signed the document, then Neel drove her and Cody to their hotel.

# Chapter Twenty-Four

Two pictures accompanied the front-page story in the *Fort Worth Star-Telegram.* In addition to Miles Bondurant being arrested, another photo depicted the barrel sitting in the medical examiner's open van. One-inch-high headlines screamed: "Body found in barrel leads to arrest." The lead paragraph read: "A Fort Worth businessman was arrested early yesterday after police, acting on a tip, found a young woman's body stuffed into a barrel on the patio of his fashionable duplex in west Fort Worth."

After answering questions from the media who still loitered in the front yard, the homicide supervisor, Sgt. Paul Kratz, went inside to check out Bondurant's home. In the den he noticed Bondurant's Texas Christian University plaques, and frowned. Kratz was also a TCU grad.

Kratz had been awakened at 3 A.M. by Detective Neel. They would bounce ideas off each other, but Kratz always had the final word.

The investigators had no trouble finding the recorder Bondurant used to tape his last words. Kratz saw it on the sofa, and one of the investigators told him they had listened to it and heard Bondurant say that Underhill committed the murder.

Part of the belt from a gun holster protruded from under the couch. When the detectives picked up the sofa, they found two weapons—a High Standard .22-caliber semi-automatic pistol that had live .22 long rifle rounds inside, and a Rossi .38 special revolver. It also contained bullets.

He went upstairs to the master bedroom and found crime expert Officer Prince Ray photographing a .12-gauge loaded shotgun.

"I saw this leaning against the wall by the bed," Ray told him. "You can see how the gun's sight scratched a trench on the wall each time Bondurant replaced it." He picked up a .9-millimeter handgun. "I found this under Bondurant's bed, and there was a .22-caliber rifle in the closet."

Kratz shook his head thinking how the house looked like an arsenal, and stepped down the hall to Coppinger's bedroom. Staring at the scene, he wondered what on earth ran through Bondurant's mind. Sheets and pillows from the bed had been thrown over the carpet to hide a massive puddle of dried blood.

He noticed a crime scene tag on a baseball bat with an ace bandage wrapped around the head. If Bondurant had shot this woman with a gun, why the bat?

Taking in the entire crime scene, Kratz thought that if it hadn't been so tragic, Bondurant's futile efforts would have been comical. He had covered the blood upstairs with sheets, set a couple fans on the patio to blow away the barrel's odor, and scattered air freshners in every room. It was like sprinkling a garden hose on a forest fire. Kratz shook his head again. How ludicrous that Bondurant thought no one would notice this. The stench was always so recognizable. The screaming, hellish smell would stay in nose hairs, clothes fibers, or anything near it. Kratz knew when he got home to Granbury, he'd be sending his suit to the cleaners.

* * *

It was almost noon—six hours since the police had brought Miles Bondurant to their headquarters. Thus far, his circuitous conversation had not produced anything the detectives could take to court.

Neel had moved Bondurant into Kratz's walled-in office, which provided more privacy.

In a confidential yet cocky tone, Bondurant said, "Frankly, I'm not really comfortable making a statement to a secretary and having it typed out."

"What would you prefer, Mr. Bondurant?" Tired, Detective Eddie Neel propped his chin on his hand, and played the charade that had gone on with several detectives since they had first brought in the suspect. Neel had ordered Bondurant's handcuffs removed, knowing any suspect would talk more freely if he weren't constrained.

Bondurant said, "Actually, Eddie, I think I could explain this thing better on tape. Then I could give more clarification as to how this happened."

Everyone referred to Detective Neel as "Detective." Other officers joked that it was his first name. But Bondurant called him Eddie, and if calling him Eddie gave the detective any answers, he wouldn't object. Also, Bondurant didn't call him "sir." He pretended to be too important to take Neel seriously.

Bondurant had flatly stated that Sandra Underhill had killed Carri Coppinger, but the detectives soon found holes in his story.

"I thought you said Sandra worked for your company. Wasn't she at work that day?"

"Ah. I can't remember."

"We'd only have to call the other employees to find out."

"Now that I think of it. Well, actually. To tell you the truth . . ."

Kratz walked in. Both men had been there on and off for hours, and neither of them felt they had yet heard the truth. The two detectives glanced at each other. Neel sighed, wearied by Bondurant's game-playing. It was past noon and they had brought in hamburgers. Kratz left to talk with the medical examiner.

Neel knew that getting a statement from a suspect was nothing but a mind game. He had cried with them and prayed with them, but he never found it advantageous to yell and holler. He had learned that rage was only met with rage.

"Okay. Let me start over," Bondurant said. "Honest, to God, this is what really happened. It was an accident. I had no intention of hurting that girl. It was only an accident."

"I've got a recorder right here, Mr. Bondurant. Why don't we get started?" Neel wasn't sure what he'd get. He had interviewed many cool, Texas bullshitters, who thought they could talk themselves out of any rap, even murder.

Bondurant took a breath. The gray and blond stubble on his face caught the glow of the overhead fluorescent lights and he looked older than when he had first been arrested. Reluctantly, he said, "Okay. I think I'm ready."

Neel put a tape into the recorder and slid it on the table. He reached over and pushed a button, and soon the reels began slowly turning. Bondurant's pale eyes looked dull as he started to answer Neel's questions. For the record, Neel again asked everything contained in the Miranda Warning so it would be on tape along with the statement.

Then, left to speak uninterrupted, Bondurant began, "It's July 16, 1994, 2:10 P.M. Eddie Neel, homicide officer, is with me. I am Warren Miles Bondurant. I understand that I am under arrest for murder. Neel read me my Miranda Warning and I know that any statement I make can be used against me. I waive my right to have an attorney present."

Using Sandra Underhill's maiden name he said, "I met Sandra Lee Coburn while she was in prison through a friend of mine from Louisiana. I became infatuated with her talent, her way . . . I visited her for six weeks on Sundays when she was in the Gatesville Prison." He went on to detail how he had worked to get her released.

Most of Bondurant's statement centered on what Sandra Underhill had done illegally. "I covered her hot checks . . . She went to Como and tried to rip off a crack dealer, then didn't lock my car . . . I was aware she was doing narcotics. In the summer of 1993 she became pregnant with my baby. She traded all of the furniture I bought her for cocaine . . ." Bondurant looked up at the detective who intently listened to him. "She went to Pinestreet Rehab and that's where she met Carri, whose mother told me they were lesbian lovers . . .

"Sandra stayed with me after the baby was born. I was fond of the baby once I found out it was mine. I thought he was a cute little guy. I was proud of him. After all, I was almost sixty years old."

He told the detective how Underhill and Coppinger ran off with his baby to Granite City, and admitted to sending an intimidating letter to Sandra to force her return.

"Once they came back," Bondurant told Neel, "I drove Carri back and forth to her job everyday." During the questioning, he even presented an excuse to the detective. "If I had wanted to get rid of Carri, why wouldn't I have done so during one of those late-night drives?"

Then later on, he contradicted himself. "After Carri came back from Illinois . . . it became a nightmare. I wanted Carri to get a job and move. It wasn't that Carri was in the way, but I was perturbed when she didn't hustle a job more. I was mad at her and told her to come into my bedroom to talk about the problem . . .

"Carri wasn't listening to me and went back to her bedroom. I took a bat in first to intimidate her. Then when that didn't work I went back to my bedroom to get my target pistol. I stood by her bed waving the gun when it went off.

"I ran around like a cockroach in a kitchen when somebody turns on the lights. I put Carri in a barrel from the garage . . . Gases emitted from the corpse made the top of the barrel swell.''

The detective showed no emotion as Bondurant related the graphic episode. Neither did Bondurant.

''Sandra became frightened because of her parole status. So I took her and Cody to the Residence Inn. I went to the house to get some things, and when I returned, Sandra had smoked some marijuana. Then she said she was going to call her stepfather.''

Bondurant looked at his heavy gold Rolex. It was almost three in the afternoon. ''I made a mistake. I panicked. I didn't mean to hurt Carri Coppinger. It was an accident. I didn't mean to hurt that girl.''

Neel asked, ''How long did you have the gun?''

''About a week.''

''Where did you buy it?''

Bondurant shook his head. ''I can't think.''

''Has anyone promised you anything? Intimidated you?''

''No.''

''Am I wearing a weapon?''

''No.'' Bondurant became silent, and Neel turned off the recorder.

At 3:30 P.M., Detective Neel dropped Miles Bondurant off at the Tarrant County Jail for processing. Ironically, it was the same jail where Sandra Underhill had been taken when Bondurant had her arrested for assaulting him. The police took him to the same counter to be photographed holding a number in front of his chest. And they told him to pass his hand over the same scanner for fingerprints, precisely as Underhill had done.

Steve Noonkester, the assistant police chief of Mansfield, Texas, was in his pasture when his wife walked out to tell him that she had just seen Miles Bondurant on a television newscast being arrested for murder.

"No! Are you sure?"

"They showed his picture on TV coming out of his house with his hands up. He supposedly shot some woman and put her body in a barrel."

The police chief looked shocked. "Miles Bondurant? I can't believe it. He's the most mild-mannered person I know." Noonkester kicked mud from his lizard boots and pondered how to help his friend without compromising his position. He had known Bondurant for 15 years, and Bondurant had frequently given lavish parties when he was married to Kimberly. They invited the policeman in gratitude for his advice on real estate codes governing Bondurant's many rental properties.

Noonkester followed his wife into their house and called Bill Lane, a noted criminal defense attorney in Fort Worth who was also his friend. Years ago, Lane had defended policemen charged with civil rights violations until he found more money defending murder suspects. Once Lane came on the phone, Noonkester asked him if he would send someone to help get Bondurant out of jail.

Bondurant's bail was only $100,000 since he had no prior criminal record, and a bond costing one-tenth of that would release him until the trial decided his fate.

Lane sent his private investigator, Janie Brownlee, who had contacted a bondsman she worked with. They advised Bondurant to use the titles to his two vehicles as collateral. Bondurant signed the $10,000 bond and walked out of the police headquarters. He squinted in the bright sunlight and smiled. Freedom felt wonderful.

Saturday evening, Miles Bondurant returned home and called Noonkester. "I can't thank you enough for sending that gal down to help with my bail. I had just finished with the police when she walked in. Now what I need to know, if *you* needed a criminal defense lawyer, who would you call?"

Noonkester said, "That woman you mentioned works

for Bill Lane, the top criminal defense lawyer in Tarrant County."

"Then I'll give him a call," Bondurant said. He hung up, feeling much better. Just how many murder suspects would have a chief of police trying to help?

# Chapter Twenty-Five

Sandra Underhill checked her watch—11 A.M.—and felt the warmth of the July sun on her skin as she walked to the entrance of the Ramada Inn.

After she fed and changed Cody, she picked up the phone. Using Bondurant's credit card, she booked a flight to Illinois. Then she called Joe Davila.

"Hey, girl, I hear all hell's breaking loose over there."

"How'd you find out?"

"Miles called a few days ago and told me about all that crap."

"When exactly?"

"Oh, shit, I don't know. Maybe last Wednesday morning. Called me from a pay phone. Anyway, it was right after he fuckin' shot Carri."

Goosebumps tingled on Sandra's skin. "What did he want?"

"That's just between me and Miles."

Underhill's shock silenced her for a few moments, then she said, "I'm feeling awful, Joe. Would you come sit with me?"

"No, girl. Don't think I should get into that shit."

Underhill hung up, realizing she had just lost a friend, and Bondurant had gained one.

As soon as Detective Neel delivered Underhill to the Ramada Inn, he contacted Glen Wilson, a FWPD crime scene detective, to meet him at the Residence Inn. It had been 13 hours since Neel's phone rang at three that morning, but he wanted to scope out the secondary crime scene before anyone tampered with the evidence. Even tired, Neel didn't look old enough to have been with the department 24 years, but he had entered as a cadet at 19, then graduated from the Fort Worth Police Academy six months later.

The men entered Room 813. Neel picked up two used glasses and an empty wine bottle. He customarily looked for drugs, marijuana, or drug paraphernalia, but found none. He gathered up Underhill's clothes and belongings.

Wilson examined the contents of the bathroom wastebasket and his findings proved more interesting. He first dug out receipts for Cokes, flea foggers, and air fresheners, then discovered small pieces of torn paper at the bottom of the wastebasket. He shook them out and reassembled a note written on Bondurant Corporation stationery that read: "Sorry, it was an accident. Had to make peace with God. Give cars to Suzie and Sandra." Bondurant's attorney, Calvin Jacobs, was given as a reference.

After Sandra Underhill recovered from the shock of Joe Davila's words, she called Jenny Campbell.

"Oh, Sandra, I saw it on the news," Campbell said. "It's just dreadful. The television showed the police rolling that barrel out on a dolly. It was godawful. We all loved Carri so. But I've been worrying about you. How are you doing?"

"I'm all strung out," Underhill told her. "Those were the three worst days of my life. You can't imagine what I've been through."

"I don't even want to. Let me pick you up and I'll have some friends of Carri's meet us at AA."

"That would be great. And could you drive me to the airport? I'm going back to Illinois at four this afternoon."

Campbell agreed to take her.

A few minutes later, Detective Neel was at her door with all her things from the Residence Inn.

"These have been cleared by our investigators," he said, as he walked in and unloaded the bundles.

As he started to leave, Underhill asked, "Whatever happened to our dog?"

Neel gave her an absent look. "Dog? We didn't find a dog in your room."

She looked at him, puzzled.

"Oh, by the way," Neel said, "there's a Majestic Liquor store across from Jack's in Weatherford. The street Jack's is on is the dividing line between the wet and dry areas."

"Good. I knew that's what you'd find." She smiled and exhaled a long stream of cigarette smoke.

Bondurant's friends and family were horrified. They had trouble reconciling the man they knew with the news coming over their television sets.

His stepbrother, Hugh Harbert, called him. Bondurant talked about the charges against him, but told Harbert that something else would come out. However, Bondurant couldn't tell him what it was right then. Hugh Harbert hung up thinking Miles must have gone off the deep end. They had known each other since childhood, and Miles had never shown any meanness.

Jenny Campbell put her arm around Sandra Underhill's shoulders and walked her into the AA meeting room. Sandra's friends couldn't control their emotions.

A girl named Susan said, "Carri and I worked our twelve-step program together. She actually made it fun."

Any story of Carri contained humor, so intermingled with grief, the women laughed at the tales while tears rolled down their cheeks.

At three, Campbell announced that she and Sandra had to leave for the airport, but everyone wanted to go along. Eight women, worn out from sobbing, scrambled into Campbell's car, sitting on laps and trying to be with Sandra one last time. Most of them took turns holding Cody. Underhill knew she'd be back for Miles' trial, but except for Jenny, this would be the last time she'd be with these people.

However, at the airport Jenny Campbell walked Underhill to her gate and would hand her a bitter surprise. At first Campbell's words were almost inaudible as she avoided Sandra's eyes and looked through the terminal's large plate glass windows. Finally, she said, "I can't give you a reason right now. But I don't think we'll ever see each other again. Maybe we can't even talk on the phone. I know that seems harsh and you won't understand."

Sandra Underhill stared at the woman who had been her strength at so many pivotal points of her life. Jenny was right, Sandra couldn't understand.

# Chapter Twenty-Six

Dr. Gary Sisler pulled into his reserved parking space in front of the Tarrant County Medical Building. An hour ago the assistant medical examiner had been called at home, which was most unusual for a Saturday. He had been alerted to expect an unusual situation—a barrel with a woman stuffed inside that would soon be arriving for autopsy.

As he pondered the postmortem examination, he ran his hand over his head, which had been shaved as smooth as an ostrich egg. He thought he had heard of everything in a career that began at 18 in Korea, then as an army doctor in Viet Nam. But after 40 years of investigating death, he knew this one would be memorable.

Sisler walked into the examination room, shortly before a medical aide rolled the barrel in on a dolly. Sisler flipped the lock and removed the lid. After taking a quick glance inside, he said, "Stick around, Ken, it looks like I'm going to need you." Then he picked up the phone and called for three more aides.

Quietly, five men peered into the barrel, and four of

them held their breath and swallowed hard, trying to avoid the putrid odor. Nothing bothered Sisler.

Carri Coppinger had slumped into a fetal position with her head bent to one side and pressed hard against the lid. Now she seemed to look up at the men, asking why they hadn't arrived sooner.

Sisler sensed that with her body so swollen, she would be difficult to remove.

With gloved hands, Sisler reached in to slide his hand under Coppinger's left armpit. "Grab under her other arm," he said to an aide. "Get your hands around her shoulders," he told another. They bent over and tugged with all their strength while the remaining aides grasped the barrel and pulled in the opposite direction to hold it down. Coppinger's compact 5′-2″, 148-pound body remained inside.

"Maybe it would be easier if we laid the barrel on its side," one aide suggested.

"We can't do that," Sisler said. "There will be several inches of body fluids in the bottom. We don't want to be swimming in that." Then Sisler had the men help him rotate the body in order to loosen it so it would come out more easily. Sisler and two aides eased their hands between Coppinger's shoulders and the barrel.

They tried to ignore the smell of the decomposing body as perspiration trickled from their foreheads and dampened their clothes. Periodically an audible gag could be heard. After wrestling another half hour, the men were able to free Coppinger's shoulders. Now two aides pulled on her arms while a third supported her back. The men raised her from the barrel while the liquids she had floated in dripped from her body. Then they placed her on a stainless steel gurney.

Once Coppinger lay on the flat surface, Sisler no longer saw a person, instead he saw a project. He leaned over to study her shattered left eye, and didn't have to guess at the cause of death.

An aide stayed to take notes as the doctor meticulously

went about the business of examining the entry wound made by the .22-caliber bullet. The blank eye, with only a fragment of the pupil remaining, held a milky opaque appearance. Sisler found the wound to be typical whenever someone received a .22 shot to the head. The gun's velocity was too low to send the bullet through the skull and out the other side, allowing no exit wound to help determine projectory. The bullet always stayed inside the skull, twirling, ricocheting, and doing its damage.

After some probing, the doctor discovered the spent bullet hiding just inside Coppinger's skull. He extracted it with forceps and dropped it with a "ping" into a metal bowl. He measured its entrance point to the exact place where the bullet had been discovered. "Note that the bullet sat two and a half inches higher than the entrance wound," he said to the aide recording his findings. "So we know the gun had been fired in an upward projection."

A week later, lab tests arrived that showed no hard drugs, but did indicate a trace of marijuana. It didn't surprise Sisler to find marijuana; he saw it in three-fourths of his autopsied clientele, even grandmothers. Tests on the fluids also indicated that Carri Coppinger had taken Prozac shortly before her death.

The doctor thought back to the woman's decayed condition and, knowing she had attempted to block depression, he thought it a sad dissertation on her life.

Sisler remembered the brightly colored tattoo on Coppinger's ankle. The tattoo depicted a yellow rose attached to wings on each side. Wings that would be flying nowhere.

# Chapter Twenty-Seven

On July 20, in Chattanooga, Tennessee, Linda Coppinger and her mother waited at the funeral home for Carri's casket to arrive. Chattanooga was Carri's birthplace and the home of her grandparents.

Linda said to her mother, "They say it's Carri, but we won't see her. Somehow not getting to see her body, I may never believe she's dead. Oh, Mom, this is so hard."

"I know," her mother said with her arm around her. "It's the worst thing you'll ever have to deal with in your life."

Linda Coppinger thought about the phone call from Detective Neel telling her that Carri would arrive in a disaster bag inside a sealed casket. Linda knew it was all necessary, but with no identification of the remains, there would be no closure, no final goodbye.

Linda thought about Carri as a little girl, when they would buy hamburgers from Crystal's Drive-In and drive to the duck pond in the Chattanooga Memorial Park Cemetery—an area that looked more like a park. She remembered Carri playing by the pond, eating hamburgers, and feeding the ducks.

Linda Coppinger told the cemetery officials to find a place by that pond, but they assured her that no plots were available. Overwhelmed by the tragedy of her daughter's death, she told them to continue searching. She had to do something she thought would please Carri.

After more probing, the officials discovered a single plot under a beautiful tree located next to the pond. Carri would be buried there.

Two days later at Carri's funeral, Linda Coppinger stood inside the First Presbyterian Church of Chattanooga greeting families who had known Carri as a little girl, as well as neighbors and friends of hers and her parents.

She was heartened to see over 200 mourners. Her good friend, the Reverend Patricia Maze, took the pulpit to tell about a teenaged Carri. "She would come to my house and talk to me about Jesus' love and concern. Before long, I started listening to that young girl, and then one day she converted me to Christianity. However, my being a Christian wasn't enough for Carri. She encouraged me to attend the theological seminary and become a minister. Carri has changed my life, and I'm sure there are many of you here today whose lives she has also touched."

Three days later at River Legacy Parks in Arlington, Texas, Linda Coppinger, her husband, Warren, and son, Chuck, flew in for another memorial to Carri. As they arrived at the park, they saw pink ribbons tied to more than 100 trees. They were told that a woman who did not know Carri read the newspaper account of her death and, touched by the circumstances, purchased many yards of ribbon to tie on the trees before the service.

Carri's friends from Lamar High School and AA had organized the memorial. Linda Coppinger again looked out on a crowd of more than 200 mourners who had braved the stifling July heat. As she stood before them, she said, "The gun did not win. Carri is now free, and she has no more frustration, no more pain. And she cares about you.

Carri's heart was bigger than her brain. If she could have done as much for herself as she did for others, we wouldn't be here today."

White balloons were distributed that had notes attached for Carri's friends to write messages of love and remembrance. At the end of the memorial, everyone released the balloons that floated into the blue sky while "Amazing Grace" played over loudspeakers. Linda Coppinger could never again hear that song without crying.

# Chapter Twenty-Eight

When the police received a report from Crimestoppers, they gave it immediate attention. The call came in one week after Carri Coppinger's death. An anonymous woman told them that Miles Bondurant had offered to pay Joe Davila to murder both Carri Coppinger and Sandra Underhill. The police had heard Davila's name on Bondurant's tape in connection with Davila being able to verify information about Underhill. His name had never been mentioned in any of the extensive media coverage the case received, so it had to be an insider who made the call to Crimestoppers. When the police called Davila, he readily admitted knowing both women in addition to Miles Bondurant.

Davila stomped into police headquarters, clearly upset to be there. He had been described to the police as having long shaggy hair; today his hair was short, but his temper was even shorter.

When Davila entered Neel's office, the detective nodded toward the vinyl and chrome chair across from his desk. Davila plopped down on it like a kid sent to the principal.

Detective Neel leaned back in his chair and gave Davila

a knowing smile. "We hear you've gotten tight with one of Fort Worth's movers and shakers."

"What are you talking about?"

"Had a call from Crimestoppers. Some gal said Miles Bondurant offered to pay you to kill Carri Coppinger and Sandra Underhill. What do you think about that, Joe?"

"That's so much shit! I can't believe you people would drag me in on crap like that."

"Are you saying Mr. Bondurant never contacted you about killing those women?"

"Mr. Bondurant's too good to even think about such bull. No, he never asked me to do none of that shit."

"Not even buying the barrels, or hauling them for him?"

"Nah. None of that crap."

"Joe, why would a guy go out and buy two barrels, kill a woman, and stuff her body into one? Why does he need the second barrel?"

"How the fuck would *I* know?"

"That was Sandra's barrel," Neel stated, and fixed his eyes on Davila's to gauge his reaction.

Davila only stared back with contempt, and said nothing.

Finally realizing he'd get neither information nor cooperation, Neel said, "Get your ass out of my office."

Neel didn't expect an outright confession, but Davila's loyalty to Bondurant surprised him.

Davila's visit made the detective anxious to get back to the Coppinger case. Neel knew that if he could find time to sit down and work on the murder without running off to a dozen other cases, it would probably be easily solved. But in order to take Bondurant to court, all the evidence had to be locked up in the police evidence room, and they still had no idea where Bondurant bought the barrels or the gun. However, they were averaging two murders a week, so the investigators were stretched thin.

Neel had taken Officer Haley with him the previous week to look at Bondurant's new Ford. The dolly Bondurant used sat in full view in the rear of the vehicle. They had found the papers for the truck sale from Hooks Ford and the Allstate car insurance. That evidence substantiated Sandra Underhill's story. Probably most important, they found Bondurant's checkbook and a box of .22 bullets. Six were missing.

Neel had taken his findings to the crime scene investigators. They tested one of the newly discovered bullets against the bullet Sisler took from Carri Coppinger and found it a perfect match.

Neel picked up the phone to make an appointment with Bondurant's landlady, Christine Logan. She had been only one thin wall away when Bondurant shot Coppinger.

Logan opened the door to her duplex, looking as nervous as she had two weeks ago when the police discovered the body. She led the detective to her living room where they sat on matching floral loveseats.

In a soft Georgia accent she said, "This shooting has been the worst thing in my entire life."

"Had you noticed anything unusual that week?" Neel asked, taking out a pen and tablet.

"I've been out of town. Just got in on the eleventh and Miles called to welcome me back. He was real thoughtful like that."

"Do you remember anything the day of the shooting?"

"Miles called. He wanted to know if I had heard a noise. Said he had dropped a Pyrex dish and knew it must have sounded like an explosion."

The detective stopped writing for a moment and looked up, surprised by the news, and remembered that Bondurant didn't bother to call 911. "*Did* you hear anything?"

"No. I really hadn't. I was busy watching *The Young and the Restless* about the time I think he meant. My program comes on right before the noon news. Also, we talked about some trouble he had with his garage door. I told him I had called A-1 Door, but I know they hadn't come by yet. Miles said not to worry about it because he had a friend who could fix it for him."

Neel wrote faster, knowing why Bondurant didn't want anyone in his garage. Then he asked, "Did you know Sandra Underhill?"

"I knew her as Sandra Coburn. Guess she went by several names. I didn't know her personally. Used to see her with that little baby. I know she lived with Miles sporadically, but I don't tend to other people's business."

Christine Logan pulled out a lace handkerchief and blotted her forehead. "I'm just drained by all that's happened. I've had to sleep at a friend's house for the last two weeks. Then I decided what I had to do."

"You're moving?"

"Oh, no. I own this place. I gave Miles an eviction notice along with a bill for $8,000 to repair the damage to the duplex. Now, every time I see that man, he reminds me of what happened."

Neel walked out to his car, musing Bondurant's excuse for the sound of gunfire.

Neel had the tenacity to work long, hard hours on cases even when the odds were stacked against him. But this time he got lucky. On August 8, before he could request a check by the Bureau of Alcohol, Tobacco, and Firearms on the gun Bondurant bought, he received a call from Detective Fulton of the Weatherford Police Department.

Fulton said, "Thought you'd be interested in what I just learned. I know you arrested that guy for murder, but did you know he bought a gun over here from Bert and Ernie's Gun Sales?"

"Haven't heard a thing," Neel said. "Do you have any paperwork on it?"

"I've got his ATF forms that he filled out for the permit. Here, I'll read what's on the form: 'Warren Miles Bondurant on July 5, 1994, submitted an application with the intent to purchase a High Standard .22 pistol.' The person who sold the gun was Ernie Gumble, and he stated he could ID the subject if you needed him to."

"Great. Can you fax me those papers?"

"They're on their way. If I can do anything else, call me."

Minutes later, Neel stood holding the ATF forms, and his smile broadened with this leap in the investigation. Both the crime lab records and the autopsy report indicated that the .22 found at Bondurant's house was the gun used to shoot Carri Coppinger.

Although Neel had folders from 13 pending cases on his desk, he knew he had to check out the gun purchase. He took his partner, Officer David Sears, to Weatherford.

Ernie Joe Gumble greeted the detectives as they walked into his plain, sparsely inventoried gun store in a modest shopping strip. Neel noticed that it didn't have the folksy earmarks of a gun enthusiast's hangout, but Gumble's dark ponytail that fell to his waist added some atmosphere.

Neel identified himself and Sears, then slapped five mug shots on the counter of Bondurant and four other men who had similar features and coloring.

Gumble didn't hesitate. "That's him right there," he said, pointing to Bondurant's photograph.

Neel smiled and showed him the faxed ATF forms. The salesman nodded again, "Yep, that's what he filled out."

"Had you seen Mr. Bondurant before you sold him this gun?"

"Yeah. I've known Miles for three or four years. First met him through Foreign Motors where I worked. He got his Mercedes repaired there."

"How did you get around to selling him guns?" Neel asked.

"I kinda did guns on the side at the car repair place, and Miles indicated an interest, so we'd talk about them. Then my brother-in-law and I started this business and Miles brought in a Browning .9 high-power semi-automatic handgun for me to clean.

"Later, I sold him a Rossi .38 revolver. Then I recently

sold him that High Standard .22 semi-automatic pistol. I remember it was blue.''

"Do you have a copy of Bondurant's receipt?''

"Yep, I should.'' Gumble scrambled through a box of receipts, then handed one to Neel. "Here's what I gave Miles when he bought that .22. 'Course he had to come in about a week prior to do the ATF paperwork.''

Neel read the receipt and was astonished to see that Bondurant had picked up the gun on the 12th, the day before he shot Coppinger. Neel said he needed to take the receipt for the police files. He'd mail a copy back to Ernie.

On the way out, Neel thought it all seemed strange. If Bondurant planned to commit murder, why would he buy a gun he had to register from someone he knew?

Two weeks after the gun fell into his lap, Neel finally found time to check out the barrels.

As he hurried to the evidence room, he thought of the many hours his department spent giving the Coppinger family updates on the case. The good families were always concerned, but it took time away from homicide's research. It further galled the family that Bondurant was free to go as he pleased. Neel usually talked with Carri's brother, and he could hear Chuck Coppinger's disappointment every time he reported they hadn't finished their investigation. Neel knew the family didn't think the police took the case seriously, which was far from the truth. Neel considered telling them about the problems of a number of the officers who discovered the body. Several admitted to being awakened with nightmares of that night, and one officer was forced into weeks of counseling sessions because of the trauma. The only one unscathed was Officer Philip Woodward, who had opened the barrel. He went home and ate a big meal.

Neel hoisted several pieces of evidence out of the way, and finally reached the plastic barrel. He grasped the barrel's sides and already saw one clue—ICC on the front—knowing it had to stand for something. Flipping the barrel upside down, he found an 800 phone number as well as a name: Industrial Container Corporation. He grabbed the phone and called. He was amazed to learn that the barrels were manufactured and sold in Fort Worth, Texas.

Debbie Alexander thought her company sold the most boring product in the whole world. The pretty young woman with long brown hair parted in the middle had only worked at Industrial Container Corporation for four months. Her job included customer relations and inside sales. She received the bulk of her orders from big industrial users who bought hundreds of barrels every week.

Alexander searched for a plausible explanation why a Detective Eddie Neel called her on Thursday, August 25, but she couldn't think of any. His voice had been polite when he told her that he wanted to come by to ask a few questions and show her some pictures.

When she pressed him for details, he wouldn't give her any, saying that he didn't want to prejudice her before she saw the pictures.

When Neel walked into her office the next day, he arranged the same five photographs on Alexander's desk that he had shown Gumble. The two other women in the office, as well as the office manager, came over to look, but none of them chose Bondurant's. When Neel told Alexander the suspect had purchased only two barrels, she felt she should have remembered him, because she seldom sold that small a quantity and it consumed as much time as a transaction involving an entire truckload.

Detective Neel said, "The police have checked the suspect's credit records and bank checks, but haven't found any barrel purchase."

"We aren't set up for credit cards," she explained. "It would have to be cash or a check. So you're telling me this was probably cash?"

Neel nodded.

"We give each customer a receipt which the customer signs and then takes to the shipping dock so the men there can load the barrels into the customer's vehicle."

Neel's interest piqued. "Then you always get the customer's name?"

"Usually. We're not computerized yet, and it's our only way to keep track of sales."

"Do you recall someone in a Mercedes?"

"I wouldn't see their car. I'm always in the office and it doesn't face the parking lot, but we can ask the guys at the dock. A Mercedes would definitely be out of the norm."

They left the comfortable air-conditioned office and trudged out into the cruel August sun. Debbie Alexander led the detective to the rear of their office building. As they neared the dock she said, "These barrels can easily fit into a car trunk or back seat because their diameter is only twenty-two inches and they're thirty-five inches tall. Since they're made of polyethylene, they can bend. I know we've squeezed them into little bitty cars before."

When they arrived at the raised, concrete shipping dock, Alexander explained the reason for the detective's visit to the four men there. Neel interjected that the car would probably have been red on the assumption that Bondurant would not have brought his yellow sports car.

The men glanced at each other, shaking their heads. None had remembered loading barrels into any Mercedes.

Neel's enthusiasm faded. He looked around at the sea of barrels and wondered how Bondurant had been able to pull it off. He turned to Debbie Alexander. "Please do me a favor and go through your cash receipts. It'll probably have been in the last couple of months."

She agreed to look, and walked back to her office. However, she hoped she wouldn't find anything. Knowing that someone might have used one of their barrels for a coffin horrified her.

She pulled out the cash receipts for the last two months

from a file and took them to her desk. Neel had told her to look for any variation of the name, Warren Miles Bondurant.

Debbie Alexander shuddered at the thought that she might have actually talked to the murderer. With only two months of product knowledge at the time he would have come in, she tried to remember what she might have told the man. She knew the barrel was liquid-tight, but not air-tight. She hoped she hadn't told him it was air-tight and now had some killer mad at her.

Alexander had flipped through receipts for less than 20 minutes when one in her handwriting caught her eye. It was for two barrels, dated July 1, 1994, and signed by a "Miles Jobe."

# PART IV

# Chapter Twenty-Nine

All during the flight to Illinois, Sandra Underhill could only think of Jenny Campbell's hurtful words and see Carri Coppinger's smiling face.

But now 24 hours later, the parade of people and arguments at her mother's house started to take its toll. After a few days of living in chaos and filth, she moved in with her sister, Allyson, in Hazelwood, Missouri, just outside of St. Louis.

Underhill found her sister's home considerably more peaceful especially since her mother was raising three of Allyson's four children. Here Sandra could remain anesthetized with liquor, rock her baby, and try to forget how much she missed Coppinger.

Underhill called her parole officer, Maggie Rhiner, as she had promised Detective Neel. She gave Rhiner her sister's phone number and asked if she needed to do anything.

Rhiner said, "Detective Neel told me all about Carri. That's just horrible. He also said you've been cleared of any murder charge so you have nothing to worry about."

* * *

After a month of grieving for Carri Coppinger, Sandra Underhill was excited to receive a letter from Jenny Campbell. As she hurriedly opened the envelope, she hoped Jenny had changed her mind about never seeing her again. Underhill unfolded the page, thinking she needed her support more than ever. She read:

> "Dear Sandra,
> There's no way I should become involved with what happened to Carri. I don't want people asking questions about things we discussed in confidence, and I don't want to be dragged into the middle of this case. Believe me, I'm sorry.
> Maybe some day I can explain it to you. Jenny."

Underhill fell into a chair at the kitchen table; her eyes filled with tears. At the airport Campbell thought she wouldn't be seeing her; now she knew for sure. She couldn't understand how the rock she had relied on had crumbled to sand. She was still staggering from the blow an hour later when the phone rang again.

A rush of familiar emotion engulfed her and she had trouble hiding her surprise when she heard Miles' voice.

"How long were you in jail?" she asked.

"A hell of a long time. Just giving the statement took ten hours, and the detectives were downright shabby in how they treated me. My hands were cuffed behind my back until my arms ached, and they just let me sit there in all that misery hoping they could intimidate me into giving some kind of confession."

"You didn't have any problem getting out after your statement?"

"I only stayed there long enough to take care of the paperwork. I'm no criminal. You're not going to find *me* in jail. After I paid my bail, I was out of there in a flash.

Of course I'm innocent of this whole thing. And I have a great lawyer. I'm feeling good about this."

"So you think you'll get off?"

"Sandra, I can't have you questioning me. This is a time when you need to stand behind me, just like I stood behind you. I paid for everything you ever needed for three years, and as long as I stay out of jail I'll continue to pay for whatever you need. Doll, that's something *you* need to remember."

Suddenly memories flashed through Underhill's mind and she knew Bondurant was right. Countless times he had taken care of her when she drank herself into a vodka stupor. His numerous possessions she had sold, given away, or destroyed probably totaled over $50,000. She owed him dearly. She would stand behind him and do whatever she could to keep him free. She heard him clear his throat.

"You know that statement you gave Neel? Well, we can't get a copy of it yet and my attorney, Bill Lane, would like to have an idea of what you said."

"I told the truth."

"Of course you did, sweetie. We were wondering if you'd give a statement to my attorney's investigator? I'd fly her up there."

"Sure."

"You just tell her what you told that detective." Then he paused. "But you know, Sandra, you were really tired when you talked to him. Probably up for two days with no sleep."

"Yeah."

"I would never put words in your mouth, but isn't Neel kinda pushy? Didn't you think he wanted things put a certain way. Like in *his* words?"

"He seemed all right to me."

"Well, I'm not telling you what to say, but I sure would think it over, honey. I understand he can be really strong with a witness."

"Okay. Who's the investigator?"

"Her name's Janie Brownlee. She'll give you a call and you can decide when it's best for her to come."

The first week in September, Brownlee flew to St. Louis then rented a car for the drive to Allyson's home to interview Sandra Underhill. Until then, Sandra had had no opportunity to discuss the case with anyone since she had left Fort Worth.

She asked Brownlee, "Do you think Miles shot Carri on purpose?"

"No. I really don't think so."

Sandra wanted to believe her, but she was suspicious since Bondurant was paying the investigator.

Janie Brownlee, middle-aged, blonde, and hyper, owned a private investigation business in Fort Worth and frequently worked for Bill Lane. Now, exuding nervous energy, Brownlee wanted to get on with the statement.

Underhill took the pen Brownlee handed her and began printing her recollections of the circumstances surrounding Carri Coppinger's death. Her statement essentially mirrored the one she had given Detective Neel. However, this time, she added an addendum:

"On the day I had been taken to the police station . . . I had been up for two days, and in my own opinion, I believe I was in a state of shock. I cannot remember if I even read what I signed. I also felt very intimidated by Detective Neel and felt urged by him to say certain things or exaggerate. There were two statements where he wrote while I talked and the other where he would tell me what to put in my own words . . . I let things go on the statement that he said."

Sandra Underhill felt happy to be helping Bondurant, and his pledge to financially support her again gave her a warm, secure feeling. Obviously he hadn't meant it when he said he'd kill her. He had only been upset because he had accidentally shot Carri.

* * *

Everything seemed to be revolving back to normal until the St. Louis County Sheriff knocked on Sandra Underhill's door with a warrant.

The wheels of justice had churned slowly. It had been over three months since Bondurant invited Sandra Underhill's parole officer into his home and exaggerated Sandra's drug abuse. Maggie Rhiner investigated his assault claims and found that Underhill had been arrested on February 4, 1993. The warrant stated that the Parole Board would now investigate her for a parole violation which could send her back to prison. Once she returned to Texas, the possibility remained strong that she would be arrested.

Later, Underhill cried as she explained the warrant to Bondurant over the phone. "But Maggie sounded so nice when I talked to her right after I came to Illinois. I can't imagine what could have happened."

Bondurant tried to sound sympathetic, but his voice strained with manufactured surprise.

A week later, Judge Don Leonard in Fort Worth invited Sandra Underhill to testify at the grand jury hearing that would investigate Miles Bondurant for murder. The summons spelled out the court's offer to pay for the flight, lodging, and expenses. She would have no excuse not to attend, so Bondurant, unsure of what she would say, had to come up with one.

Tarrant County asked the Circuit Court of St. Louis County to grant Underhill protection against arrest of either civil or criminal charges while en route to Texas to testify before the grand jury.

Concurrent with receiving the summons for the grand jury hearing, Underhill received a phone call from Janie Brownlee. "This is really important, Sandra. Miles doesn't want you talking with the D.A. in Tarrant County."

"But I have this parole warrant now in addition to the summons for the hearing. Legally, I'm suppose to turn myself in until this parole violation is cleared up."

"That's right, and we can't tell what the D.A. will do when you refuse to testify. Just in case, let me tell you the plan. When you get into town, I'll take Cody and give him to Miles to take care of should you have to go to jail."

"I don't like the sound of this," Underhill said, thinking that losing another child would be her worst nightmare. "I'll agree only if I can have Cody back as soon as I'm out."

"Of course, Sandra. On the offhand chance you'd have to do any time, Cody would be with Miles only until you're released. But don't worry, we have a plan about your testifying. Miles will call you tonight."

"Hi, sugar," Bondurant said, his voice sounding artificially sweetened.

"I really want to help because I don't want to see you go to prison," Sandra said.

"You bet your sweet neck you don't want me going to prison." Then he resorted to his customary litany; "Who'd support Cody and the new baby we're having? I'd hate to leave you out there on the streets like when I first found you." Then he softened his tone. "But we don't need to worry about that. I know how to take all the pressure off you to testify."

Bondurant went on to explain that since they had lived together for three years, they could be considered married in common law. With Sandra as his common-law wife, she'd have spousal privilege and wouldn't have to testify against him.

She said, "I did sign a divorce waiver from Robert Underhill. I guess it depends when the judge signed it."

"That's just a technicality. You hadn't seen Underhill for four years. He wasn't supporting you. I was. Really, I think this will fly. I've been talking with Sam Bonifield, a real cracker jack lawyer about you. With the cost of lawyers, I'm getting drained real fast, especially since the damn judge denied my business bankruptcy."

Underhill had heard Bondurant frequently complain about money, so she ignored his remark. She had something more important to settle. "Janie promised that if I give Cody to you in case I have to do jail time, I'll get him right back when I get out."

"Don't worry about that, honey."

"Miles, I want you to promise. If not, I'll just leave him here with my sister."

"I promise. I'll keep Cody only until you're out. And Sandra, Bonifield will be your lawyer to see that the state doesn't revoke your parole. Stick with me, doll. I'll take care of you. And when the D.A. flies you in, you go. And when you get to their office you refuse to speak. Got that?"

# Chapter Thirty

On September 22, Sandra Underhill's plane passed over sprawling Texas ranches and large man-made lakes before touching down at the Dallas-Fort Worth Airport. She had barely stepped foot inside the American Airlines terminal, balancing Cody and her carry-on bag, before Janie Brownlee and Sam Bonifield rushed up to her.

Brownlee introduced Bonifield and said, "Give me Cody. I'll take him over to Miles."

Sandra hugged Cody tightly before handing him over. "Now remember," she said to Brownlee, "you and Miles have both promised."

Janie Brownlee nodded and carried off the baby, while Bonifield took Underhill's suitcase and walked her out to the parking lot.

Once seated in his Cadillac Seville, Sandra declared her willingness to help Miles any way she could.

Bonifield reminded her that he would do all the talking when they were inside the D.A.'s office.

* * *

The Tarrant County District Attorney shared a new contemporary building with the district courts near downtown Fort Worth. Bonifield ushered Underhill into the granite and carpeted offices of the D.A. The long-legged assistant D.A., Mike Parrish, shook hands with the visitors and introduced them to one of his investigators, Celeste Rogers.

Parrish started outlining what would be expected at the grand jury hearing, but Bonifield interrupted him.

"We feel it's in my client's best interest not to testify."

Rogers looked surprised, but Parrish's mood veered sharply to anger. "Will you please tell me why we flew your client down here?" he asked.

"There's been a change of plans," Bonifield told them.

"There certainly has," Parrish said. "We could slap Ms. Underhill in the county jail this very minute."

"No, you can't. She has a statement from St. Louis County guaranteeing her immunity from any charges while she's here."

Parrish took a deep breath. "We gave her that immunity to testify. Now she's reneged on that. Therefore, her immunity is canceled. Here's the original of the immunity waiver," he said, pulling the paper out of his file. He shoved it toward Underhill. "She needs to acknowledge she gave up her immunity. Sign it."

"You want my client to surrender her immunity?"

"She already has by not testifying. Sign it."

"I need to make a phone call."

Parrish slammed his file drawer shut and told Bonifield he could find a phone in the hall.

After making a call Bonifield and Underhill returned to the D.A.'s office and Sandra signed the document. Then Parrish slipped it back into his file. Not trying to hide his annoyance, he said, "I think this calls for a trip back to the airport."

"I'll drive her there to make sure she gets on the plane," Celeste Rogers offered.

Before the women left, Sam Bonifield whispered to Sandra, "Don't you say one word to Celeste on the way to the airport."

As they drove, Rogers looked over at Underhill. "I wish you'd cooperate with the D.A. Won't you talk to us?"

Sandra continued looking straight ahead.

Rogers shook her head and appeared puzzled. "I don't understand why you're doing this. You're risking your own arrest."

Special Crimes Detective Celeste Rogers had paid her dues by working as a Fort Worth police officer, then became a detective for the D.A. Her long, tightly-curled blonde hair looked inconsistent with her thin framed glasses that confirmed her serious side.

Rogers pulled into the sprawling airport, parked, and walked Underhill into the terminal. After Underhill boarded, Rogers stood by the window until the plane had pulled away from the gate and taxied down the tarmac.

The D.A. ushered Sandra Underhill out of Fort Worth so quickly that she had no chance to pick up Cody. Bondurant, of course, could have offered to deliver him to the airport, but didn't. As a result, Sandra called Bondurant daily to get a report on the baby she missed so terribly.

After two weeks of pondering her situation, Underhill knew that as long as she refused to testify for the grand jury, she would have no immunity and could be jailed on her parole violation. Her main concerns were Cody and the baby she would give birth to in four months.

She called Bondurant to discuss her dilemma and told him she didn't want to be separated from Cody any longer.

"Sweetie, just think about your record with raising children. Cody and I are doing just fine here. He loves living with me. Besides, you've already lost three. Legally, you had two of them taken away."

"No, I didn't! I got Nicole and Joshua back and you talked me into giving them up for adoption."

"Honey, just for once, think of what's best for the little guy. I've been a parent. I've raised three wonderful children. I hate to say this, but there's no doubt that I'm the better parent."

Intimidated, she did not refute his comments. Instead she reverted to silence as she always did. Five minutes later, Janie Brownlee called.

"Sandra, you should see Cody. He's so happy. He just loves living with Miles. He gets so much attention with Miles' other children around. This is definitely the best place for him."

Underhill mulled over their suggestions and decided to turn herself in on her parole violation, but only so she could get it over with, get out, and raise her children.

Barely three weeks since she had left Fort Worth, Sandra Underhill flew back. Janie Brownlee met her and drove her directly to her parole officer, Maggie Rhiner. Only minutes later, the police retrieved Underhill from the parole office and escorted her to jail.

Sandra Underhill stood in line to collect her prison uniform. The trustee in charge took one look at her pregnant body and gave her a huge blue cotton dress. Sandra told her she wore a size five shoe. The woman handed her rubber flip-flops double that size. She allowed her to keep her own underwear and socks, but no makeup. Sandra wanted to hide.

Underhill's first parole revocation hearing was held

three weeks after her incarceration, and a bailiff clamped leg irons around her small ankles and locked handcuffs on her wrists before leading her along the underground walkway that traversed under the courthouse, past the kitchen, and up an elevator to a room where her parole officer waited.

With the clank of her leg iron chain hitting the floor, Underhill walked in for the hearing. Sam Bonifield and Maggie Rhiner sat at a long Formica table, along with a regional representative from one of the city's parole districts. A different representative would attend each of the three hearings. Rhiner looked up at Underhill and smiled sympathetically, then inserted a tape into a voice recorder.

Once Underhill sat down, Rhiner reiterated the story about Underhill assaulting Bondurant. She defended the revocation, saying, "It's not the severity of the offense we need to consider, it's the fact that she did it. She should be stopped now in fear of what she *might* do in the future. And remember," Rhiner said as she frowned at Underhill "Sandra didn't report her arrest, and that made the offense all the more severe."

The regional director turned to Sandra. "Were you provoked?"

"Well, not really," Underhill said, choosing not to tell them that Miles' temper and his calling her white trash prompted the slap, since she feared the revelation would be detrimental at his trial.

Bonifield pulled out his file. "I think it needs to be recognized that Sandra has never done anything to violate her parole in the past. She's never hurt anyone. It's obvious that she's pregnant. What a dismal stigma for a child to be born in prison. You both need to take all of that into account when you consider whether to revoke her parole."

Maggie Rhiner listened to him, but apparently preoccupied with Bondurant's manufactured tale of Underhill's temper and drug abuse, she couldn't agree. She also couldn't divulge the story because she had learned it covertly. Without further explanation she said, "Your request is denied. I think Sandra should go back to prison."

Underhill looked at the woman who less than three months ago had told her she had nothing to worry about. Now she pondered if that wasn't just a ploy to get her back to Texas.

# Chapter Thirty-One

Sandra Underhill lived with twelve other female inmates in a room known as "the tank." It contained 13 single beds, three picnic tables, a shower, and three toilets with no partitions to provide privacy from the rest of the room.

Her fellow inmates were jealous that she had Sam Bonifield for an attorney. They told her they thought he was the best-looking lawyer in Tarrant County, with his thick dark hair and magnetic blue eyes.

Underhill didn't care that he had movie star good looks; she was only interested in his legal ability. She knew Bonifield wanted to be involved with the Bondurant case for the publicity he would garner. Initially, the *Fort Worth Star-Telegram* ran daily articles with colored photographs of Bondurant, and even now periodically mentioned the progress of the case. The newspapers of Dallas and other cities around the country also picked up the bizarre story.

Bonifield telephoned Underhill in her tank to discuss the upcoming grand jury hearing. He told her that when she went into the hearing she was *not* to answer one question, and only to claim spousal immunity. If for some rea-

son that didn't fly, she could invoke her Fifth Am
rights.

She tried to remember all his instructions because
knew that lawyers couldn't accompany clients to grand jur
hearings.

A week after her first parole revocation hearing, Underhill clanked into the large grand jury room in small steps dictated by the chain connecting her ankles. The bailiff directed her to the witness stand that was equipped with a microphone. The 12 jury members sat at three tables arranged in a horseshoe while Mike Parrish sat in a chair behind the jury. With him was another assistant D.A., Mickey Klein, and the investigator, Celeste Rogers.

Sandra Underhill stared at the 12 strangers on the jury. They stared back at the 31-year-old pregnant, shackled woman, who shook visibly. But the D.A., for whom she had refused to testify, scared her most of all.

Once Parrish started asking questions, Underhill became so nervous she forgot Bonifield's restrictions. The first question simply asked her name. In a natural response, she answered, "Sandra Underhill."

To the second question, "To whom are you married?" she said, "Miles Bondurant."

But when Parrish asked her the third question, "Can you prove you are divorced from Robert Underhill?" she told him she couldn't. Suddenly, the entire magnitude of the situation hit her; she had admitted bigamy. Too late, she recalled Bonifield's instructions, and raised her hand to stutter, "I evoke the spousal privilege."

Parrish stood up. "I'll ask the bailiff to escort Ms. Underhill to a hearing on spousal immunity. Until we get that cleared up, I don't think we can proceed."

Then Underhill declared, "Oh yes, I also claim my Fifth Amendment rights."

The D.A. rolled his eyes and left the room.

* * *

Even though Underhill sat safely next to Bonifield at the spousal hearing, she still shook. Her experience of an hour earlier had left her rattled.

Judge Harry Hopkins presided, and asked her to swear to tell the truth. After hearing of Underhill's previous performance, the judge asked, "Mr. Bonifield, have you informed your client that lying under oath could bring an indictment of aggravated perjury?"

Bonifield assured the judge he had, then led Sandra along a verbal path, trying to establish her common-law marriage to Bondurant. Through a maze of questions, he established that Underhill and Bondurant had lived together on and off since August of 1991, and they had one child. He asked her the child's name.

"Cody Lee Miles Coburn," Underhill said, using her maiden name.

Now her lawyer appeared startled. "Cody who?"

"Coburn."

Perplexed, he asked, "Why isn't his name Bondurant?"

"Miles wanted a DNA test before he'd put his name on Cody's birth certificate."

"What were the results?" Bonifield asked. His raised eyebrows suggested he didn't know the answer.

"Positive. Miles is the father."

The lawyer exhaled audibly. "Are you pregnant at this time?"

Underhill adjusted the big tent around her extended middle and said, "Yes. I'm pregnant by Miles."

Then Bonifield allowed her to admit that she had been married to Robert Underhill, but had signed a waiver of appearance in June, 1994, declaring that she had not protested Underhill's divorce filing.

"Did you and Miles Bondurant hold yourselves out as being husband and wife?"

"Yes, absolutely."

"Who did you hold yourselves out to, and how did you show you were married?"

"We told everybody we knew. Whenever we went anywhere. Out of town. At hotels."

"Whose idea was it for you to assert the privilege of spousal immunity?"

"Mine."

"Has anyone promised you anything to assert that immunity?"

"No."

"It is my understanding that you are claiming to be the common-law wife of Mr. Bondurant?"

"I am."

Without any documents or one substantiated fact, Bonifield turned the hearing over to the assistant D.A. for cross-examination. Mike Parrish's delivery proved direct and cutting.

"Are you aware of allegations that you are somehow involved in this [murder] case?"

"Yes."

"Do you know who made those allegations?

"Yes. Miles Bondurant," Sandra Underhill said, without a trace of bitterness.

"When you signed the waiver to divorce Underhill, who were you living with at the time?"

"Miles Bondurant and Carri Coppinger."

"Do you have any credit cards in the name of Sandra Bondurant?"

"No, but sometimes he lets me use his."

"Do you have any bank accounts in that name?"

"No. It's against my parole to have checking or bank accounts."

"Do you know the date you signed the divorce waiver and where it had been notarized?

Judge Hopkins cut in and asked Bonifield, "Do you have a copy of the divorce decree?"

"I do."

"Has Mr. Parrish seen that?"

"No, Your Honor."

The judge frowned and said, "Show it to him. Maybe we can get this divorce thing over real quick."

"I didn't want to show it to him, really."

The judge looked flabbergasted.

Bonifield said, "Ms. Underhill testified that she is divorced, and a lawyer in Illinois said she's divorced."

"That doesn't mean she's divorced," the judge said heatedly. He pointed his finger at the decree Bonifield held, indicating that the lawyer better give the paper to the assistant D.A.

Bonifield hesitantly handed the document to Parrish. After a brief perusal, Parrish said, "She did not divorce Mr. Underhill until a month after the killing. The document counsel has just provided is dated August 15, 1994."

Mickey Klein sat beside Parrish assisting him, and now hurriedly flipped through the legal tome sitting on the table in front of him to search for a case proving their point. When he found the information, he quickly gave the passage to Parrish, who shared it with the judge: "Spousal immunity cannot be allowed when the subject in question [Carri Coppinger] is proved a member of the household."

Parrish asked Sandra Underhill, "At the time of Carri Coppinger's death was she living with you and Mr. Bondurant?"

"Yes."

"That answers our question, gentlemen," Judge Hopkins declared. "The victim was a household member, so Ms. Underhill will not be held immune from testifying."

Immediately after the hearing, the bailiff escorted Underhill to a holding tank, and told her she'd have to wait to testify because one of Bondurant's three children was on the stand. Her confining leg irons and handcuffs became all the more uncomfortable as she sat cramped in a 6 x 6-foot cell.

She felt angry that Bondurant freely walked the streets

while she remained in jail. True, he kept sending her money, but now she began to see it as a bribe.

Underhill sat in the small cell for four hours, but the day's allotted time ran out and court recessed before she could testify. Tomorrow she'd be brought back to wait again in the confining quarters.

Sandra Underhill trudged back to her quarters and noted her 12 roommates staring at her. Whenever anyone left to testify, the other inmates in their living group became suspicious. The person testifying had the opportunity to divulge facts about the others to get her own time shortened. In addition, an unwritten jail code held inmates in low esteem who testified against murderers. The idea that you could help put someone away for life or send them to the electric chair didn't fare well for the informer, and some found themselves the next day with purple bruises they were afraid to explain.

Sitting by herself on her cot, Underhill avoided the eyes that gazed upon her. She felt relief when one of her fellow inmates, Greta, smiled sympathetically and sauntered across the room.

"When's your baby due?"

"Late February."

"We'll both be out by then. I'd love to see your baby when it's born. Give me a call." Greta wrote her mother's name and phone number on a piece of paper.

Sandra wrote Bondurant's phone number and the women exchanged notes. It was a common thing to do in jail, a way of coping. To think about the future and having a life after jail helped soothe the confined souls of the women. Underhill promised to call Greta, but realistically, she thought it unlikely she'd ever see the tall, thin redhead again.

* * *

The next morning, October 24, 1994, Sandra Underhill lingered two more hours in the holding cell before she finally had her long-awaited chance to testify in front of the grand jury. Now, with a parole violation over her head, she felt forced to testify, tell the truth, and hopefully not do any damage to Bondurant

At the hearing, Parrish questioned every aspect of her life with Coppinger and Bondurant, especially the two days after Carri's death.

A repetitive theme evolved around Bondurant having a relationship with both Coppinger and Underhill. The question of a *menage à trois* came in a variety of forms, but the meaning was always the same—was Bondurant also having an affair with Coppinger?

To all the questions, Sandra Underhill answered, "No. Absolutely not. Miles and Carri were never lovers." She inwardly shuddered thinking how repulsive that would have been to Carri.

Then Parrish asked her, "Did you have a lesbian relationship with the victim?"

Underhill looked down at the gray carpeted floor and struggled to come up with a satisfactory answer without perjuring herself. In the end, her embarrassment at admitting the affair won out. She looked up at Parrish, and said, "No. We never had a lesbian relationship." She hoped her heated face did not betray her. Otherwise, her secret was safe. Only she and Carri knew the truth.

At Sandra Underhill's second parole revocation hearing, she saw a different regional representative, but heard the same accusations from Rhiner.

Sandra sat quietly, always trying not to cast Bondurant in a negative light.

At this session, the police officer who had arrested Underhill testified, "The house looked like a mess. The stories I heard from Mr. Bondurant and Ms. Underhill didn't match, but they had quite a struggle according to the looks of everything." He shrugged his shoulders. "I had to arrest someone."

At the revocation hearings, the three regional representatives had a collective 50 percent vote on the outcome. Rhiner had the other 50 percent and she never wavered. After the third hearing, where Maggie Rhiner told yet another area representative that Sandra's parole should be revoked, the outcome of a final hearing at the State Board of Parole in Austin seemed a foregone conclusion—Underhill would return to the penitentiary. As it turned out, all the other inmates she lived with, save Greta, had lost their freedom.

Sam Bonifield watched the swift proceedings. Although he realized his first priority was to Bondurant, he thought the hearings were terribly unfair. At each one he stood to speak on Sandra Underhill's behalf. "Remember that once she's free, she's guaranteed a job at the Bondurant Corporation. Remember too that Mr. Bondurant never filed charges on her. Returning her to prison would be ludicrous!"

Rhiner turned a deaf ear to his pleadings, but she would live to regret it. Following Rhiner's pronouncement that she would refer Underhill's parole case to Austin with the recommendation that parole be revoked, Bonifield stood up again. Pointing a finger at Rhiner he said, "I want this board to know that last year Ms. Rhiner illegally accepted a registered Shih Tzu puppy from Sandra Underhill."

A hush fell over the session and all eyes turned toward the parole officer. The seriousness of the charge rested on the strict parole policy that an officer could accept nothing from a parolee.

"Is this true?" the regional representative asked.

One glance at Rhiner's red face answered his question. She quickly nodded. A week later, the parole board held an embarrassing hearing for Maggie Rhiner. She was fired.

* * *

Sandra Underhill tried to mentally prepare herself for prison. If the guidelines prevailed, she would be locked up for one year as a penalty for losing her parole status. Plus she would serve a percentage of her remaining sentence. In total, she'd be in prison for three years. Worst of all, she would give birth in prison.

Prisoners are not allowed to be in Austin for their parole revocation hearings. So Underhill tried one last plea for leniency on November 8, 1994, by composing a letter to accompany the evidence sent to the Austin Parole Board, although she was still careful not to blame Bondurant for any of her problems:

> "To Whom it May Concern:
>
> I understand that it is not acceptable to go around slapping anyone and I am more than willing to comply with any special conditions attached to my release on parole status once again. I apologize for any inconvenience resulting from these hearings. I realize that I have cost many people time and money concerning these matters, but am willing to work hard at reconciliation by going to counseling, paying additional fees and costs, returning to month-to-month supervision, or even week-to-week, being put on electronic monitor and/or any other possible way to accommodate the Board of Pardons and Paroles.
>
> I am asking that the board show mercy and see fit to discharge me from custody so that I may return to my place of employment and be able to be with my eight-month-old son and prepare for the birth of my new baby.
>
> Thank you for your time and consideration in this matter."

She signed her name and gave it to Bonifield.

In Austin, the questions, accusations, and answers were

the same, but in the absence of Maggie Rhiner's testimony, the State Board had trouble finding sufficient evidence to revoke the parole. So after a total of three parole revocation hearings, a spousal immunity hearing, a grand jury hearing, and three months of confinement, Sandra Underhill, now seven months pregnant, was ecstatic to be set free two days before Christmas 1994.

# Chapter Thirty-Two

The court insisted that Sandra Underhill have a place to live and a job before her release from jail, so Bondurant rented her a depressing one-room apartment in the hospital district on Eighth Street and gave the Bondurant Corporation as her place of employment.

The apartment, in a large old house that had fallen into disrepair, had been revamped from a single room and was sparsely furnished. The tiny kitchenette had old, small appliances, and the bathroom featured only a toilet and a mildewed shower stall. Adding to Sandra's frustration, the owners banned smoking.

On the way back to Bondurant's house she complained about the dirty place. He said, "Honey, you know you'll be at my house with Cody and me most of the time."

"What do you mean at your house with Cody? You promised you'd return Cody to me as soon as I got out of jail."

Bondurant's eyes opened wide. "I don't remember agreeing to that."

* * *

On the day after Christmas, Miles Bondurant accompanied Sandra Underhill to Janie Brownlee's office to discuss Bill Lane's trial strategy.

Underhill said, "Janie, you promised me that you'd return Cody when I got out."

Brownlee's surprised expression resembled Bondurant's. "Sandra, you must be joking." Underhill argued with both of them, but finally let it drop for the time being because soon she'd be busy with the new baby.

Brownlee, eager to get on with Lane's plans, looked sternly at both of them and told them that she wanted them leading separate lives. She told Sandra that was why Miles rented her the apartment. Heatedly, Janie said there was some electric current running between them, and before Bondurant went to trial, they couldn't afford to get into fights and call the police. And Lane didn't want any ruckus that would cause neighbors to call Child Protective Services.

Regardless of Brownlee, Underhill spent time at Bondurant's new quarters although they didn't measure up to his luxurious duplex. After his eviction, he had moved to a smaller, more modest house on Misty Meadow Road that had three bedrooms and a single garage. Any extra money he had went to his attorneys. He even sold his beloved Mercedes sports coupe for $15,000 to raise funds.

When Sandra Underhill stayed overnight, she slept on the couch in the living room while Bondurant and Cody occupied bedrooms. Any amorous feelings Bondurant might have had were replaced with worry over his approaching trial. When the two of them were together, he only wanted to talk about his legal problems and how he could get out of, as he saw it, "that ridiculous murder charge."

"You have a good lawyer," Underhill reminded him. "Isn't he coaching you on how to testify?"

"When I call him, his secretary tells me he's busy and can't talk."

"Will he tell me what to say?"

"I'll tell you what to say," Bondurant assured her. "When you get on the stand, tell them that you knew about the baseball bat."

She nodded, and tried to remember a baseball bat. She didn't know he played baseball.

As the weeks drifted toward Bondurant's trial, he tried to transfer the responsibility for his troubles to Underhill, and feeling physically drained in her ninth month, she became even more vulnerable to his schemes.

Bondurant sat in the same leather chair he'd had on Collinwood while she lay on the couch. "Doll, the time's going fast. Bill Lane said the trial will open in mid-July. Only six months away. Thank God I'm free on bail. Otherwise Lane would have demanded a speedy trial. This way we don't care if the trial ever opens." He stood up to get two beers from the refrigerator.

"I shouldn't," Sandra said, reaching for the bottle. She took a big swallow. "What can we do?"

"Here's what I've decided," Bondurant said. "My life's terrible. It's not worth living. My friends don't call any more. People treat me like a joke. I don't see any way out for me." He paused and took a big breath. "I need to commit suicide."

"Oh, Miles. You've said that before. Now think. Who'd support the children?" She frowned at his words.

Then as Bondurant sat quietly nursing his beer, Underhill pondered her own question. Who would take care of the children? Her mind raced for a way to save him.

Ten days later, Sandra Underhill had been on Bondurant's couch, supposedly sleeping. Instead, she had spent a fitful night trying to invent a solution for him, and in the wee hours of the morning, she finally devised her drastic plan.

When Bondurant walked into the living room the next morning, she told him, "I've found the answer to our problem."

Sarcastically, he said, "Sure, sweetie, how are *you* going to make everything right?"

Lines of tension stayed in her face. "I'm going to take the blame for Carri's death."

Bondurant stared at her in astonishment. "And just how are you going to do that?"

"I'll write a confession and say I did it. Believe me, I could deal with prison a lot better than you."

"Really?" Bondurant's mouth opened in shock. "You'd really do that?"

"With how your life's been, prison would just kill you. I couldn't stand thinking about you being locked away somewhere. I'll say that you're a very good person and you've been protecting me all this time."

Bondurant sat stunned for a few moments before his elation began to show. He threw his arms around Sandra. "You'd really do that for me? I can't believe it. Frankly, I don't know what to say."

"Well, you're right. It's my fault. I never should have insisted that Carri come back to Fort Worth."

Bondurant did nothing to dissuade Underhill from thinking otherwise. His shock at her taking responsibility soon turned to acceptance, then to eagerness for her to write her confession. He told her not to go into a lot of detail because she might get tripped up if she gave too many facts. Then he'd take the confession to Brownlee tomorrow.

His face broke into a smile. "Here's a good idea. You should mail a copy to the *Star-Telegram.* They'll be the most important people to send it to, because everyone in Fort Worth would see it and think I'm not guilty. I bet my friends would respect me again," he said, with a brightness in his eyes that hadn't been there in months. "Also, send a copy to the D.A. and Bill Lane." The more Bondurant planned, the more enthusiastic he became. Then his face became serious. "Sandra, don't ever tell anyone I had a thing to do with this."

Underhill worked for an hour, and finally came up with her confession. She handed it to him.

> "To Whom it May Concern:
>
> I couldn't live any longer knowing that I am the one who really killed Carrington [Carri] Coppinger. Miles has only been covering for me because of his love and loyalty. This is a confession and I so hope that I can redeem myself and clear Miles and that justice can be served. Sandra Lee Coburn."

Bondurant read her confession, and his smile broadened in approval. "Sweetheart, this is perfect."

The telephone rang the next afternoon and Sandra Underhill immediately recognized Janie Brownlee's stern voice. "What is this statement all about?"

"I don't think we should discuss it on the phone," Underhill told her.

"Then I'm sending Miles over this minute to pick you up."

Thirty minutes later, they sat in front of Brownlee in her office.

"This statement is just plain crazy," she began.

"Miles didn't have a thing to do with it," Underhill told her,

"Right," Brownleé said, her voice dripping with sarcasm. "Miles, this is unconscionable."

"It's what Sandra wants to do."

"He didn't buy those barrels, either. Didn't you find them somewhere?" Sandra Underhill asked.

Brownlee frowned. "Miles, you told me where you bought them."

"Sandra's mistaken. I never told her I found them. Yes, I bought them."

Underhill looked baffled.

Brownlee glanced down at Sandra's confession. "Well, there just happens to be a flaw in this," she said, looking at Sandra. "Where was Miles supposed to be when you killed Carri? Weren't you at the office with Charles all day? He'd be a witness who'd say you were there."

Underhill looked at Bondurant. "Gosh, we didn't think of that."

"What about on your lunch hour?" he offered.

"I didn't have a car. Besides I couldn't have taken Cody with me."

"Right. It would have to be before you left home."

"That's it," Underhill said. "I could have shot her while you were at the store buying flea bombs."

"Doll, that's a great idea," he said.

Brownlee gave Bondurant another look of disgust. "This is not only crazy, it's unethical."

"I just want to help Miles," Sandra told her.

Then with a resigned shrug, Janie Brownlee said, "We'll see what Bill Lane has to say about this."

A week went by, and they heard nothing from Lane about the confession, so they assumed he wouldn't dignify it with a response.

Sandra told Miles, "The trouble with that confession is that we're still alive. I'll go ahead and sign a statement saying I killed Carri, and also add something about how you were covering for me. We'll find someone to adopt the kids—maybe your brother's daughter, Madison, would do it. I know she loves them. Then we'll die together."

Bondurant was silent at first, then said, "I need a cigarette. Let's go out in the garage and sit in the truck." Bondurant now smoked as much as Underhill, but he didn't want Cody inhaling secondhand smoke.

They piled into the Ford Explorer with their cigarettes,

two glasses, and a bottle of Scotch. Underhill had become so depressed that suicide didn't sound half bad. Her dependence on Miles convinced her that she couldn't have a life without him. She figured that she'd wither away or live on welfare as her mother had all her life.

Bondurant poured them both a drink.

"Let's think," she said. "Where could we commit suicide?"

Bondurant thought for a moment as he looked around the darkened garage. "Here, honey, in the garage. We'd plug up everything and sit in the Explorer. Then we'd turn on the engine. And wait. It would be completely painless."

It became a nightly habit to sit in the garage, smoke, drink, and talk about their suicide plans.

Sandra Underhill asked, "Have you talked with Madison about adopting the children?"

"Doll, I just don't think a double suicide's going to work. Yeah, I talked with my niece. I asked her if she'd take the kids in case anything happened to me. I said it that way, letting her think it was in case they found me guilty, but I didn't want to say the word suicide. She'd get all shook up if she knew I planned to kill myself. She agreed to take the kids and raise them. Really a bright lady. But she's a lawyer and totally into her career. I don't know . . ." His voice trailed off.

"Then I got to thinking. They're my kids. I want some say in how they're being raised."

Soon the idea of a joint suicide dissipated and they went back to trying to find a solution to save Bondurant.

Then one night it all changed. Underhill sat in her dingy one-room apartment when Bondurant called. She could tell he had been drinking, and in no time he started screaming at her. "Sandra, you are a no-good, low-life. If I hadn't tried to get you out of prison, there wouldn't be a murder rap hanging over my head. Just knowing you has made a disaster out of my life! You are one hundred percent responsible for everything that's happened!"

Underhill didn't refute what he said, because over the months he had convinced her she was responsible. Once Bondurant had finished ranting, Sandra said, "What am *I* supposed to do, kill myself?"

Only silence greeted her words. "Miles?" She waited a few more moments, then finally his voice came back abruptly.

"Yes!" he shouted at her. "You should kill yourself."

# Chapter Thirty-Three

The following week, Bondurant's voice sounded as sweet as honey when he called Sandra. He hadn't been this congenial since they first met, and he kept pushing her to let him bring over more beer and cigarettes.

She assured him that she had plenty for right now. What she really wanted was to see Cody, since it had been three days since her last visit.

Bondurant readily agreed and offered to pick her up around noon for lunch, then they'd go back to his place to fine-tune their plans.

Underhill walked into his house and looked at his collection of firearms. "I know you have a bunch of guns," she said. "But there's no way I could shoot myself."

"Sweetie, I'm not asking you to do anything like that. Do what you're comfortable with. Probably the most painless way is sleeping pills."

"Yeah. Sleeping pills," she said. "I'd just have to work up my nerve to take them."

"You're a different person with alcohol. Don't you know, sweetie?" He playfully elbowed her side. "Just start drinking early in the afternoon, then by ten or so, you'd be ready for the pills. What do you think?"

She nodded, and they continued planning over the next several weeks. They decided on a time frame of three or four months after the baby's birth.

In the meantime, life went on as normal. Bondurant kept custody of Cody and Underhill visited his home as often as she wanted. Not a word of criticism left his lips as she drank one beer after another, even though she would soon deliver his child.

Bondurant repeatedly sought reassurance that Sandra would stick with their arrangement. He'd say, "I know at least one of us should be here to raise the children."

Underhill would automatically reply, "And I know that someone is you." Then she'd cry and he'd walk over and pat her back.

Bondurant's eyes would shine. "You'd take the dive for me?"

She'd nod.

"Do you think they'd believe that you did it?"

"An ex-con? They'd believe me."

"Darling, would you really do that?" His ears couldn't hear enough of her affirmation. Only when she continually promised would his mind be at ease.

"Sure I would. You haven't been to prison, so you'd be a much better role model."

Bondurant would put both arms around her and with tears in his eyes he'd say, "You are so noble."

One day after seeing Bondurant's appreciation, Underhill thought he'd at least divulge the last moments of Coppinger's life. She needed to hear that before she died, so she asked him if Carri had said anything before he shot her.

"She was indignant. Showed me absolutely no respect."

"Did she mention me?"

"Yeah. Said she'd always be your friend and wouldn't leave without you."

But Sandra's continued requests of why he shot Carri were met with Bondurant's same words. He still maintained the shooting had been an accident.

She wanted to tell him that she and Carri only had a brief physical relationship, but knew he couldn't handle it. Even though their fling ended long ago, she was positive it still blazed brightly in Bondurant's mind.

On Sunday evening, February 26, 1995, Sandra Underhill stood at the front door and watched Miles Bondurant leave with Cody bundled up for his birthday party at Marian's house. Cody's blue eyes peeked through the small opening allowed by his hood. He would turn one tomorrow. Marian had said, "Bring Sandra if she wants to come," and it may have been sincere, but Sandra thought Marian felt forced to ask. She opted to stay home.

No one would tell Underhill how it happened, but somehow Pebbles had materialized at Marian's house after the dog had last been seen at the Residence Inn.

Underhill went back into the house to clean since she didn't have to tend Cody. She eyed Bondurant's 4-foot square coffee table of thick metal with big swirls cut into the top. It sat on a heavy wrought iron base, and had taken two men to carry into the house. She decided to move the massive piece so she could clean underneath. She knelt on the floor and tried to shove it, but it sat as defiantly as a boulder. Then she stood and forced her weight against it and the table actually moved a discernible inch. Suddenly, pain shot through her body. She was in labor.

Two hours later, at almost nine, Bondurant walked in the door and found Sandra lying on the couch.

Perspiration covered her body although the night was cold. "Get me to the hospital," she moaned. "Fast."

Bondurant grabbed her suitcase. He'd drop off Cody at Marian's on the way to All Saints Hospital.

They hurried to the garage and piled into the Explorer. Bondurant started the engine, threw the gears into reverse, and crashed into the closed garage door. The crunch of wood and metal jarred them. He pulled the car forward and got out to survey the damages. He shoved his body against the bent metal while Underhill moaned in pain. Using a crow bar, he banged away at the bulging door and finally straightened it enough so it would open, then they were on their way.

At 11:20 P.M., Sandra Underhill gave birth to another boy. Had he waited 40 minutes, he would have been exactly one year younger than Cody.

Bondurant stood by Sandra's bed when she was rolled back into her room. "I've got a great name for him," he said.

She looked up, still sleepy from the anesthetic.

"Let's call him Warren Clark Bondurant. We'll call him Clark after my brother. I wish you could have met him. Wonderful, brilliant anesthesiologist. He died at forty-eight of a heart attack in his car on the way to work.

"He used to fly down to Mexico every year with a bunch of other doctors and gave his time to those people. After my dad left, Clark became the man in the family. He kept us all in line." Wistfully, Bondurant added, "My life would have turned out a lot better if Clark had stayed around."

Bondurant looked down at Sandra, who had fallen asleep. She had given him another son and then she would give him her life. He thought about the wretched one-room apartment she'd have to return to with the new baby and decided to rent her a nicer place. He'd do that tomorrow.

# Chapter Thirty-Four

In three weeks Sandra Underhill had recovered from the delivery. She looked out the window of her new, freshly painted duplex near the TCU campus. She couldn't mask her surprise when Bondurant had picked her up from the hospital and brought her to this comfortable place.

Now her only problem was that she had so little time to enjoy it. It was March 17, 1995, and she had promised to commit suicide on June 17.

Bondurant had told her that would allow plenty of time before his July 16 pre-trial hearings. He knew he'd have to deal with being charged an accessory to the fact, aiding and abetting, that sort of thing, but those charges didn't compare to having a murder rap hanging over his head.

Suicide constantly occupied Underhill's thoughts. She resigned herself to it as if a doctor had announced she had cancer and only three months to live. Frequently, she cried during the day, and always cried herself to sleep at night.

* * *

In a few minutes, Bondurant would come by her duplex to take her to her monthly meeting with her parole officer. He would baby-sit the boys while she was gone. This meeting and the weekly one with her therapist were the only times she left home. The parole board had forced her into anger therapy for slapping Bondurant.

A half hour later, Underhill walked lethargically into the office of her parole officer, Mr. Brevig. He was on the phone, so she sat down and read the framed professional certificates on the wall behind him. She wasn't particularly listening to his conversation, but one name caught her attention.

"Greta had better not miss her next appointment," Brevig barked, "or she'll be in hot water up to her red hair." He slammed down the receiver.

Underhill knew the name and hair color were too much of a coincidence not to be the red-haired Greta she had shared a cell with in the Tarrant County jail. She hoped she still had the phone number of Greta's mother in her billfold.

Then she pulled out a picture of Clark and proudly showed it to Brevig. Bondurant had made her promise not to give the slightest hint about her pending suicide. He told her that her parole officer would probably revoke her parole and throw her back into prison if he learned she was planning anything like that.

That night Sandra Underhill reached for the phone to call Greta's mother. She pulled her hand back. Why should she? She barely knew the woman. To Sandra, it seemed that she always looked out for other people with little regard for herself. And where had it gotten her? Still, she sighed, if she could help Greta stay out of trouble with just one phone call, why not? She punched in the number and left a message with Greta's mother.

* * *

Clark gurgled as his mother gave him his bath. She loved his plump little body. He looked so much like Cody—same blond hair and blue eyes. After she dressed him, she held him close. He became all the more dear to her knowing she would leave him in a matter of weeks. She'd write letters to both boys. Certainly Miles would agree to give them the letters when they grew up, so they could understand the sacrifice their mother had made.

She no longer saw Miles in the evenings as they had before Clark's birth, and since Miles had become so consumed by the trial, they never spent their nights together. He only brought Cody over for a few hours during the day so Sandra could baby-sit while he went to the office or ran errands.

Underhill had sat down to give Clark his bottle when the phone rang. She rarely talked to anyone these days, not even her mother or sisters. The phone rang for the fifth time before she finally answered.

"Sandra, it's Greta. What's going on, girl?"

Sandra explained the conversation she had overheard at the parole office and Greta promised to call Brevig the next day.

"Did you have your baby?"

"I had a beautiful little boy. His name's Clark."

"You promised I could come see him."

Underhill's eyes brightened at the thought that Greta had remembered. "Come anytime. I'm always home." She gave Greta her address without much hope that she would visit, thinking Greta was being polite only out of gratitude for Sandra's having told her about her possible parole problem.

The next night Sandra's doorbell rang. The only person who ever came to see her was Miles. She couldn't imagine why he didn't use his key and walk in.

As the bell continued to chime, she peeked out the window and saw Greta with a man she didn't recognize. Hesitantly, she opened the door and invited them in.

Greta introduced her friend, Mike Lester, a lean, 6′-4″ blond, whose thick hair hung down on his forehead. Lester sauntered in and immediately headed toward Clark. He pulled the toothpick out of his mouth and picked up the 4-week-old and hugged him and talked to him until they both cooed.

"Oh look at that," Greta said, and laughed. "I think Mike's in love."

"Who wouldn't be in love with this precious baby," Lester said, and started dancing around the living room with Clark in his arms. The women laughed at the capers. But Underhill was particularly taken with his gentleness. She offered them a beer. Lester asked for a Coke instead. He didn't drink much. That's just how his Jehovah Witness parents had raised him, he explained.

"I wanted Mike to meet you," Greta said. "I told him, you can't believe this gal. She's so sweet—sure doesn't belong in jail."

Greta and Mike stayed for over three hours, time enough for Sandra to give Clark two bottles. After they left, Underhill realized how she liked talking to someone other than Bondurant and the people associated with her parole. She thought Mike Lester was the kindest, most polite, and compassionate man she had ever met. She was impressed, too, by his work ethic. Ever since Lester had graduated from high school in Tennessee, he had always worked. He had helped manufacture and transport trailers, and now he removed the kinks from new trailers before their owners took possession. His two older brothers were in the same line of work.

Underhill had been buoyed by Greta and Mike's visit, but after a couple of days, she sank back into depression. Then the following week, her doorbell rang again. She opened the door to find Mike Lester standing there alone. She smiled broadly at him and looked puzzled not to see Greta.

He read her mind. "Ah, Greta couldn't make it," he grinned, and his face reddened. "Actually, I missed Clark. How's my buddy doing?"

"Come in and see."

She offered him a beer, and this time he took one. They didn't really know each other, and she assumed he accepted a beer just to break the ice. Lester went over and plopped down on the floor by Clark's infant seat, which sat in front of the TV.

"Where's Greta?" Underhill asked.

"She left town and we broke up." He grinned. "Didn't want you to think I was running around on her."

Lester tucked his t-shirt into his jeans, and said, "I stopped off after work and rented a couple movies."

She took his *Batman* cassette and slid it into her VCR. "Greta was the only person I talked to in prison."

"She said you knew about a murder."

Lester was open and unpretentious. Underhill found him so easy to talk with that she filled him in on Carri Coppinger's death.

His blue eyes never left her face as she described the three days before she called the police.

"I can't believe how much you've been through. You make me feel like I don't have a problem in the world."

He looked around the duplex. "What do you do here with just Clark?"

"That's what I do—just Clark."

Mike Lester hated to think that Sandra Underhill was stuck in her duplex without any adults to talk to. He was soon drawn to her, thinking he had never met anyone quite like her.

Over the following weeks, Lester listened to her stories about Bondurant, her family, and her ex-husbands. At first he had difficulty believing the more bizarre things that had happened to her, but eventually he accepted those as well.

At 44, Lester's track record with women rivaled Sandra's with men. He decided not to tell her that before Greta moved, she had stolen his money, VCR, and television, leaving him with only pawn tickets.

Mike Lester came over every night, usually with rented movies. Conversation became so easy for them that they talked a good deal, and played gin, their favorite card game.

Lester thought Sandra was the sweetest, prettiest girl he had ever met. From the first week, he was hooked.

During one of Bondurant's phone calls to Underhill, he heard Mike Lester jabbering with Clark in the background, and wanted to know who was there. Once he learned about Lester he called more frequently, seeking assurance that Sandra still intended to take her life and free him from his burden.

On one occasion he told her, "You know you're not a good person, Sandra. Basically you really aren't. Both boys are going to be much better off with you out of the picture. You didn't have a decent childhood yourself, so you're incapable of giving the children one.

"Now remember how we planned this. I certainly hope you do it right."

After that particular call, Underhill walked back into the living room where Lester sat. Tears streamed down her face.

He looked at her and frowned. "What on earth? Who was that on the phone?"

She didn't answer. She sat crying and shaking her head, trying to convey that she didn't want to tell him.

Lester persisted. "Sandra, what's going on?" He put his arms around her and held her close as she sobbed.

"Promise me," she said hesitantly. "Promise you won't get involved."

"Involved with what?"

"With my plans."

He took hold of her shoulders and held her away from him so he could look into her eyes. "What plans?"

"I made a promise to Miles. He's really the better person, and I feel so badly that I took Carri to his house. It's really my fault that he killed her. I promised him . . ." She started crying again.

"Sandra, tell me what you promised."

After a long time, she finally said, "I promised him I'd leave a note saying that I killed Carri, then I'd commit suicide. He shouldn't go to prison. He'd just die there."

Lester slumped on her sofa. Disbelief deepened the lines around his eyes. "You can't be serious. This is like what you'd see in the movies. I don't believe this."

Sandra went to her bedroom and pulled out papers, then showed them to Lester. One was a copy of her confession, the other held Bondurant's specific details on how she should kill herself.

"It's suppose to happen on June 17th."

Lester shook his head and looked lost.

She took his hand. "Forget about me and let me go on with what I'm about to do. I don't want you to get tangled up in this."

Lester let many silent moments go by before he felt he could speak. "Sandra." He swallowed hard. "Let's go back to what you said about this guy being a better person. You're talking about someone who'd let you take your life for something *he* did. That's not a good person. That's a self-serving, terrible person."

"You really don't know Miles like I do. He's done a lot of good things in his life. He's been generous to lots of people."

"I know you. *You* are a good person. You deserve to live. Sandra, you didn't make Miles kill Carri. You are one of the kindest, nicest persons I know. I've seen you with your son. I've never known a mother so patient. You never get angry with him." He reached down and picked up Clark, who was asleep in his infant seat on the floor. "See this little guy? Don't you think he'd miss his mother?"

That was difficult for Sandra. Leaving Clark would be the hardest thing she'd have to do.

"You mean in six weeks you're going to kill this little boy's mother?"

Sandra hadn't thought about it that way. But she still remained committed to her promise.

Mike Lester became a man with a mission. He vowed to keep Sandra Underhill alive, despite her determination to go through with her suicide. Recognizing that she was mixed up, he continually told her how much he cared for her and that she didn't deserve to die. On many occasions he witnessed her phone calls with Bondurant. Currently he sat in the living room burning with anger at Bondurant as Underhill talked with him on the phone.

"Okay, doll, remember our plan," Bondurant said. "I've bought you the sleeping pills. I'll bring them over sometime this week. I'll also bring some more beer.

"Then remember to turn off the pilot lights so your place won't blow up before you turn on the gas. I want you to do this right. Understand?"

Friday night, June 16, Mike Lester was reluctant to leave Sandra Underhill. "Did y'all decide on a time for . . ." He hesitated. Saying "suicide" was too difficult for him. "What time are you supposed to carry out your plan?"

"No special time. Just late at night. I'm supposed to get good and drunk, and then when I'm drunk enough, I'm supposed to take the pills."

Lester shook his head and found it very hard to leave after he kissed Sandra goodnight.

* * *

Giving Clark his bath on June 17 proved almost impossible for Sandra. She cried so hard, her tears kept dropping into his bath water, making little expanding circles as they fell. After she dressed him, she sat in the rocking chair and fed him. Then she held him for the rest of the day.

Around 5:30 P.M., Bondurant came over and brought Cody along. He pulled sleeping pills out of his shirt pocket, then went back to the Ford and carried in two six-packs of beer. He didn't stay long and he didn't say much. Looking anxious to leave, he picked up a bag Underhill had packed with Clark's clothes.

Sandra hugged Cody and Clark, but her head was numb from depression. In her confused state she went through the motions of handing over Clark to his father. She had heard Bondurant's curt, "See ya. 'Bye," then saw the door close. All of a sudden, the reality of her loss rushed to her and she fell against the door sobbing.

She was still crying 15 minutes later when Mike Lester knocked on the door. He had come directly from work.

He walked in and picked Underhill up from the floor where she had fallen and hugged her tightly. She couldn't stop crying. She cried for Carri, Cody, Clark and her wasted life.

Over the last six weeks, he had tried desperately to convince her of her worth as a human being; she couldn't imagine he had anything more to say.

Underhill blew her nose and, still sniffling, said, "Remember, you're not supposed to get involved. It would be better if I didn't see you tonight."

"I care too much about you to *not* get involved."

Lester had brought over two movies: *Alaska* and *Forrest Gump.* He thought they'd help take her mind from her troubles. She cried through both of them.

At intervals as frequent as 30 minutes, Bondurant called. "You haven't done it yet?"

"Not yet."

"Are you drunk enough?"

"I'll do it, Miles, don't worry."

"Well, get on with it."

Underhill hung up the phone, realizing she had cried the entire evening.

Lester used every minute to convince her, chanting over and over that she deserved to live.

By 11 p.m., she was very drunk. Lester knew not to leave her alone.

"Let's go for a ride," he suggested. "Fresh air will do you good."

In her condition, Sandra didn't resist. He put his arm around her and guided her out to his truck. She sat in a trance as he drove her to his apartment. They went in and talked. After a couple hours they left and drove back to her place, where she stretched out on her couch. Around two in the morning, she finally fell asleep. Lester sat beside her in the rocking chair; he would take no chances.

The sun was streaming into Underhill's living room when the telephone rang. Lester jumped up to get it.

Sandra shook sleep from her head and quickly realized it was no longer June 17. "Oh no, you know who that's going to be. I better get it." She fought to stand up, but her head pounded. Slowly she made it to the phone as it rang, eight, nine, 10 times.

Hesitantly, she said, "Hello."

"Sandra!" Bondurant's angry voice told her everything. "I should have known. You promised you'd help me, but you let me down. You were just leading me on. I can't believe this. I had counted on you, and you were lying to me the whole time."

Underhill felt guilty to be alive. Bondurant's words stabbed her heart and all of her desire to please him rushed back to her.

"I'll bring Clark back today," Bondurant continued.

"But mark my words, you will not get another cent from me. Not one red cent. And the main thing, Sandra"—Bondurant paused for emphasis—"you will never see Cody again!"

# Chapter Thirty-Five

To commemorate the one-year anniversary of Carri Coppinger's death, her mother wrote an open letter to Miles Bondurant. The *Dallas Morning News* published it July 14, 1995, as its lead letter on the editorial page. She had sent the same letter to the *Fort Worth Star-Telegram,* but since the trial had not been held, they refused to print it.

Linda Coppinger graphically detailed how Miles Bondurant had shot her daughter in the head, stuffed her in a barrel, and left her to rot. She told of the family's suffering and revealed that she had to change jobs and move as anything familiar heightened her grief. Then she ended her letter by suggesting he confess his sins or he would "live in hell where it's hotter than inside a barrel sitting in the heat of a Texas July sun."

Now that a year had elapsed, the Coppingers wondered how much longer Bondurant's trial would be delayed and they became all the more distrustful of a justice system in which the wealthy frequently went free, even with murder. They recalled a similar situation several years earlier in

Fort Worth. A rich man was accused of killing two people. Although eye-witnesses testified to seeing him carrying a gun the night of the murder, the jury found him not guilty. His lawyer had convinced the jury that the witnesses's drug-tainted testimony couldn't be believed.

The Coppingers feared the same argument could be made to free Bondurant if Lane made Sandra Underhill's previous drug abuse an issue.

Mike Lester visited Sandra Underhill every night, and when the lease on her apartment terminated, he urged her to move in with him. She readily agreed and they moved to a two-bedroom, second-story apartment in the Haltom City area of Fort Worth.

Lester loved Clark, and with Bondurant not around to remind him otherwise, he began thinking of himself as the baby's father. In no time he had Clark calling him "Da Da."

But in other areas, Mike Lester had his work cut out for him. He worried that Bondurant still held Sandra's written and signed confession to Carri's murder. He tried to convince Underhill that she needed to clear things up with the DA. because her last statement blamed Detective Neel for pressuring her into questionable comments. She couldn't see that it mattered.

"Look at it this way," Lester said. "If Miles wanted to get both boys, he could show CPS your confession. Even if he couldn't convince them you killed Carri, he could make you look unstable for having written it, then he could take the kids. Either way, it's not good for you."

Underhill finally realized Lester was thinking more clearly than she was. She agreed to talk with the D.A.'s office, but she'd speak only with Celeste Rogers. After she had refused to testify at the grand jury hearing for Mike Parrish, he still intimidated her to death.

* * *

On Wednesday, June 21, 1995, Underhill and Lester went to see Celeste Rogers. Underhill already felt better about this visit because she came on her own accord.

"I have something to tell you," she began, "especially because the trial is to start in three weeks."

"Wrong," Rogers said. "Judge Leonard called us yesterday. Bill Lane convinced him that Miles was too ill to stand trial. It's been delayed until October."

Underhill slumped into the nearest chair and Lester sat down next to her. "October? We have to wait that long?"

Rogers nodded. "It's not unusual for a murder trial to go on and on, but don't worry, the judge won't put up with this forever."

"What did you come to tell me?" she asked.

"I need to straighten out some things about my previous testimony."

Underhill began confiding everything that had happened since she gave her statement to Detective Neel, including her testimony to Janie Brownlee in Illinois. "Miles had pushed me into saying things that weren't true about Detective Neel. I need to clarify all that."

Celeste Rogers smiled, then asked for a court reporter to come into her office to take Underhill's statement.

Underhill elaborated on the details of trying to help Miles Bondurant avoid a murder trial and all the scenarios they planned, even her suicide.

"Oh, Sandra, how could you?" Celeste asked in disbelief.

Sandra herself now wondered how she could have sunk that low. "I was so depressed. Miles took advantage of that and convinced me I was a low-life and couldn't take care of the children. Fortunately," she said, reaching toward Mike Lester, "I met a friend who helped me see that that wasn't true."

Lester took Sandra's hand while she continued. "I was sad about Carri, and the idea that the father of my children might go to prison that I suggested taking the blame. It was my idea to write the confession."

Lester explained that Bondurant still had a copy as well as Brownlee, because Underhill thought up Bondurant's alibi in her office.

"You did this in front of Janie?" Rogers' mouth opened in astonishment.

"Yeah," Underhill said. "My suicide was the only way my confession would work."

"Did he ever say why he shot Carri?"

"She had been indignant to him."

Rogers rolled her eyes. "I mean anything other than that?"

"Well, several times he told me that he didn't want lesbians raising his children."

Celeste said, "That's interesting. The *Star-Telegram* ran an article recently on how no investigator had come up with a motive."

"But we weren't lesbian lovers at the time. At the grand jury hearing I told them that we were *never* lovers, but that wasn't true. We had three sexual encounters during November 1993, and after that we were just friends."

Sandra Underhill began her statement at 1:10 P.M. and as the words began to flow she gathered new strength. When she finished at 3:20 P.M., the statement contained four single-spaced pages. In that time, she had erased all of the lies she had told the D.A.'s office, in addition to clarifying her bogus confession. She was ecstatic with relief.

# PART V

# Chapter Thirty-Six

In 1977, Miles Bondurant had crashed his Jaguar into a retaining wall. He broke his hip, leg, and ankle. He also strained his neck, and the whole calamity left him in a body cast. In order for him to walk, the doctors removed a tendon from his foot, leaving him with a slight but permanent limp.

His hospital stay lasted six months and his mother flew in from Lubbock to hover over him for an additional six months.

Then in 1986, Bondurant fell and broke his knee. The combination of those two mishaps left him with acute arthritis in his knee, hip, and neck.

If Bondurant could no longer count on Sandra Underhill's help during his trial, he had to rely on his worn-out body to delay matters. Bill Lane asked for a postponement of the July 16 trial, assuring the judge that Bondurant's physical condition wouldn't allow the rigors of a trial at that time. The judge rescheduled for October 1995.

As the new trial date approached, Bondurant called Lane again. "I've got this terrible problem with my neck. The doctor says the only thing that will help is surgery and his first opening is in October.''

Lane again called the judge, who reluctantly postponed the trial until May 20, 1996, with the pre-trial hearing set for May 14, 1996.

Judge Don Leonard of Tarrant County's Criminal District Court Number Three presided over Miles Bondurant's trial, which ultimately opened on May 14, 1996, almost two years after Carri's Coppinger's death.

Leonard had been familiar with the case since he signed Sandra's Underhill's petition to appear before the grand jury in September 1994.

Bill Lane made a pre-trial motion to suppress both taped confessions of his client. He complained that ''Both statements were made as the result of an illegal arrest and detention of the defendant. The statements were not voluntarily given and were obtained in violation of the defendant's constitutional rights.''

At the end of the session, Leonard announced his decision. ''I think that Mr. Bondurant's confession was the most voluntary and admissible that I have ever heard. As far as signing the consent to search, the signing of the written consent is just evidence that there was consent.''

On Monday, June 20, 1996, Judge Leonard pounded his gavel on the peach granite of his bench top and called the court to order. Then he asked Bondurant to stand as he read the indictment in Case #055833D: ''Warren Miles Bondurant on or about July 13, 1994, did there and then intentionally and knowingly cause the death of Carrington Elizabeth Coppinger by shooting her with a deadly weapon.''

He asked Bondurant how he pled.

''Not guilty, sir.''

The defendant had already admitted to shooting the

victim, and the weapon he used sat safely locked in the police evidence room. Whether or not Lane could convince a jury that Bondurant did this accidentally became the question.

Sixty men and women were selected from the jury pool and herded into the cool, light-paneled courtroom that they found a respite from the 90-degree heat outside. Judge Leonard asked if anyone felt they could not serve, telling them he got paid to listen. Several hands went up. The judge excused a woman who knew Bondurant's daughter, Suzie. Their children had played together. Bondurant's dog groomer happened to be on the panel, as well as a man whose parents lived on Collinwood, prompting him to follow the case. They were excused in addition to a woman who thought she recognized Bondurant from church.

By the end of the first day, the lawyers had chosen a jury of two women and 10 men. It appeared to be a sharp panel as the jurors listened attentively to the judge's directions. The defense could have thought a lopsided number of men boded well for its side, but the majority of jurors were half Bondurant's age. All the jurors were white with the exception of one black man.

When the trial began the following day, reporters from radio stations, as well as the *Fort Worth Star-Telegram* and the *Dallas Morning News* sat scattered in the courtroom, while television cameramen remained in the back with camcorders mounted on their shoulders.

Bondurant listened but only occasionally glanced at the jurors. His dark business suit, blue and red silk tie, and deeply-grained alligator shoes portrayed him as a successful businessman.

As the session opened, Bondurant's family and friends were happily confident. His supporters sat on the far left of the courtroom behind the defense table. Bondurant's first wife attended the trial, as well as his two daughters and their husbands. Between those regulars and an assorted group of designer-dressed friends who dropped in to watch the proceedings, at least a half dozen people were there for him at all times.

Assistant District Attorney Mickey Klein opened for the prosecution in a direct, no-nonsense manner very similar to that of Mike Parrish. The red-haired, slightly-built attorney shared equally with Parrish in questioning the witnesses. He began with the statement, "We are going to bring you a woman named Sandra Underhill." He outlined every point that would be aired later in the trial. He also divulged the lesbian relationship to dilute its shock value before the defense brought it up.

Klein described Bondurant's obsession to control, mentioning the demand letter sent to Underhill in Granite City.

When Klein spoke, Bondurant appeared disinterested. He sat at the defense table to the left of Lane, resting his face on his hand, and infrequently glancing at the D.A. as if he were talking about someone else.

Klein laid out his entire case, previewing each piece of evidence they would present and announcing specific witnesses they would summon.

Mike Parrish called Linda Coppinger, Carri's mother, as the first witness for the state. Parrish was more than ready for the trial after its many delays.

Linda Coppinger had been sequestered in the Victim/Witness Lounge on the fifth floor. Now she walked in looking like an older fashion model, with stylishly coiffed dark gray hair. A whiff of Georgio followed her into the courtroom.

Linda Coppinger remained poised during the questioning. Her black and white, unwrinkled linen suit mirrored her smooth, calm demeanor.

Parrish said, "Do you know Sandra Underhill?"

"I know of her, but I have never laid eyes on her," Coppinger answered.

"Do you know Miles Bondurant?"

"I have talked to him on the phone, but I had not seen him before today."

When Parrish asked her about her husband, Edward Warren Coppinger, Linda said he couldn't attend because he was a diabetic and confined to a Nashville hospital. Although an ordained minister, his health allowed him to preach only part-time.

Linda Coppinger candidly testified that Carri had been in AA as early as her senior year at Lamar High School in Arlington, Texas, and later at Pinestreet where she met Sandra, but Parrish never asked questions that required the word "lesbian" to escape her lips.

Parrish asked her to describe the circumstances of the arrival of her daughter's body in Chattanooga. For the first time Linda looked distraught. Frowning in anger, she said, "It was dreadful." She glanced at the jury. "Carri was sent to us in a disaster bag inside a sealed coffin. I couldn't even buy my daughter a new dress for her funeral. There was no closure because we couldn't identify her remains."

With the words hovering in the courtroom that Carri Coppinger had been returned in a disaster bag, Parrish entered Carri's high school graduation picture into evidence. The portrait was that of a pretty young woman with curled hair, artfully applied makeup, and her chin demurely posed on her hand. Linda proudly identified the photograph, and the bailiff showed it to the jury.

Linda Coppinger's family sat surrounded by her daughter's friends in the courtroom's large center section on wooden benches that resembled church pews. Linda's son, Chuck, had his mother's brown-eyed attractiveness. Carri's tall, gentle grandparents sat holding hands, and her grandmother's eyes remained red-rimmed throughout the trial.

Bill Lane wisely passed on questioning Linda Coppinger, knowing he wouldn't gain points cross-examining the victim's mother He refused, however, to excuse her from future testimony, which would have allowed her to sit in the courtroom and be a constant source of sympathy for the jury.

The next witness, Debbie Alexander from Industrial Container Corporation, had sold Miles Bondurant the barrels. When Mike Parrish handed her the receipt Bondurant had signed, she nodded in recognition. Parrish asked her to read every word of the receipt. The D.A. folded his arms over his chest and stood smiling as he waited for the punch line: "Miles Jobe."

After questioning Alexander, the prosecution placed the 55-gallon drum in evidence. The bailiff hauled in the big, vivid blue container that dramatically impacted everyone as they looked at the temporary tomb.

For the best effect, Parrish shoved it directly in front of the jury.

Now it was the defense's turn to cross-examine. As he would with every witness, Bill Lane introduced himself and said, "I don't believe we've met before." He wanted to present himself as someone who wouldn't influence a witness's testimony before the trial.

Lane asked, "I suppose you frequently sell a barrel or two to ranchers for storing feed or whatever?"

"No. That would be rare," Alexander said. "We normally sell in large quantities."

Her answer forced Lane to shift tactics, indulging in a lighthearted banter about the various uses of barrels. He tried to make them seem commonplace, and claimed to have two of their barrels himself.

Forty-seven-year-old Ernie Joe Gumble strode into the courtroom in his striped shirt, suspenders, and cowboy-cut jeans. His long ponytail had been braided for the occasion. Bert and Ernie's Gun Sales no longer existed and

Gumble stated he was unemployed. He went into detail describing Bondurant's pistol. Parrish had him discuss the ATF forms, how guns worked, and what damage various types of guns do. When he finished, everyone in the courtroom had a thorough understanding of the murder weapon.

But when Bill Lane cross-examined Gumble, he wasn't at all interested in firearms. Lane asked about Gumble's previous job at Foreign Motors where he first met Miles Bondurant, and if he remembered Sandra Underhill stealing Bondurant's car.

Gumble squinted, then his dark eyes darted around the courtroom as he tried to think. At length, he thought he had heard something about it. To refresh his memory, Lane handed him the work order for $4,690.35 that Bondurant had paid.

Lane's questions had nothing to do with the murder of Carri Coppinger, but for a few minutes they shifted the spotlight from his client to Sandra Underhill.

Mickey Klein questioned Christine Logan, Bondurant's landlady, who still lived in the duplex on Collinwood. Even now, she appeared nervous and upset as Klein led her through her two phone conversations with Bondurant on the day of the murder.

When Lane had his opportunity to quiz Logan, he introduced himself and started with his trademark, "I don't think we've met before."

She immediately corrected him. "Oh yes, many times. I've met your brother, too."

Lane removed his wire glasses and glanced down, smiling to himself. Although likable, he unfortunately didn't ascribe to the legal maxim that you never ask a witness a question without first knowing the answer.

He recovered and said, "That's right. You know Jim." Then he took Logan through Bondurant's relationship with Underhill, and again tried to discredit Bondurant's live-in girlfriend.

Charles Arnspinger, Bondurant's office manager, had a stable background of marriage, one child, a steady work record, involvement in church activities, and wore conservative clothes. He stood in sharp contrast to Miles Bondurant. Perhaps some members of the jury wondered how the two had been able to maintain a long-time business association. Although Arnspinger was president of the company, he always referred to Miles as Mr. Bondurant.

Klein led him through the comings and goings at the office on July 13, 1994, and Arnspinger precisely repeated everything he had told the investigators.

On cross, Bill Lane tripped himself again with his "We've never met before" line.

"Oh, yes," Arnspinger corrected, "I've talked to you a couple times when you called Mr. Bondurant."

"Well, other than that," Lane said, then essentially put Sandra Underhill back on trial. "I don't think that you were ever a fan of Sandra Underhill's, were you, Charles?"

"No, sir, I was not."

"After she went to work for Mr. Bondurant, did it become apparent that she was bleeding the company dry?"

"Actually both the company and Mr. Bondurant."

Arnspinger admitting that initially Sandra was efficient in her work, but later her performance declined. Then the questioning shifted to Underhill's taking Bondurant's car to Como, using drugs, and practically giving away all the furniture Bondurant had bought her.

"Did you have any communication with Ms. Underhill about the furniture?" Lane asked.

"Yes. I have a copy of a letter we wrote regarding her theft of the furniture."

Quickly, Parrish jumped to his feet. "We object to this letter—it's all hearsay. The defense is trying to introduce the defendant's words through another source without having the defendant testify."

The judge agreed. "Objection sustained. It would be like writing a letter to Santa Claus saying he's been stealing furniture."

Lane was forced to hit on another subject no one had yet mentioned.

"Are your office doors locked during the day?"

"No, the doors are always open during business hours."

"Charles, tell the jury how close your office is to the west sector substation of the police department."

"It's no more than a block."

Is it difficult to get to the police from your office?"

"No. There's no fence. Just an empty lot, then a parking lot. It's easy to get to."

"And how long was Sandra at work that Friday?"

"From 9:30 A.M. to around 5 P.M."

"Did Sandra Underhill attempt to go to the police during that time?"

"Not that I know of. She was there all day."

Lane had established that Sandra had every opportunity to report Bondurant to the police if she really thought he had deliberately killed Carri Coppinger.

Arnspinger's testimony concluded the first full day of the trial.

That night, three officials from the D.A.' s office decided to visit Sandra Underhill.

# Chapter Thirty-Seven

Mike Parrish toted a satchel of papers into Underhill's apartment. Celeste Rogers had told him that he made Sandra nervous, so it was decided that he would play an inactive role. If they wanted a successful meeting, Rogers knew she had better handle it. Mickey Klein came with them and they all pulled up chairs from the kitchen and sat in a circle.

They planned to show Underhill that both Parrish and Klein could be pleasant, important since one of them would be questioning her at the trial.

"I understand Miles has let you see Cody in the last couple of months." Rogers said, hoping Sandra had questioned Bondurant's motive.

"Yes. I'm so glad he has decided to be nice again."

Celeste Rogers winced at her words. The entire D.A's office knew Bondurant only wanted to secure sympathetic testimony for his trial by allowing Underhill access to her own son.

Realizing Underhill's information of the murder had been varnished by Bondurant, Rogers showed her their documents proving when he purchased the plastic barrels and the gun. Then she asked, "Did you know that Miles had signed 'Miles Jobe' to the barrel receipt?"

Underhill looked mystified. "How strange. Maybe he's had too much Prozac and seen too many detective movies," she said, and laughed.

"We wanted to bring copies of your statements so you could look them over," Rogers told her.

Underhill took the papers. "I remember what I said and I'll tell the truth even if it doesn't help Miles. I know it will come down to my doing the right thing, getting it over with and walking away. Or lying to protect him, then going to prison for perjury."

"That seems like an easy decision," Klein said.

"If I had to choose between Miles and the boys, I'd take the boys every time." Then as an afterthought, she said in all seriousness, "But Miles isn't a threat to society."

Parrish, Klein, and Rogers registered stares of disbelief. If only she'd take off her rose-colored glasses and see Bondurant the way they did.

Rogers handed her a subpoena to appear in court.

Underhill smiled. She had received a similar one a couple of years ago and had flatly refused to testify. "Don't worry. I'll be there this time, and I'll tell the truth."

When the trial resumed on Wednesday, the barrel became a target of the lawyers. Lane tried to hide it by making it a table and placing legal documents on top. Parrish countered by nudging the barrel with his foot, sliding it closer to the jury.

The prosecution brought in everyone Miles Bondurant had talked with from July 13, when Coppinger had been murdered, to July 16, when police found her body. The first two witnesses were Bondurant's car insurance salesman and the sales manager from the Ford dealership. They both remembered Bondurant's rush to get everything transacted quickly.

* * *

Margaret Templeton, the elderly, heavy-set night clerk from the Residence Inn who had dialed 911 for Sandra, entered the courtroom. She hobbled slowly to the witness stand and settled herself in the chair. Age had dimmed her hearing, making it necessary for her to lean forward as she listened to the lawyers. She frowned with concentration and frequently requested that a question be repeated.

Klein asked her to describe the events in the lobby that night.

"Sandra Underhill came in carrying a baby and she looked frightened. She was shaking all over and wanted me to call her a cab. She feared for her life."

"Objection, Your Honor," Lane said. "This witness can't testify to what she *thought* Ms. Underhill felt."

Templeton didn't bother to wait for the judge to rule on Lane's objection. "It's not at all what *I* thought. She told me herself she was afraid. Said someone killed a woman and put her in a barrel, and if she told anyone he'd kill her too."

Lane screamed, "Objection," and waived his arms as his face flushed to scarlet.

The judge asked the jury to retire to its quarters. He waited until the last juror had closed the door, then leaned forward and in the kindest voice explained, "Ms. Templeton, you need to tell only what you've been specifically asked and wait until you're asked before responding."

"I intend to do that," she said with authority.

The jury came back and Klein completed his questioning and nodded to Lane.

Lane wanted to establish the ground rules before beginning his cross-examination. "Now, Ms. Templeton, we don't want to know what you thought or overheard, we want you to tell us exactly what Ms. Underhill told you."

The witness frowned again. "I *didn't* overhear her statements. She said them directly to me. And it scared the *heck* out of me."

Mild laughter rippled through the courtroom, and Lane had already heard enough. He excused the witness and shook his head in disgust.

Judge Leonard rose from his bench and walked over to Templeton. Taking the elderly woman's hand, he escorted her down the two steps from the witness stand. Then smiled and thanked her for coming.

Dramatic testimony was guaranteed by the next witness, the assistant medical examiner, Dr. Gary L. Sisler. He sat down and unbuttoned his well-cut blue sports coat. After establishing his credentials, he went into detail regarding his problem of extracting Carri Coppinger from the barrel.

Some of the spectators glanced over at the Coppinger family to see how well they were handling the graphic information. The family kept their eyes on the witness, but most of those eyes were moist.

In order for Sisler to detail the damage made by the bullet, Assistant D.A. Mickey Klein offered his skull for demonstration. As the two men stood in front of the jury, Sisler pointed with a pen to the side of Klein's head showing how the bullet had entered at eye-level, then veered two-and-a-half inches upward. He noted Coppinger could have lived 20 minutes to two hours after being shot.

When Lane had a chance to cross-examine, he did an admirable job, considering the witness and the nature of his testimony.

"Dr. Sisler, we *have* met before," Lane said to courtroom laughter. Sisler had testified at hundreds of cases in Tarrant County.

Wanting to clear up the baseball bat scenario, Lane asked, "Did you see any indication of a skull fracture that would indicate Carri had been hit with a blunt instrument?"

"No. There was no fracture."

"How can you be sure that this was a distant gunshot wound?" Lane asked.

"There were no powder burns or tattooing that would indicate she was shot at close range. The victim did have a cerebral laceration because the bullet hit her face, but I believe that she sustained a distant gunshot wound."

"One last question, doctor. You said previously that Carri could have lived twenty minutes to two hours. Isn't it also possible that she could have died immediately?"

"Yes," Sisler conceded, "with a head wound like this, death could have been instantaneous."

Now the most difficult part of the trial had arrived for the victim's friends and relatives. The judge sent the jury out of the courtroom while Sisler removed six autopsy photos from a large brown envelope he carried.

After the jury left, the judge said, "I assume there are family members present."

Members of the Coppinger family raised their hands.

"We're going to present some pretty gruesome stuff. You are welcome to leave at this time if you wish."

An unidentified voice said, "We're prepared, judge."

"Okay, let's proceed. I always want to preview the pictures. We'll show the jury just one."

The attorneys approached the evidence table and began sorting through the photographs with the judge. Lane objected to the most graphic picture—a full bloated face view, and said, "The picture depicted in Exhibit Fifteen is extremely gross and inflammatory and would not be offered for any probative issue but to prejudice the minds of the jury against my client."

Parrish argued, "It shows the death wound. It doesn't show any other body parts."

Lane favored Exhibit Nine, which showed only Coppinger's eye. "That's the proper one. It shows the wound without showing the gory details the state's trying to get before the jury, which the doctor has already testified to."

While the 8x10 photos were being passed back and forth in front of the courtroom, the family could easily see them.

During this time, Bondurant sat with his elbows on the defense table and his large hands totally covering his face. He chose to see none of the pictures.

The jury was summoned back and the judge announced that he agreed with the prosecution to show the full face view. Lane's arms flapped to his sides in resignation.

While the graphic evidence passed from juror to juror, the only sound in the courtroom was the soft crying of Carri Coppinger's grandmother. Several jurors looked over at Miles Bondurant, but they only saw him hiding behind his hands.

At 5:40 P.M., it was well past time to end the day's session. Judge Leonard announced that court would reconvene at 9 A.M., and closed in true Texas fashion. He patted the top of his bench and said, "That ropes the calf!"

Sandra Underhill would be the first witness the next morning. Given what had been said about her for three days, interest was piqued as to what she would add to the proceedings.

# Chapter Thirty-Eight

Since Carri Coppinger's death, Sandra Underhill had ignored Miles Bondurant's wishes for short hair and now appeared in court with her long dark hair piled on top of her head. However, the teachings of the Neiman-Marcus makeup consultant were still evident and she looked very pretty. Her softly toned face and light blue dress gave no hint of her ex-con status.

Mike Parrish led Underhill through her life with Bondurant from answering his ad, their on-again, off-again relationship, and through the multitude of places she had lived. Underhill was normally an open book, and under sworn testimony she gave minute details. When she told about Bondurant's tossing her out to various apartments and his expectation for her to return on weekends to provide maid service and sex, the two women on the jury shot irate glances at the defendant.

Sandra Underhill kept a smile on her face during the entire questioning, and discussed her addiction to drugs in the same unemotional voice as she did taking classes at Tarrant County Junior College.

The jury had to believe Underhill because she confessed

such detrimental things about herself. She talked of being in prison, buying drugs in Como and leaving Bondurant's car there, smoking and injecting cocaine, stealing Bondurant's jewelry, and pawning the furniture he bought her.

She talked about meeting Carri Coppinger at Pinestreet, and when asked to describe her, Sandra said she was "outgoing, friendly, boisterous, loud. Wonderful."

The courtroom hushed as Parrish questioned Underhill about taking the blame for the murder so Bondurant could go free.

"Had you and Mr. Bondurant sat down and wrote out a document saying you were the one who killed Carri?"

"Yes. I agreed to take the dive because he's the better person. At first he was bumbuzzled [flabbergasted]. Then he became ecstatic that I would help him like that."

"Do you think he's the better person now?"

Underhill smiled. "That's a hard question to answer."

Many on the jury looked puzzled at the odd response.

Underhill further discussed how their plans drifted toward her suicide. She looked down at her lap and smiled again. "I know. It sounds silly now, but that's what I was willing to do at the time."

"So while you were doing that, what was the defendant doing?"

"Miles was furnishing me cigarettes and liquor."

"You're a recovering alcoholic and Mr. Bondurant was buying you liquor?" Parrish threw a sour look at the defendant.

"Yes, sir."

"Those statements about you shooting Carri aren't true?"

Underhill smiled again. "No."

Throughout Sandra's two hours of testimony, Miles Bondurant seldom glanced in her direction, and when he did, it was as if he were looking at a stranger.

* * *

Bill Lane had a lot at stake in cross-examining Sandra Underhill. He had to make her look as bad as possible while helping his client nourish the image of a generous patron wanting to help a hapless young woman.

Lane first introduced himself and asked his standard question. He literally had never met Underhill although she had fully expected such a meeting to take place. She had watched enough television mysteries to know that the defense attorney usually took depositions from the important prosecution witnesses.

Underhill never objected to Lane's attempts to discredit her background or her actions.

He asked her to describe her mother's present living conditions in order to suggest the same squalid environment where Sandra was raised.

Underhill said, "My mother lives in a housing project. There are no blacks, just your normal, everyday, poverty-stricken people."

Lane accused her of using Miles Bondurant to get out of the penitentiary.

"That's not true," she said. "I was still legally married to Robert Underhill, so I could have gone to his house in St. Louis, but I wanted to stay in Texas where my two children lived."

Lane veered into Underhill's taking Cody to Illinois without telling Bondurant. "Did you speak to the defendant when you were in Illinois?"

"I didn't talk to him before receiving the blackmail letter."

Blackmail was not a word Lane wanted to hear. "You stole $30,000 worth of jewelry from the defendant and you thought the letter was blackmail?"

"He collected insurance on his jewelry."

Lane let that go and asked, "How did you get to Illinois?"

"In Carri's truck, but Miles had Ford Motors come pick it up."

Lane frowned. It was obvious he had no control over the words coming from Sandra's mouth, perhaps regretting that he had not met with her beforehand. "You know that for a fact?"

"Yeah. Ford told us."

Now Lane had to do some serious damage control, and the people he wanted to protect most were himself and his investigator, Janie Brownlee. "Whatever it was you dreamed up to say in that letter of confession, I didn't have anything to do with it, did I?"

"No."

"Janie Brownlee didn't have anything to do with it, either, did she?"

"No."

"When you gave it to her, she told you that it was crazy."

"Yes, and unethical."

Lane excused Underhill. He would stop while he was ahead.

Once Sandra Underhill had left the courtroom, Bill Lane grasped another opportunity to discredit her. "Your honor, I think Ms. Underhill is under the influence of some kind of narcotic or medication."

The judge asked, "What is it you want me to do, counselor? She gave you the information you asked for."

Lane further tried to prejudice the jury by saying, "I suspect she needed a little help getting in and out of the courtroom today."

Angrily, Parrish jumped to his feet. "That's absolutely untrue!"

Judge Leonard told Lane, "I see no evidence that her testimony was affected. Whether she took aspirin or whatever, her answers were appropriate."

For the remainder of that day and the next, the many investigators from the Fort Worth Police Department and the crime scene experts paraded through the courtroom relating the results of their investigations.

The last crime investigator of the day was Officer Prince C. Ray. The 13-year veteran had spent eight hours combing the crime scene and now brought to court his extensive pictures, diagrams, fingerprint records, Bondurant's gun, caulking gun, and a large piece of blood-spattered carpet cut from Carri Coppinger's room.

When the prosecution sought to enter all of Ray's items as state's exhibits, Lane objected to every one. It was now time to use the ploy Lane had been planning for two years. Bondurant had told him he asked the officers if he should call an attorney before he signed the consent to search. Bondurant had heard the police say they could get a warrant anyway and interpreted their remarks as a threat, making him feel forced to sign.

Judge Leonard said, "Your objections are noted, considered, and overruled," and allowed all the evidence to be admitted.

Court recessed for the day, but that night, Sandra Underhill received a phone call from an angry Miles Bondurant. "I thought you were going to help me instead of hurt me in court. I'm not too happy about your testimony today, but you probably did that because you're so mentally messed up."

"I told the truth."

"You didn't need to call that letter a blackmail letter. That really put me in a bad light."

"That's what you were doing. Blackmailing me to come back to Fort Worth."

"I was not. I had full legal justification. You know why I wanted my son out of that situation. That was no way to raise a *boy!*" He slammed down the receiver.

The crime lab administrator, Wade Thomas, testified as the last witness of the week. He had a master's degree in science and once worked at Dow Chemical. As a firearm specialist, he tested the .22 caliber pistol that had killed Carri Coppinger.

First, Thomas explained that guns uniquely mark the bullets fired from them. Investigators could trace bullets to a gun as dependably as fingerprints to an individual. He described the test bullet as having six lines and grooves with a right-hand twist.

"Did you compare the test bullet with the death bullet?" Mike Parrish asked. The D.A. tried to stress the terms death and murder at every chance in order to contrast Bill Lane's calling the whole thing an accident.

"Yes," Thomas answered.

"How did the death bullet compare?"

"It had the same six lines and grooves with a right-hand twist. The width of the lines and grooves were exactly the same."

Parrish next tried to establish that the gun wouldn't fire accidentally. He asked the investigator, "What steps did you take to make sure the gun was safe?"

"First I pulled the trigger with the safety on. Then I hit it with a hammer. After that, I got up on a ladder and dropped it down on a concrete floor."

"What were the results?"

"Nothing happened," he said, shrugging. "The only way we could get that gun to fire was to release the safety and pull the trigger."

With that conclusive report, the court recessed for the weekend.

When the trial opened Monday morning, the prosecution had only two more witnesses. A fingerprint expert had examined the arches, loops, and whorls found on the barrel and ascertained they belonged to Miles Bondurant.

A handwriting expert declared that the signature, "Miles Jobe," was the same handwriting as Bondurant's on the contract with Hooks Ford and the business documents the police had collected from his office.

At 10:30 A.M. on May 28, the state rested. Bill Lane had expected the prosecution to carry on until noon and had told his first witness not to report until one.

Judge Leonard became impatient with the delay. "Make some motions, Lane. Make an opening statement. Make something happen."

Lane said he had to call some people and asked for a short break.

During the intermission, Bondurant's supporters appeared to have taken the prosecution's testimony in stride, knowing Bill Lane would have an opportunity to strengthen the defense. They laughed and joked with the defendant.

The Coppinger family watched their gaiety with somber faces. They were well aware that without a criminal record, Bondurant could get probation. The fact that he had managed to stay free for the last two years seemed to justify their fears.

After the recess, Bill Lane stood to begin Bondurant's defense. Lane's reputation as a successful criminal defense lawyer accompanied stories about his appearance. He didn't own a pair of shoes, but he did have an impressive collection of cowboy boots that gave all of his suits a western flair. His wavy gray hair fell well past his suit collar.

"Ladies and gentlemen, it now becomes our opportunity—I say opportunity because we are under no obligation whatsoever to present evidence to you twelve folks.

"I'm going to bring you Detective Eddie Neel who took the defendant's oral statement. He will show you how my client fully cooperated with the police. He will show you that Miles did a number of things to help Carri . . . The evidence will show it is no more than what Miles told everybody it was—a horrible accident. Even though he did a lot of stupid things, he did not intentionally kill this girl."

Detective Eddie Neel had an office in police headquarters across the street, so Lane was able to pull him in quickly as his first witness.

Lane asked the detective, "Did my client provide information that was helpful in your future investigation of this case?"

"Yes," Neel answered.

"Did he provide you with information as to where the blue barrels were bought?"

"No."

Lane's eyes showed surprise, but he quickly went on to his next question.

"Did my client indicate to you during his statement that this was an accident?"

Mike Parrish stood up to object. "This is going into the statement. That statement is the state's evidence and does not belong to the defense. He can't introduce it. It's hearsay and self-serving."

Parrish had a plan to force Bondurant to personally testify. The D.A. eagerly wanted to visit face-to-face with the defendant, and he did his best to see that Bondurant's testimony would not be introduced through any other source.

Lane had no recourse. If he wanted Bondurant's words heard in the courtroom, they would have to come from Bondurant's mouth. Lane dismissed Detective Neel, then walked over to his client and put his arm around his shoulders as he usually did when he spoke confidentially to him. Reluctantly, he called the defendant to testify.

# Chapter Thirty-Nine

Miles Bondurant shuffled to the witness stand. Other than a slight limp, his body gave little hint of his 61 years. He still maintained ramrod straight posture, and thanks to years spent lifting weights in the gym, he had the physique of a much younger man. His makeup gave his skin a healthy glow and a convincing light brown color clung to his hair.

He passed the blue barrel by only inches on his way to testify. Bill Lane continued edging it with his foot, sliding it farther away from the jury.

Bondurant had expected to be coached for the trial. He wanted Lane to orchestrate some magical testimony for him; instead, the only thing Lane told Bondurant was to be humble. However, Lane didn't know that he had given Bondurant an impossible task.

Lane looked compassionately at Bondurant. "I've explained to you since the day you hired me on July 16, 1994, that you don't have to testify. You understand that the burden of proof is on the state and you have an absolute Fifth Amendment right to not testify in this case."

"I understand that," Bondurant said, his voice relaxed and confident.

"Are you testifying now because the State of Texas saw fit not to produce your oral statement to the jury that you gave to Detective Neel?"

Bondurant nodded.

"Also, you understand this is the only way to get your side of the story before the jury?"

"Exactly." As Bondurant's testimony proceeded, a hint of aloofness crept into his manner and he raised his chin.

Lane sought sympathy for his client. "I noticed when you walked to the stand you have a bit of a limp. Do you have some medical condition?" It was a stretch for Lane to place such emphasis on Bondurant's health problems, but it was worth a try to make the jury think twice before convicting a kindly, older man with a limp.

Bondurant answered, "I have acute arthritis in my right knee, left hip, and my neck."

"You've been treated surgically and medically for quite some time?"

Bondurant nodded, and Lane led him through his two accidents. Throughout the questioning, his attorney kept reminding him that he didn't need to testify.

Then Lane said, "Miles, I want you to look that jury straight in the eye and tell them whether you killed that girl intentionally or not."

With posture as wooden as a ventriloquist's dummy, Miles Bondurant turned toward the jury and said, "I certainly did not. It was an accident."

In order to preempt future questions by Mike Parrish, Lane asked Bondurant how he met Sandra Underhill.

He described advertising in the *Star-Telegram*. I don't know whatever possessed me to respond to her. I guess I thought I was Henry Higgins of *My Fair Lady* and she was Eliza Doolittle. I thought I could help her."

"Did that ad have anything to do with sex or trying to lure someone into having a sexual relationship?"

"No. Not at all."

"You simply contacted Sandra to fulfill your part in the bargain. To send her to school?"

"Sure."

Bondurant would spend the better part of two days on the witness stand, and the bulk of his testimony to Lane recounted all of Underhill's misdeeds. "Her whole life was collecting food stamps and Medicare. She smoked crack and lost her children." Bondurant said he was a naïve kind of person, and didn't realize she reverted to drugs until she took his 450 SEL and left it with a dope dealer.

Lane asked, "What did she do for your corporation?"

"She was vice president of operations."

A voice of one of Bondurant's supporters said, "She wishes," and muffled laughter followed from that section.

Bill Lane wanted to establish Bondurant's familiarity with guns and asked if he had grown up with them.

"I inherited my love of firearms from my father and older brother. They were big hunters. I had been weaned on hunting as a little guy. Then around 1970, I bought a ranch between San Saba and Goldwaite, Texas, on the Colorado River. I used to have big hunting parties there—had lots of deer and quail on the ranch."

Lane asked a question many people wondered about: "Why did you continuously invite Sandra back to live with you?"

"Sandra promised to go to rehab. I was just bringing her back to give her another chance."

Miles Bondurant's version of the September 20, 1993, birthday party given by his older children differed from Underhill's. "My daughters invited Sandra, but she declined. Then that very same night she took my jewelry worth $30,000 and spent it on cocaine."

Although Bondurant testified he had never visited Sandra at Pinestreet, he also testified that she repeatedly shot dope there. He gave her addiction as his reason for kicking her out of his house right before Christmas in her seventh month of pregnancy. "For the first time I wised up to the whole situation. I realized that all along she had been using me."

"I understand you finally received the DNA results on Cody around May," Lane said.

"Yes. I was so excited about the results that I mailed copies of them to thirteen friends. Then only two days later, Sandra shocked me by taking Cody to Illinois."

"Did you have a problem with Sandra and Carri's relationship?"

"Yes. They were lovers."

"Did you want your baby growing up in that atmosphere?"

Parrish objected, but the judge overruled.

"I did not."

Lane wouldn't let the lesbian relationship drop. "You knew that Sandra and Carri were lesbian lovers for quite a long time?"

"Yes. Ever since Pinestreet."

The jury may have wondered how Underhill became pregnant being Coppinger's lover because Bondurant testified that Sandra had slept with Carri instead of him.

Having exhausted his efforts to malign Underhill, Lane led Bondurant through the events on July 13, 1994.

Bondurant's rendition of the story lacked emotion as he said, "I asked Carri to come into the master bedroom to discuss when she would be leaving.

"Carri told me that she, Sandra, and the baby would be going soon. She was indignant to me and became hostile and went back to her bedroom. So in order to persuade her, I went to my car and got a baseball bat that I kept there for protection. I told her that Cody was staying but she needed to leave. The baseball bat didn't intimidate her, in fact, she became even more indignant.

"So I went back to my bedroom and got my target pistol. I took it into her bedroom to threaten her. I was scared. I began waving it at her and I said, 'Get your butt out of here.' Then I accidentally pulled the trigger.

"She dropped. I felt her pulse—nothing. I panicked. I

had no intention of killing Carri. There was quite a bit of blood." Bondurant cast his eyes down with that recollection.

"Did you panic?" Lane repeated, planting the word firmly in the jury's mind.

"I panicked good. I acted like a cockroach on a kitchen cabinet when someone turns on the light. I regretted what had happened and I certainly didn't handle the situation properly.

"I went downstairs to get a barrel I had bought to put stereo equipment in."

Since the prosecution had presented the issue of Bondurant signing "Miles Jobe" to the barrel receipt, Lane now had to answer that puzzle. "Tell the jury why you signed Miles Jobe to the receipt."

"Sandra has a very, very vicious temper. As part of her probation she had to go to temper control meetings."

"Was she jealous when other women called your house?"

"Yeah. That's what prompted the Miles Jobe situation. There were two girls that used to call and Sandra would have a fit."

"So you were protective of giving your name out?"

"Yes, I didn't want this little girl I bought the barrels from to start calling me." The jury had seen the pretty young saleswoman, who could have been Bondurant's granddaughter.

Bondurant testified that he put Coppinger's body in a barrel, took a shower and changed clothes, then went back to the office in shock. Lane led him through his plans to commit suicide and finalize his estate.

Before Lane passed the witness, he had Bondurant reiterate for the jury's sake, "This was only an accident."

Mike Parrish had waited through 10 days of trial for the opportunity to question Miles Bondurant. Parrish didn't wave his arms and use hand gestures as Lane did. He preferred a more understated style—usually standing with his arms folded across his chest and staring into the eyes of the witness. But his razor-sharp words and almost theatrical timing worked effectively.

"When you shot Carri Coppinger, did you run to the phone and call 911?"

"No, I didn't."

"Did you call anybody?"

"No, I didn't."

"Now think about that for a minute." Parrish patiently waited for an answer while the defendant sat and fidgeted. "Didn't you call Christine Logan and say, I just dropped a hot bowl?"

"I hit star-69 on the phone and heard Christine's voice. I guess I said something to that effect. I dropped a Pyrex bowl."

"You were covering up for the gunshot?"

"No. In my mental state, I just don't recollect everything I did at the time."

"When you were talking with Mrs. Logan, where was Carri?"

"Upstairs."

"And where were you?"

"Downstairs."

"Carri is lying by her bed?"

"Yes, sir."

"You go downstairs and immediately tell Christine Logan a lie?"

"I'm not sure what I did in the meantime."

"We know for sure that you didn't call for help."

Bondurant sat silently, trying not to meet Parrish's eyes.

The D.A. handed Bondurant the receipt for the barrels. "Did you tell Ms. Alexander that your name was Miles Jobe?"

Bondurant nodded slightly.

"You're such a hot number that you're afraid women are going to chase after you?"

Bondurant puckered his lips and looked around the courtroom, but didn't answer.

Parrish wanted to paint a mental picture for the jury of Bondurant being at the scene. "Where did you put Carri into the barrel?"

"I took the barrel up to her bedroom."

"Exactly where was she?"

"Carri was lying on her right side. She was between the bed and the wall, with her head facing the wall."

"How did you get her in the barrel?"

"I laid the barrel down at her feet and edged her in a little at a time."

Parrish showed him a picture of the crime scene that had duct tape on the bed, but Bondurant couldn't remember the tape.

"What did you do with the casing of the bullet?"

"I don't remember."

"Where did you get the live rounds of ammo?"

"I don't recall."

"Where's the .357 [gun] normally kept in the Mercedes?"

"I don't remember."

"How come the empty casing was in your new Ford Explorer?"

"The casing belonged to someone else."

Parrish's face reddened. "How did it get into your *new* Explorer?"

"I don't know."

"Is your memory conveniently gone on these points?" When Bondurant didn't answer, Parrish let the silent moments tick by. He stood staring at Bondurant, who shifted in his chair and became more uncomfortable by the second. His two defense attorneys looked helpless and sat frowning.

"Tell us what happened after you put Carri in the barrel."

"I stood the barrel upright and put on the lid. I tightened the metal band to seal it, then I slid the barrel on its side down the carpeted stairs and took it out to the garage."

"When did you load the gun?"

"I don't remember."

Now Bondurant's cheering section became ghostly quiet. The Coppinger family sat erect and listened carefully.

Finally Mike Parrish said, "Do you murder someone every day?"

Bill Lane jumped to his feet, yelling, "Objection." But Judge Leonard overruled, forcing Bondurant to answer.

"No, sir."

Leonard called another "calf rope" and the court adjourned. Until the next morning, the jurors were left with Bondurant's words that he didn't murder someone *every* day.

# Chapter Forty

The next morning opened with Miles Bondurant still on the witness stand. Parrish immediately attacked. "You killed Carri because she said she wouldn't leave since you'd just throw Sandra out again—like you always did when you couldn't control her. Carri also said she wasn't leaving until she saw Sandra. Isn't that true?"

"I don't remember."

"Has your memory conveniently disappeared?"

Bondurant didn't reply.

Parrish shifted to a series of unpredictable questions. "You bought that gun one day before you killed Carri?"

"I played with it the night before."

"Do you recall where you loaded the gun?"

"No."

"You've lied to this jury."

"I haven't told a lie."

"What did you tell Christine Logan?"

"I call that panic."

"On Friday, you noticed the barrel had swelled and bubbled."

"I didn't caulk the lid on Friday. I don't remember the cover-up for the murder."

Parrish jumped in the air waving his arms. For someone so extremely controlled, it made a spectacular impact to see him that excited. He shouted, "*You just used the word 'murder' for this incident.*"

"No, I didn't."

"Think *real* close." Parrish said nothing while he stared at Bondurant. Bondurant and his attorneys squirmed at the amount of time Parrish let elapse.

When it became apparent that Parrish wouldn't be getting an answer, he moved on. "You went back to the house to let some air seep out of the barrel."

"I was making plans to turn myself in."

"And buy a new Explorer." Parrish's spitfire delivery lent drama to the courtroom dialogue. Bondurant's answers, in contrast, sounded foolish.

Bondurant said, "It was a traumatic time in my life."

Parrish shot back, "It was a traumatic time for Carri Coppinger. Alive at twenty-two one minute, then," he snapped his fingers, "stone dead the next."

Parrish reminded him, "On the tape you called this a murder."

"I was inebriated. I don't remember the tape."

Bill Lane had tried to get the tape introduced before. Now that he had put his client in jeopardy, he asked to have the tape presented.

Judge Leonard allowed the tape to be played that recorded Miles Bondurant saying Sandra had killed Carri.

After the tape, Parrish reiterated, "You used the word murder on that tape. You said everything that you did only you said Sandra did it. You told how *she* planned the murder. How long did *you* plan the murder?"

"I didn't plan it."

"After going downtown did you make a statement?"

"Detective Neel questioned me about 1 P.M. I had been in custody since 4:30 A.M." Sounding abused, Bondurant said, "I had my hands handcuffed behind my back."

"Most murderers do."

"I object!" Bill Lane said. "Judge, instruct the jury to disregard that statement and I call for a mistrial." Bill Lane had objected so many times he was hoarse. The judge again ignored his plea.

"On that tape for Detective Neel, we didn't hear about buying plastic barrels, lying to Christine Logan, caulking the barrel, or buying the pistol one day before you murdered Carri. You had ten hours to sit in Detective Neel's office and think about having said, 'Sandra did it', and change it to 'It's an accident.' "

With both statements recorded, Miles Bondurant had to sit quietly or agree with the D.A. He chose silence.

"If this was an accident, why did you have to kill yourself?"

"I muffed the whole thing."

"You said you used a baseball bat," Parrish said as he picked up the bat. "Show us how you threatened Carri with this."

Bondurant took the bat and anemically waved it in the air, then placed it on his lap.

Parrish became quiet and planted a foot on a chair while he rested an elbow on his raised knee. He stared at Bondurant and said, "That second barrel was for Sandra, wasn't it?"

Bondurant looked down at the floor and didn't answer.

Parrish took advantage of the silence and entered Bondurant's statement into evidence. He also tried to enter the receipts from the wastebasket at the Residence Inn, but Lane asked that the jury be excused.

As the last juror left the room, Judge Leonard leaned forward and with an impatient voice said, "Why do you want the jury out this time, counselor?"

"I still have a problem with my client being asked to sign a consent to search."

In exasperation, the judge said, "Counsel, you said Miles Bondurant was *ever* so cooperative with the police. Now I have ruled and ruled and ruled. And this evidence *will* be heard."

The jury members quietly filed back in and took their seats.

Parrish stood in front of the court sorting through receipts for flea foggers and other items. "You signed all these receipts with 'Miles Bondurant'?"

Bondurant nodded.

"But you signed 'Miles Jobe' on the receipt for the barrels."

Bondurant sat quietly, looking lost.

Having made that point, Parrish eyed the murder weapon. "You told us you were very familiar with guns," Parrish said, picking up the .22 pistol. "Can we have him step down here in front of the judge?"

"You may," Judge Leonard replied.

Parrish's real intention was to place Bondurant directly before the jury and he pulled up a chair for the purpose.

Lane jumped to his feet in exasperation. "Objection, Your Honor. He's going to have *my* client sit right in front of the jury and do this? No other expert witness had to testify in this manner.

Parrish said, "The jury couldn't see as well."

The judge agreed, "The procedure he's going through would not be visible from the witness stand."

"You mean my objection is overruled?" Lane asked in disbelief.

The judge glanced over his reading glasses and nodded.

Parrish handed Bondurant the gun. "Here, take this and show us how you loaded it.

Obediently, Bondurant took the gun and said, "First I put shells in the clip. Then I took the clip and pushed it in. I pulled back the slide to put a bullet in the chamber."

"Once a bullet's there," Parrish asked, "what would you have to do to fire the weapon?"

"Pull the trigger."

Lane twisted uncomfortably in his chair.

"Okay. Put your finger on the trigger. I want it to be

just like it was when you shot Carri Coppinger. Using me, show the jury where Carri was standing."

Bondurant stood up and positioned the D.A. He then shoved the D.A.'s face into the angle Carri's had been. "We were having a heated discussion." With one hand in his pants pocket, he began waving the gun, then he suddenly stopped. He looked down at the gun and clicked open the chamber.

The assistant defense attorney flopped his head on Lane's shoulder

"What did you just do?" Parrish asked.

"I just checked to see if there was a bullet in there. I don't want to hurt these nice people," Bondurant said, nodding to the jury.

Parrish glared at Bondurant. "You know all about guns, don't you? You had that gun leveled at Carri."

"I said she was sitting on the bed."

"Then why did that bullet take an upward projectory?"

Bondurant hung his head. "I don't know."

"You knew that gun was loaded."

"Yes, but I didn't pull the trigger on purpose."

# Chapter Forty-One

Now that Mike Parrish had finally finished grilling Miles Bondurant, Bill Lane could play the tape his client had made for Detective Neel. The 30-minute tape of only Bondurant's words described how Sandra Underhill robbed him, used him, and disgraced him.

Lane brought in Bondurant's civil attorney, Calvin Jacobs. The pleasant, heavy-set man had been the attorney Bondurant talked with while police pounded on his front door.

Lane quizzed him about how Bondurant sounded that morning.

Jacobs replied like a concerned friend, "He was upset, despondent. He sounded suicidal to me."

Lane wanted to establish that typically, Bondurant wouldn't have premeditated a murder, much less anything else. He asked the attorney, "Would you describe Miles Bondurant as a planner?"

Smiling and shaking his head, Jacobs said, "No, Miles is not an organized person. He accomplished what he did in business because of Charles Arnspinger."

When Parrish cross-examined Jacobs, he wouldn't let him off that easily. Now that the tape had been played, it became fair game. The assistant D.A. hammered on Bondurant's telling Jacobs, via the tape, that Underhill planned the murder and killed Coppinger, then instructed Bondurant to buy the barrel and bury it. Parrish made Jacobs admit that he thought they were all lies.

Joe Davila testified next. The court had heard his name mentioned on tapes and in the "blackmail" letter, so all eyes were riveted on him as he strutted in with short hair and a thin goatee and mustache. In contrast to Bondurant, Davila looked like a teenager.

Bill Lane asked him if Sandra Underhill had revealed the identity of her son's father to him.

Davila sat on the edge of his chair, in a ready-to-leave posture. "Sandra told me Cody was mine. Many times."

Lane asked him to describe Underhill's temper and Davila testified, "She'd really lose it and throw things. I've seen her apartment practically destroyed."

Just as Lane's favorite theme was Underhill, the D.A.'s pets were the barrels and the gun. Parrish asked Davila about trucking in Bondurant's barrels for him.

"Yeah. He wanted me to get some barrels and take them to storage. But my truck broke down so I couldn't help."

Parrish was more than interested in the 10 A.M. Wednesday phone call the morning of the murder. "Why would Miles Bondurant have called you that specific morning?" he asked, frowning.

"We had befriended each other."

Parrish knew there was more there, but Davila kept dodging. "Didn't Miles tell you about the night before, that he heard the girls whispering like they were planning to leave again?"

"Yeah. He told me about that. But I didn't find out Carri was dead until Saturday. Miles told me he accidentally shot her."

Some have speculated that Bondurant's initial plan included having Davila on standby to pick up the barrel and bury it. Why else would he have called him that morning? In any case, Davila's truck proved as undependable as its owner. If he had been part of Bondurant's plan, he was the weak link.

Bondurant had testified that Linda Coppinger told him her daughter was having a lesbian relationship with Sandra Underhill. The D.A. called Mrs. Coppinger back into court and she firmly denied saying that.

Linda Coppinger was the first and last witness. The court rule allowed witnesses to remain in the courtroom once they had completed their testimony, so she walked over to her family and squeezed in with them to listen to the conclusion of the day's session. The next day, she'd be back to hear the final arguments and await the verdict.

Sandra Underhill could also be a spectator during this next-to-last day of a trial that had consumed the better part of two weeks. But too nervous to sit, she preferred to smoke and walk the corridors with Mike Lester and collect snippets of the trial during breaks. At one point when Lester had returned to work, Celeste Rogers let her sit in her office.

Underhill strolled in and started to place Clark's diaper bag on the desk, but had to move a brown envelope first. When she did, all of Coppinger's autopsy photos fell out and scattered on the desktop. Underhill put the bag on the floor and picked up the pictures. She saw the bloated face with her protruding right eye and tongue. The next one showed Coppinger in the barrel, the top of her head bald from where her skin had slipped. Devastated, she threw down the pictures and ran crying from the room.

Wednesday, May 29, 1996, began slowly because the 12th juror was late and no alternates had been selected. Nervous attorneys, with details of final arguments in their heads, paced the courtroom.

Enduring the wait, Judge Leonard commented that he didn't have to do this forever. He had 557 days until his 60th birthday. Then he could retire.

Mike Parrish, who had worked with the courthouse staff for years, was rubbing tension from the court reporter's shoulders when the embarrassed 12th juror rushed into the room. An accident ahead of him on the freeway had prevented his prompt attendance.

Finally, the bailiff called the court to order, and Judge Leonard instructed the jury that they could find Warren Miles Bondurant guilty as charged with first degree murder. It had to be beyond a reasonable doubt, but he added, that the prosecution didn't have to prove guilt against *all* doubt, only that which is reasonable. If the jury failed to find Bondurant guilty of murder, it had three other options: voluntary manslaughter, involuntary manslaughter, or criminal negligent homicide.

Since the state had the burden of proof, they were allowed to go both first and last with their closing statements. That of the defense would be sandwiched in between.

Mickey Klein stood inches away from the jury box, looking into each juror's face. "Remember Judge Leonard told you that you first have to decide whether or not Miles Bondurant is guilty of murder. You don't get to a lesser charge unless you rule out murder.

"Miles Bondurant planned this murder. It started on July 1st when he bought those barrels." Then Klein went on to chronologically revisit the case.

"Miles Bondurant wants you to think it's an accident. But you know the defendant's a liar. He advertises that he's in his mid-forties when he was really fifty-seven. He shoots Carri and tells his landlord he just dropped a Pyrex dish. He tells police that Sandra killed Carri.

"The man has guns strewn all about his house, but he chooses the smallest weapon he owns to shoot her. It's easier to explain a pop instead of a kaboom. He knows about guns. Did you see him check for a bullet?" Klein had trouble hiding a grin.

"You know that Sandra is from a very poor background. You know that Carri is from a loving background. I don't know why they had to escape reality with drugs and alcohol, but that is not the issue! You have to know about their relationship because that is the *motive* for Carri's death.

"Yes, you know the defendant's a liar. The closest he got to the truth was in that suicide tape—'Sandra murdered Carri Coppinger.' Just substitute Miles Bondurant for Sandra Coburn Underhill and you have his true confession.

"He hid Carri in that barrel just like he tried to hide the truth from you. But he was done in by the hot Texas sun and nature. You should convict him of murder."

Scott Brown, Bill Lane's young, handsome assistant, spoke before the court for the first time when he began the final argument. He said, "The defense is not arguing about what happened on July 13th—we agree it was a tragedy. Your job is to decide if the state has proved beyond a reasonable doubt all that they alleged in the indictment. Beyond a reasonable doubt is the microscope that you have to use to examine the state's evidence.

"The only issue is what was in Miles Bondurant's mind

at the exact minute it happened. You cannot extrapolate what happened one month before, one day before, or one minute after. Bondurant told you exactly how it happened. Now you have to base his actions on his mental state at the exact time of the shooting."

He asked the jury to find Bondurant not guilty, then he said, "It's a hard thing to do when there's a dead body, but it's the state's burden of proof, and they haven't proved their case."

Smiling, congenial, Bill Lane solicitously thanked the jury. He explained that the first tape Bondurant created, claiming Sandra Underhill killed Carri Coppinger was the result of Prozac and alcohol clouding his mind. "After ten hours of sobering up, he realized exactly what it was—an accident!"

Lane leaned over the jury rail, and spoke conversationally. "Last night, my five-year-old daughter and I were watching a magic show on TV. My daughter turned to me and said, 'Daddy, how did he do that?' I told her it was a trick. An illusion. He's trying to make you think something happened that really didn't. At three this morning I woke up, and I said, 'That's it!' The state has tried to create an illusion for this jury—the illusion that there was some wild plan. But it's an illusion because a planner doesn't try to keep someone out of the penitentiary, doesn't drive them home at eleven, and doesn't bring them back from Granite City. A planner doesn't buy a gun from a dealer he knows when he could have gotten it from a swap deal and not registered it."

He dropped his voice to a soft pitch. "This man's life is in my hands, but in a short time his life will be in your hands. See it as a magic show that the state is trying to create. A show about what happened. Miles made every mistake he could. He acted like an old fool. And there's no fool like an old fool.

"That autopsy photo was to create an illusion.

"Would Sandra, lover of Carri, have stayed with Miles Bondurant if she thought it wasn't an accident? She could have walked that one block to the police to report him."

Lane paused and let a few seconds elapse to build for his closing. "You promised me and you promised God. Don't give up, don't go along, and don't go back on your word. Separate the illusion from the state's question. Don't buy the trick. I urge you to find Miles Bondurant not guilty because the State of Texas has not proven its case."

Assistant D.A. Mike Parrish immediately lashed out at Lane, "The state has no illusion. No trick. Miles Bondurant gave the wrong name when he bought the barrels. That's the illusion; that's the trick. He's such a hot number he thought Ms. Alexander was going to ask him for a date.

"Before you consider reasonable doubt, consider all the evidence first. The state would not allow that self-serving taped statement of the defendant because it was our strategy to let you hear the witness on the stand.

"As far as showing the autopsy photo, I heard the defendant say 'not guilty,' so I showed you what he did.

"Don't be confused. A man who's rich isn't necessarily smart. Miles Bondurant committed a known murder. He lied, planned, plotted, and fumbled the result.

"This cannot be considered an involuntary act." Parrish frowned and raised his voice. "Wasn't it a *voluntary* act to pick up the gun a *day* before he shot Carri? What changed is that he learned Sandra was pregnant. That second barrel was for her.

"As soon as Bondurant felt that pop, his lies and stories began flowing. He thought, 'Oh, oh, Ms. Logan is back from her trip, there's just a wall between us;' that lie came out good; it came out sweet; it came out clean. *There* is the illusion. *There* is the trick. That's what they're trying to get you to buy.

"I'm going to ask you for justice—flat, plain, smooth justice. This man plots. This man plans. This man kills. Give him the justice that he asked for. Give him the justice that he deserves."

# Chapter Forty-Two

It was only 10:30 A.M. when Mike Parrish spoke the last words of his closing argument and walked back to the prosecution's table. The attentive courtroom was packed with supporters for both sides, but members from the media could have filled the place all by themselves. Video cameras were everywhere, and during any break, a family member from either side was likely to find a microphone thrust in his face or see a camera lens focused on him.

Judge Leonard gave the charge to the jury and the jurors filed out to start deliberating.

The smokers in the room darted outside. Mike Lester had to return to work, so Sandra Underhill hesitantly pushed Clark in his stroller toward Miles Bondurant, who stood with his daughter, Suzie, on the outside veranda. Although Bondurant had given Sandra the cold shoulder in the days following her testimony, she thought he would welcome her today because she had brought Clark. The three pulled out cigarettes and Bondurant's hand shook as he lit his.

Bondurant reached down and picked up Clark, now a chunky 15-month old. Clark's grin showed a full mouth of baby teeth. A photographer ran up to catch the paternal scene, and that apparently gave Bondurant an idea. "You should bring Clark into court," he told Underhill. "That jury needs to see him so they'll think twice before sending a parent of young children to prison."

"I'll ask Celeste," she told him.

Bondurant stepped on his cigarette butt, grinding it into the concrete floor of the porch. "I've been thinking. In case this doesn't go right, I want you to promise me something."

Underhill knew the answer would be "yes" before he asked, for at this point she'd do nothing to upset him.

"If for some reason I'm found guilty, promise me that you'll let my niece raise Cody."

His unjust request didn't seem to register with Sandra. She had heard so many. "Sure, Miles. If that's what you want."

Suzie's mouth opened. She frowned at her father, then shot a disbelieving glance at Underhill. "That's ridiculous! Why on earth shouldn't Sandra raise her own child? You'd be taking Cody away from his brother. Sandra, don't do this."

Surprised to have Suzie take her side, Underhill was so sure that Bondurant would be found innocent, she only smiled.

Inside, the bailiff stood waiting for any summons from the jury. An hour after beginning deliberation, the foreman pushed the doorbell in their quarters. The buzzing sound zapped the attention of everyone in the courtroom. The foreman handed a note to the bailiff who took it to Judge Leonard. The judge read it aloud for the court records: "We need all crime scene photos; the receipts for the barrels and flea bombs; the testimony of the barrel saleslady, Joe Davila, and the landlady. Also send us both taped statements by Bondurant."

Judge Leonard frowned, fearing they wanted to hear the entire trial again. He sent word back that they should request only the disputed portion of the material they asked for.

The jury narrowed its request, and 10 minutes later sent another note: "We are breaking for lunch. We will return at one."

For the reporters who covered trials everyday, the case should have been routine. But even they seemed uncommonly curious about the triangular relationship. They periodically glanced at their watches, hoping something would happen in time to meet their afternoon deadline. They didn't have to wait long.

At 1:45, less than four hours after the jury began deliberating, the foreman buzzed again and handed the bailiff their third note.

The sun caught Janie Brownlee's blond hair as she rushed outside toward Miles Bondurant. "Hurry," she called. "The jury's coming back with its verdict."

Many people were already seated in the courtroom by the time Judge Leonard climbed to his bench.

Sandra Underhill had checked with Celeste Rogers about letting Clark accompany her inside the courtroom. "Absolutely not," Rogers told her. "He could make noises that would disturb the entire proceeding."

The jury filed into the expectant courtroom without glancing at Bondurant and the foreman handed the verdict to the court clerk.

The judge took the paper and instructed Bondurant and his two attorneys to stand. Peering through his half glasses, Leonard read, "We the jury, find the defendant, Warren Miles Bondurant, guilty of murder in the first degree."

Bondurant immediately shut his eyes and his chin fell reflexively to his chest. His makeup was the only source of color on his face, and his puckered lips showed the exasperation he felt.

* * *

The defense had the option of letting a jury determine the sentence or of leaving it up to the judge. From the beginning, the case had been politically charged because the victim had been a lesbian. The defense decided against placing the burden on Judge Leonard, fearing politics would force him to render a harsh sentence. A jury, on the other hand, unburdened by such considerations, might prove more lenient.

The defense could make one more attempt to lighten the sentence during the trial's punishment phase. With a sentence of 15 years or less, probation was a possibility, so Bill Lane assembled four of Miles Bondurant's friends to speak on his behalf.

Ray Shipp had known Bondurant since seventh grade and had served as best man at his wedding. He had driven all morning from east Texas to testify for his friend. Shipp told the court, "Miles and I were both considered weenies in school because we were so non-confrontational. We would run from a fight. I can't imagine Miles would do anything harmful to anyone."

Mike Parrish asked, "Do you know what he did to Carri in the July Texas heat?"

Shipp nodded somberly.

Next Bondurant's faithful ex-wife, Marian, who had known him for 30 years, testified. "Miles and I were married for seventeen-and-a-half years. It was my fault that we're divorced. He was a wonderful father. Always full of hugs and kisses for the children. Don't destroy more lives by taking Miles out of the lives of his children." She generously offered to let Bondurant live at her house if he were paroled.

Marty Cook, president and director of the Arthritis Foundation for 26 years, spoke of Bondurant's unselfish dedication to the board. She said, "Miles absolutely shouldn't go to prison because he is a kind, generous human being."

Parrish asked, "Do you think that the feelings of the Coppinger family are important?"

"Yes, the family is important. But Miles is punishing himself right now."

Bondurant listened attentively and smiled at the affirmations.

Last, and most surprisingly, Assistant Police Chief Steve Noonkester took the witness stand. Bill Lane first discussed with him how difficult and compromising it was for him to testify.

Noonkester agreed, then said, "Miles is a person who deserves probation, which must sound odd coming from a man who has been a police officer as long as I have. For justice to be served, it doesn't always mean that someone has to be in prison. Miles is a compassionate person with a passive personality."

In closing this last part of the trial, Lane told the jury, "Consider Miles' 60 years that he gave to the community. Any prison sentence at his age would be a death sentence."

Conversely, Parrish argued that, "Miles has taken a life, so why not a life sentence? Miles had stolen fifty years from Carri Coppinger."

Judge Leonard read the charge to the jury. "The punishment authorized for this offense is confinement in [prison] for life, or for any term not exceeding 99 years, or less than five years." He explained to the jury that, ". . . before this trial, the defendant filed a motion that in the event he be convicted, that he be granted probation."

While the jury left to deliberate Bondurant's future, the court allowed him to roam freely and he walked outside. Noonkester accompanied him along with Sandra and Suzie.

Bondurant, buoyed by the positive comments of his character witnesses, smiled with confidence as he lit his cigarette. "No problem. I'll get probation," he said as he heartily exhaled.

"Oh, I know you will," Underhill said earnestly.

Noonkester nodded. "When you can get an ex-wife to testify for you, that says a lot."

As Noonkester spoke, Sandra looked up at the handsome man, almost a foot-and-a-half taller than she, and felt proud that someone so distinguished would speak on Miles' behalf.

At 5:30, the jury sent out its fourth and final note: "We have reached a sentence."

Soon everyone convened in court, and Bondurant and his lawyers were instructed to stand. The solemn-looking judge read: "We the jury sentence Warren Miles Bondurant to fifty years in the state penitentiary with no parole until he has served twenty-five years."

Gasps met the announcement. Bondurant's hand flew to his mouth. Color drained from Bill Lane's face.

Ten minutes later, the bailiff slapped handcuffs on Bondurant and rushed him out of the courtroom. He was immediately put on a suicide watch.

Sandra Underhill had been peeking through the courtroom door. Now after the sentence, she stood in disbelief and wanted to go home. She had tried to escape the media who had pestered her for two weeks, at one time even following her into the ladies' room. She hurriedly walked down the corridor pushing Clark in his stroller.

"Miss, were you surprised at the sentence?" a female reporter asked.

Underhill slowed down and nodded. "I didn't think the jury would be so hard on him."

"Do you still love him?"

Sandra stopped and turned around. "I once loved him. I still care for him very much."

"Do you think the killing was accidental?"

She again nodded, and sniffling she said, "Yes, I think it was an accident." She still couldn't bring herself to hurt Miles. Then she collected her thoughts and tried to control her sobbing. "Miles is a good man. He's worked hard all his life. He wouldn't hurt anyone."

She started to walk on, then turned around to face the reporters one last time. "I'd be nowhere today if it weren't for Miles."

# Chapter Forty-Three

Now both Cody and Clark belonged to their mother.

Four months after Bondurant's trial, his niece Madison, a very bright attorney, cleverly drew up a child custody agreement forcing Sandra Underhill to take both boys to the men's state penitentiary every month for a visit. Judge Frank Sullivan's 322nd Judicial District Court put teeth into the order by threatening Underhill with prison and a fine of $500 for not obeying.

Even from prison Miles Bondurant manipulated Sandra Underhill to do his bidding. On September 22, 1996, he wrote pleading for her to "recall way back in 1991, when you were incarcerated in Georgetown and then in Gatesville, how I went out of my way to see to it that you were at least as comfortable as I could possibly make you. Money, visits, letters, kindness, you name it." Now he demanded the same courtesies.

Underhill still held an unexplained loyalty to Bondurant, for she showered him with money and letters. In late September 1996, she planned her first visit.

* * *

After spending the night in Houston, Mike Lester, Sandra, and the boys climbed into Lester's truck and headed south for the hour's drive to Rosharon.

They turned onto a two-lane asphalt road leading to the Ramsey I Unit of the Texas State Penitentiary for Men, and Underhill inhaled deeply. The heavy air smelled salty, floating in from the Gulf of Mexico, only 36 miles to the east.

The prison guard held a clipboard with names of approved visitors and Lester and Underhill had to show identification and allow themselves to be searched.

Sandra Underhill's heart raced as the four of them were steered to the visitor's room, which looked exactly like the room where she first saw Miles. They waited in the murky atmosphere that reeked with familiarity.

Bondurant hobbled in on a cane. In prison, he had twice complained of chest pains which earned him several days in the infirmary. The cane provided support, protection, and sympathy.

Underhill initially spied him through the heavy metal mesh that divided inmates from visitors. Leaning on his cane, he stood in his rough, white cotton shirt and pants that had been laundered, but not ironed. His hair had reverted to its natural gray, and without makeup he looked as pale as winter.

All of Sandra's previous prison experiences rushed back to her when she made eye contact with Miles, and she cried. She cried for the good times they had had, for her best friend he had taken from her, and for Miles, who was now experiencing everything she had endured in prison. Only for Miles, it would be for the rest of his life.

# Epilogue

Sandra Underhill and Mike Lester have purchased a new home and are raising Cody and Clark.

A few months after the trial, Jenny Campbell revealed to Underhill that she began living with Janie Brownlee's brother around the time of the murder, and since Brownlee was working for Bill Lane, it would be a conflict of interest for her to get involved with Sandra. Jenny and Sandra are once again friends.

A month after the trial, Miles Bondurant went back to court to declare himself a pauper, enabling him to receive a court-appointed lawyer who recently announced he had found grounds for an appeal.

# READ EXCITING ACCOUNTS OF TRUE CRIME FROM PINNACLE

**A PERFECT GENTLEMAN** (0-7860-0263-8, $5.99)
By Jaye Slade Fletcher
On October 13, 1987, the body of 16-year-old Windy Patricia Gallagher was found in her home in Griffith, Indiana, stabbed 21 times and disemboweled. Five months later, 14-year-old Jennifer Colhouer of Land O'Lakes, Florida, was found raped and also slashed to death in her own home. But it was the seemingly unrelated cold-blooded murder of a Beaumont, Texas police officer that sparked a massive, nationwide manhunt across 5 states and 2 continents to apprehend one of the most elusive—and charming—serial killers who ever lived.

**BORN BAD** (0-7860-0274-3, $5.99)
By Bill G. Cox
On a lonely backroad in Ellis County, TX, the body of 13-year-old Christina Benjamin was discovered. Her head and hands were missing. She had been sexually mutilated and disemboweled. A short distance away was the badly decomposed corpse of 14-year-old James King face down on the creek bank. He had been brutally shot to death. This ghoulish discovery would lead to the apprehension of the most appalling torture killer Texas had ever seen. . . .

**CHARMED TO DEATH** (0-7860-0257-3, $5.99)
The True Story of Colorado's Cold-Blooded
Black Widow Murderess
By Stephen Singular
Jill Coit spread her lethal web of sex, lies, and violence from one end of the country to the other. Behind the beauty queen smile was a psychopathic femme fatale who took a fiendish delight in preying on innocent men. With fifteen aliases, countless forged birth certificates, and a predatory allure, she married ten men, divorced six, and always stayed one step ahead of the law in a poisonous spree of bigamy, embezzlement, and murder that lasted nearly 35 years.

*Available wherever paperbacks are sold, or order direct from the Publisher. Send cover price plus 50¢ per copy for mailing and handling to Kensington Publishing Corp., Consumer Orders, or call (toll free) 888-345-BOOK, to place your order using Mastercard or Visa. Residents of New York and Tennessee must include sales tax. DO NOT SEND CASH.*